APPLIED ELECTROMAGNETISM

Books by Susannah Nix

Chemistry Lessons Series:

Remedial Rocket Science

Intermediate Thermodynamics

Advanced Physical Chemistry

Applied Electromagnetism

Starstruck Series:

Rising Star

Fallen Star

APPLIED ELECTROMAGNETISM

SUSANNAH NIX

Haver Street Press

This book is a work of fiction. Names, characters, places, incidents, tirades, opinions, exaggerations, prevarications, and dubious facts either are the products of the author's imagination or are used fictitiously. Any resemblance to actual events or persons—living, dead, or otherwise—is entirely coincidental.

FIRST EDITION: July 2019

ISBN: 978-1-950087-02-0

Haver Street Press | 448 W. 19th St., Suite 407 | Houston, TX 77008

Edited by Julia Ganis, www.juliaedits.com

Ebook & Print Cover Design by www.ebooklaunch.com

Chapter One

It was Friday afternoon, and Olivia Woerner was engaged in a battle of wills with herself.

Just get up and go talk to him.

She stared across the office at Adam Cortinas. All she could see over the walls of his cubicle was the very top of his head, but that hadn't stopped her from staring at him for the better part of an hour.

Just go over there.

It didn't have to be a big deal. It was a simple ask. The odds of him saying no were pretty slim.

Probably.

All she had to do was walk up to Adam and say one sentence: *Will you write me a reference for the Future Leader Development Course?*

It was a new program the company had announced last week, and Olivia wanted to be a part of it, more than she'd wanted anything professionally since she'd first started this job.

Aside from the obvious leverage it would provide when year-end review and bonus time rolled around, it would be nice to be officially recognized finally as someone with leadership potential. A person worth developing into something more than a junior analyst on the commercial systems team at an independent power producer, which was where she'd been stuck for the last four years.

Jesus tap dancing Christ, her job sounded so boring she was putting herself into a coma just by describing it.

It pretty much *was* boring, except the part where she was on call at all hours and sometimes had to get up in the middle of the night to fix some code in a system that had gone offline, or else Very Bad Things happened—like hospitals and airports losing power, or grandmothers either freezing or dying of heatstroke, depending on the time of year.

That was what Brad, the CIO, always told people when he thought they might be slacking off: imagine if it was *your* grandmother without heat in Nebraska in the coldest January on record, or without air-conditioning in Reno during the worst heat wave in a decade. How would you feel if your own beloved grandmother's power went out because someone wasn't paying enough attention to their job?

Other than *that*—the part where Olivia was helping keep grandmothers alive—her job was mega boring.

Not that she expected work to be exciting. She'd accepted that most people spent their lives doing boring work in boring jobs. Even if you had an exciting job like paramedic or bounty hunter or hostage negotiator, she imagined there were still probably lots of days where it felt ho-hum.

But Olivia had been in the same role on the same team for too long, and she was in danger of stagnating. If she wasn't careful, she'd end up as one of those people in their fifties who'd been stuck in one job their entire career, until suddenly the technology changed and rendered them obsolete.

What she needed was a challenge. An opportunity to grow into something more.

But despite raising the subject of her professional advancement multiple times with her boss Gavin, opportunities never seemed to arise. Or when they did, they always seemed to be earmarked for someone else.

This leadership course was her chance to stand out. To be noticed, finally, and taken seriously.

She'd already finished her application. All she needed now were two professional recommendations. Gavin had already agreed to provide one, but the other had to be from someone on another team.

That was why she needed Adam Cortinas.

He worked on the plant systems team and spent half his time in the field. Whenever one of the company's power plants was having an issue, Adam was the guy they'd throw at the problem. The CIO *loved* him, because Adam had saved his bacon about a million times by parachuting into a disaster and fixing whatever was broken. He was a troubleshooting rock star.

If Olivia could get a recommendation from Adam Cortinas, it would give her a serious edge up on the competition.

She and Adam interacted pretty regularly, keeping the company data systems that she maintained integrated with the plant systems that he maintained, and she *thought* he liked her okay.

Adam could be tough to read. He was a little...brusque. But he was like that with everyone, even the CIO. It was just how he was. Adam wasn't interested in small talk or making friends around the office. He was laser-focused on his work, and since he was a rock star, he could be as brusque as he wanted.

Olivia wasn't especially into making friends around the office either, but she didn't have a choice about playing nice. She wasn't a rock star like Adam. She was a woman in a predominantly male field, and if she didn't put in the extra effort to suck up and make friends, it would bite her in the ass professionally.

So now here she was on a Friday afternoon, trying to work up the nerve to talk to Adam, which she wouldn't have had a problem with under normal circumstances. If she'd needed to talk to him about an ordinary work thing, she'd go straight up to him, no problem.

But this wasn't an ordinary work thing. This was a favor she was asking him to do for her.

Olivia *hated* asking for favors.

She preferred to solve problems on her own. Asking for help felt like an admission of weakness, and she already had enough of a problem seeming weak because she was small and female, not to mention so pale, with her alabaster complexion and light blue eyes, that she practically disappeared into the industrial beige walls.

People had a tendency to look right through her, or right past her, or right over the top of her five foot three inches. It was why she always wore thick, black eyeliner and the darkest, most dramatic lipstick she could get away with in the office. To try and make herself seem tougher—or at least less invisible.

Her reluctance to ask for favors wasn't the only thing keeping her from going over to talk to Adam. There was also the small matter of her long-standing crush on him.

Adam Cortinas was the most attractive man in the office by a considerable margin.

Admittedly, there wasn't a lot of competition for the title. Most of the IT guys she worked with were a lot older than Adam, who couldn't be much over thirty, and most of them looked exactly how you'd expect middle-aged IT guys to look. A few of the energy traders upstairs were okay-looking, she supposed, if douchebags were your preferred type—but they most definitely were not Olivia's.

Adam looked more like an Instagram model than systems analyst. He would have been the hottest guy in *any* office.

For starters, he had beautiful bronze skin, piercing dark eyes, thick black hair that fell across his forehead in luscious waves, and a jawline that could cut diamonds. Then there was the matter of his body, which was practically a work of art. The guy definitely spent time in the gym. The same vendor-branded polos that hung shapelessly on everyone else around the office pulled tight across his broad chest and clung to his muscled arms like they'd been custom tailored just for him.

Adam Cortinas was the whole luscious package, and Olivia had been fantasizing about him from afar since he'd joined the company two years ago. Which was why, if this whole reference thing went well, she was thinking of asking him out for a drink.

It was the perfect opening. She could couch it as a thank-you for writing her the reference. That way she wasn't extending herself too far. It was simply a friendly drink among coworkers. A professional courtesy.

She just had to go over there and talk to him first.

Yet somehow she wasn't doing it. Her feet were two chunks of lead, and her ass was permanently welded to the seat of her swivel chair. She was never moving. She'd be excavated by archeologists eons from now, still sitting here, chin in palm, staring dreamily in the direction of Adam's cubicle.

Olivia was twenty-eight years old, but she felt like she'd been teleported back to the pubescent hell of fifteen, when she'd been too scared to ask Josh Fratangelo to the Sadie Hawkins dance. Olivia's arch-nemesis Ashley Beeman had asked him instead, and Olivia had spent the night at home alone with a tube of raw cookie dough and her *Veronica Mars* DVDs for consolation.

Get up. Go over there. Talk to him.

Just as she was about to screw up her courage, Adam got to his feet.

Olivia lowered her eyes in a panic, terrified he might have noticed her staring. What if he had spidey senses that tingled to warn him when someone was watching him and having lustful thoughts?

Out of the corner of her eye, she saw Adam carry his coffee mug into the break room without even a glance in her direction.

This was her chance. She could go get more coffee and just happen to bump into him.

Oh hey, how's your day going? she could say. *Listen, since we're here, would you mind writing me a rec for FLDC?* And once he'd agreed, she could offer to buy him a drink sometime after work.

Why not, right? Nothing ventured or some shit.

Olivia breathed deep for a count of three. Smoothed her hand over her white-blonde hair. Gathered her strength and grabbed her coffee mug off her desk before she strode into the break room.

And stuttered to a stop just inside the doorway.

Adam was leaning into the fridge, bent over, with his ass pointing directly at her.

Jesus roller-blading fuck. That was one USDA Prime cut of meat staring at her. Why did he have to have such a nice ass? And why did it have to be pointing right at her? Totally unfair.

He turned his head in her direction lazily, as if he almost couldn't be bothered to see who'd walked in. His eyes flicked over her, his expression dull and disinterested.

Olivia swallowed down her nervousness and propelled herself toward the sink. "Hey," she managed to force out, despite the fact that her throat felt like it was coated with gravel. Also, her heart was pounding in her ears and her legs felt like jellyfish tentacles.

Adam acknowledged her with a nod before turning back to the fridge.

The way he was bending over should be an occupational safety hazard. It was definitely hazardous to *her* occupational safety. She ought to report him to OSHA for bringing an ass like that to the office.

And of course she was still totally staring at his ass when he closed the fridge and turned around, holding a carton of almond milk.

His eyes narrowed slightly, which meant he probably knew she'd been staring at his ass, so that was completely mortifying. Not that it was entirely her fault. He was the one who was bending over, presenting his ass for all the world to see. She'd just come in here to have a simple conversation with him, and his ass happened to be front and center. What else was she supposed to look at?

Now that he was facing her, she realized that looking at his face posed a whole new set of challenges. She definitely couldn't look directly into his eyes. Oh no. It was impossible to concentrate when she was looking into those bottomless ebon orbs.

Which left her staring at his mouth. His lush, soft lips with an almost sulky curl to them—

Nope. Stop.

She needed to pull herself together and quit objectifying him. He was her coworker, and he probably had a gorgeous girlfriend. A model or an actress—maybe even someone famous. That could be why he was such a closed book. Because he was dating, like, Rihanna or Jennifer Lawrence, and didn't want anyone at work to know so they didn't act all weird around him.

Weird like Olivia was acting right now.

To keep from gawking at him, she tried to focus on an imaginary point just to the right of his head. But since there was nothing there but empty air, she ended up staring at the CPR poster on the wall behind him, which must have looked odd because he actually threw a glance over his shoulder like he was trying to figure out what she was looking at.

She dragged her eyes back to his, but that was *way* too much, so she let her gaze fall to his chest, which ought to be safe. Except Adam's chest was exquisite. His gray polo was made of shiny athletic fabric with a drape that would make Tim Gunn drool. The shirt was thin enough that she could see the square outline of his pecs, with just a hint of his nipples beneath.

Sweet cream-cheesy Jesus, she was staring at his nipples now.

Her eyes jumped higher, settling on his collarbone, which was only marginally better because now she was noticing the strong tendons in his neck and the graceful way they melted into his broad and apparently hairless chest. Or was that a hint of dark chest hair just beneath the open collar of his shirt? It was hard to tell from this distance.

"Did you need something?" Adam asked, appearing only mildly curious to know why she was gawping at him like an imbecile. He was probably used to being stared at. With a face and a body like that, he must get ogled all the time.

Olivia cleared her throat.

Just spit it out before this drags on and gets even weirder.

"Yeah, actually. I—uh—I was hoping you'd write me a reference for the Future Leader Development Course."

"Ah." He turned away, but not before she glimpsed his unmistakable expression of distaste.

Her heart sank to the floor, where it lay in a puddle of mortification at her feet. This was why she hated asking people for favors. Because it opened the door for rejection, and as far as her brain was concerned, rejection was a fate worse than death.

He hasn't even said no yet. Calm down and give him a chance to answer before you panic.

"So, yeah," she continued, forging ahead with false buoyancy, "I'm putting my name in the hat and you need two references—one of which has to be from someone on another team. And I was hoping you'd be willing to do it, since we've worked together for a while."

Adam stirred almond milk into his coffee without looking at her. "Can you ask someone else?"

"Oh." Her heart clattered to the floor again and smashed to bits. "Um, sure. I guess."

If she'd had a time machine, she wouldn't use it to kill baby Hitler, she'd travel back five minutes and jam a plastic spork into her eye, so she wouldn't humiliate herself by asking Adam for a fucking reference. And *then* she'd kill baby Hitler.

"It's just that I'd rather not," Adam said, still not looking at her.

So, that was that. That was her answer. He wasn't willing to write her a reference.

"Can I ask why?" She knew it was a mistake, but the question slipped out before she could stop it. She had to know. It was possible it had nothing to do with her. Maybe he just hated writing references. Or maybe he'd already promised one to somebody else.

He put the almond milk back in the fridge and picked up his coffee cup, regarding her silently as he lifted it to his lips. "Look, I'm sorry," he said finally. "But I just can't see you as a manager."

He might as well have slapped her across the face. Olivia's cheeks stung with pins and needles as if they'd been struck.

She wanted to argue. She knew she ought to speak up and defend herself, but she couldn't formulate any kind of retort. "Okay, well, thanks anyway," she forced out in a voice so small and high it was practically a whistle.

Adam gave her a jerky nod and walked out of the kitchen without another word.

On the bright side, she was no longer distracted by his hot bod.

He wasn't the least bit attractive to her anymore. He was a cockwaffle. An arrogant, hostile fecalwad who had apparently never liked her and thought she was bad at her job.

Her. The person who had sat with the users and calmed them all down when they'd had that big outage last year. And who'd solved that problem in the trading system a few months ago that no one else had been able to figure out.

How dare he? She was fucking awesome at her job.

Well, screw him. She didn't need his stupid reference. Plenty of people around here liked her. Because she was *nice*, and she'd gone out of her way to make allies. She'd have no trouble getting a reference from any number of other people.

Adam Cortinas could shove his reference and his attitude straight up his Grade A Prime ass.

Chapter Two

Olivia sat cross-legged at one end of the couch in her best friend Penny's Culver City apartment.

It was similar to Olivia's apartment in Santa Monica, only three times nicer, thanks to Penny's neat streak and flair for decorating. Whereas Olivia's apartment was cluttered with multiple craft projects in progress, old mail, baskets of laundry that would probably never be folded, and the spoils of her last Target trip still waiting to be put away, Penny's place was always tidy and immaculate, from her perfectly fluffed matching throw cushions to her dish-free kitchen sink.

The first thing Olivia had done after her encounter with Adam in the break room was send Penny an SOS text to let her know she'd be needing some wine and BFF therapy tonight after work. Penny worked from home as a patent examiner, so by the time Olivia showed up at her apartment door that evening, she was ready and waiting with not only a bottle of rosé, but also a batch of freshly baked cookies.

Penny was truly the *best* of best friends.

Over a plate of her favorite sea salt chocolate chip cookies,

Olivia blurted out the whole humiliating saga of her conversation with Adam.

"I can't believe he said no!" Penny exclaimed when Olivia was done. "What kind of person says no to something as simple as giving a reference?"

"Apparently this guy," Olivia said around a mouthful of cookie.

"I thought the rule was that you just sucked it up and tried to write something generically nice no matter how you actually felt. I mean, *maybe* you could plead that you don't have time if you really don't want to do it. But to flat-out refuse because you don't think someone's worthy? Only a sociopath would come right out and say that."

"Thank you for validating my outrage."

"Have another cookie." Penny pushed the plate toward Olivia as she leaned forward to top off both their wineglasses. "I'm right, aren't I, Caleb?"

Penny's boyfriend looked up from the cookie sheets he was hand-washing in the kitchen. "You're asking the wrong guy. I've never written a reference in my life."

Ever since Caleb had moved in with Penny last year, he'd become a de facto participant in Olivia's BFF therapy sessions too.

It had taken some time for Olivia to get used to Caleb being a fixture in her life. The last guy Penny had dated hadn't really been around all that much—because he'd been cheating on her, it had turned out—so he'd never gotten in the way of their one-on-one BFF time.

But when Caleb came in to Penny's life, everything had changed. He wasn't anything like Penny's shitty last boyfriend. He was nice, for one thing, and treated her like she was a queen and he was her loyal subject. The two of them were pretty much inseparable. But also, Caleb actually seemed to like Penny's friends and enjoy spending time with them.

Which was sweet, but also a little weird for Olivia sometimes. It meant he was suddenly a part of everything. Olivia didn't get

Penny to herself anymore. It was always Penny and Caleb. Together. A matched set.

Which was great. Good for them. It was just...for years, Olivia had been the number one person in Penny's life, and now Caleb had come along and usurped her position.

She wasn't bitter though. At least, she was trying really, really hard not to be bitter. Caleb made Penny happy, and Penny deserved to be happy. You'd have to be a real festering shitbag of a human being to be resentful over your best friend's romantic happiness.

Caleb was a great guy, which was all that really mattered. Olivia genuinely liked him, but more importantly, she liked the way he treated her friend.

"I'm right," Penny said, turning back to Olivia. "That guy's a dick." Penny hardly ever swore, so her calling Adam a dick meant she'd gone full-on angry mama bear.

"I can go kick his ass if you want," Caleb offered casually. He could probably do it too. He was even more muscular than Adam, and he'd grown up in a military family with two brothers, so he probably knew how to throw a punch.

Penny shot a disapproving look in her boyfriend's direction. "No one's kicking anyone's ass. Even if he is a big, honking jerkface."

"It's very sweet of you to offer though," Olivia told Caleb. "You're like the big brother I already have, only much nicer."

Her own brother had never once risen to her defense, even when they were kids. When Cody Briggs had called her a booger-eater on the playground in second grade and teased her until she'd cried, her brother had laughed along with his fourth grade friends, then told her she needed to grow up and fight her own battles.

Olivia would trade her brother for Caleb in a hot second. But she'd also probably trade her brother for a handful of fake magic beans and an expired Bed Bath & Beyond coupon.

Penny reached for her wineglass and looked at Olivia. "Who

else can you ask for a reference? I'm sure there are loads of other people who would be happy to do it."

"I don't know." Olivia couldn't stand the thought of extending herself all over again. She wouldn't be able to deal with another rejection. Her soul would probably depart her body, leaving the empty husk of her earthly vessel behind to crumble into dust, and it didn't seem fair to make the janitorial staff clean that up.

"It won't be this bad the next time," Penny said, reading her mind.

"Yeah, because maybe there won't be a next time."

"But you still need a reference for the leadership program."

Olivia's stomach tightened. "I don't know if I can go through this again."

Penny leaned forward and patted her on the knee. "Sure you can. You just happened to pick the biggest butthead in the office. Which, admittedly, is bad luck—but now you've gotten all your bad luck out of the way. No one else is going to say no to you. How could they? You're awesome."

"What if he's right though, and I have no business applying for this?" Olivia sagged forward and pressed the heels of her palms against her forehead. "Maybe I'm fooling myself thinking I've got a chance."

"He's not right. He doesn't know anything about you. I do, and I'm telling you you're going to make an amazing manager." There was steel in Penny's voice. Mama-bear mode was still in full effect.

"You don't know what I'm like at work," Olivia protested. "I'm a different person there than I am around my friends." Penny probably wouldn't even recognize the fake, friendly, positive person Olivia pretended to be in her professional life. She was such a fucking fake, she made herself nauseous.

"Well, duh. I'm sure you don't walk around the office calling people dickweasels or buttnuggets—even when they probably deserve it."

"They do deserve it. And I never say anything."

"Of course you don't. You have to get along with people at work, and from everything you've ever told me, you're really good at it. Don't let this miserable jackass undermine your confidence in yourself. You're smart, kind, and professional." Penny reached out and squeezed Olivia's hand. "People love you—a lot more than you think they do."

Whether that was true or not, Olivia was going to have to gather the shattered remnants of her dignity and face Adam Cortinas at work on Monday. Pretending he didn't exist wasn't an option. The two systems they managed needed to interface, which meant so did they.

But hopefully not too much. As long as their interactions were kept to a minimum, she could handle it.

Maybe.

"WHAT DO you think's going on in there?"

Olivia swallowed a sigh of irritation as Trevor, one of the other junior analysts on the commercial systems team, perched his ass on the corner of her desk.

Trevor was always coming over to chat whenever he didn't feel like doing his own work. Which wouldn't be so bad, except his idea of chatting too often involved him explaining stupid internet memes to her, as if she didn't have her own Facebook account and hadn't already seen the same jokey photo in her feed a dozen times already.

The thing about memes was that they weren't nearly as funny when someone was describing them to you—assuming they'd even been funny in the first place.

"In where?" she asked, offering Trevor a false smile.

"Conference room." He gestured with his coffee mug, which featured a cartoon of a bear pooping into a bucket for reasons that Olivia had never understood and did not care to ask about. "Gavin is in there with Cortinas and the CIO, and he doesn't look happy."

All the men around the office called Adam by his last name, like he was some kind of hero in an action movie. It was a physical effort not to roll her eyes.

"Which one doesn't look happy? Gavin?" She refused to turn and look.

"All of them. Well, except Cortinas, who looks the same as always. Nothing ever fazes that guy. He's like a robot."

Yeah, an evil robot, Olivia thought to herself.

"The CIO looks pissed, and Gavin looks like he's about to wet himself."

"Really?" That inspired her to turn around for a peek.

Sure enough, Gavin was pacing around the conference room with that constipated look he got whenever things were going badly. Brad, the CIO, was seated at the head of the table looking annoyed as fuck, which was never a good sign.

Olivia told herself she wasn't going to look at Adam, but her eyes slid over to him of their own accord. He was kicked back in his chair, either listening intently or on the verge of falling asleep. It was hard to tell from his bland expression.

As she was turned around in her seat watching them, Gavin suddenly stopped his frenetic pacing and looked right at her. Brad and Adam immediately followed suit, so all three of them were now staring directly at her.

"What the fuck?" Trevor whispered as Olivia snapped her head around again, turning her back on the conference room. "Why are they all staring at us?"

"I don't know," she said. "Are they still looking?"

Trevor stared at the conference room with the self-preservation instincts of a possum that had wandered onto train tracks and been hypnotized by the light of an oncoming train. "Yeah. Totally."

"Are they looking at you or are they looking at me?" Olivia asked.

"You, I think. Did you fuck something up?"

"Not that I know of." Not since that fiasco with the Tulelake plant, anyway. Christ on a tricycle, could that be what this was about? The one thing she'd fucked up in her four years at the company. And it wasn't even her fault. The head of the west desk was the one who'd insisted on the three-by-eight generator configuration.

Olivia had tried to talk him out of it, knowing that configuration wouldn't work with that plant, but he'd waved her concerns away. What was she supposed to do? Refuse to follow a directive from the head trader? Of course, then his way had backfired, just like she'd known it would, and the company had been fined by CAISO. But because he was a trader who made the company millions of dollars, culpability had magically bounced right off him and onto her.

"Okay, they're not looking anymore," Trevor said.

Olivia exhaled. "What are they doing?"

"Gavin's talking to Brad and Cortinas now."

"Okay." Hopefully the danger had passed. Maybe it was just a coincidence that they'd all been looking this direction. Maybe it didn't have anything to do with her.

"Oh my god, my high school buddy posted this hilarious video on Facebook this morning," Trevor said, and Olivia girded herself. "There's this little kid, and she's trying to get Alexa to play that baby shark song. You know the one, it goes like—"

Olivia's phone vibrated loudly on the desk next to her. A feeling of cold dread sank into her bones as she read the notification. It was a text from Gavin:

Come join us in the conference room.

What in the pluperfect hell was going on? Had Adam said something about her?

Trevor peered over her shoulder. "Guess they were definitely looking at you, then."

She pushed herself to her feet. "We who are about to die salute you."

"I'll pray for you."

"Thanks." When she turned toward the conference room, all three of its occupants were staring at her again, and none of them looked happy. Even Adam looked like he'd swallowed a wasp.

Olivia wended her way through the maze of cubicles and pulled the conference room door open. Maybe if she didn't actually step across the threshold, she could remain uninvolved. Maybe they just needed to ask her a quick question. Something simple she could answer quickly and then go back to work.

"You rang?" She hovered just outside the door, pointedly refusing to look at Adam or acknowledge his presence.

"Come in." Gavin waved her to the chair across from him. "Close the door."

Fuck me sideways. Olivia mustered all her resources to paste a pleasant expression on her face as she obeyed.

Brad offered her a strained smile. "Thanks for joining us. Gavin, you want to bring her up to speed?"

She'd only had occasion to speak to the CIO a handful of times before, and he always put her on edge. There was a briskness beneath the surface of his politeness, like he wouldn't hesitate to cut you loose as soon as you stopped being useful to him.

"Sure." Gavin shifted in his seat and ran a hand through his thinning brown hair. He was only in his mid-thirties, but with his pleated pants and unfashionable haircut, he looked more middle-aged than Brad, despite being almost twenty years his junior. "We've finally inked the deal on our acquisition of the Walhalla plant in Texas," he told Olivia.

"Great." It had been in the works for months, but these things had a tendency to move slowly.

"The original plan was to have the plant onboarded within thirty days," Gavin said, shifting his eyes to Brad.

It was an aggressive timeline, but not impossible for a smaller acquisition. Olivia nodded, confused why everyone seemed so worked up about it.

Brad's smile became even more strained. "Unfortunately, it's taken three weeks to do our due diligence and get the deal cleared by the regulators. But in the meantime..." He winced like he'd stepped on a Lego. "A commitment was made to the board of directors to have the plant fully integrated with our systems and operating as part of our fleet by the end of June."

The end of June was only a few days away. There was no way they would be able to make it.

Olivia couldn't help noticing Brad's use of the passive voice, which implied the commitment had somehow made itself, magically. It certainly wasn't because *he* had made an unrealistic commitment to the board of his own free will.

"Which only leaves our teams a week to do our thing," Gavin added with a grimace.

So Brad was holding them to the deadline? No wonder Gavin looked like he was going to piss himself. A week was insane. That was faster than their team had ever taken on any plant before.

"I see," Olivia said, trying to keep her expression neutral. "How can I help?"

Gavin cast a guilty look in Brad's direction before answering. "Normally, I'd go out there with Cortinas and handle the commercial systems side of the integration myself." Gavin's eyes darted briefly to Adam, whose face was utterly blank. He might not even have been listening. For all Olivia could tell, he was composing a grocery list in his head or silently reciting the *Animaniacs* nations of the world song.

"The thing is," Gavin went on, "my wife's due date is in two weeks, and the doc thinks they might need to induce early. Which means I can't leave town right now." His gaze settled on Olivia. "So I'm sending you to Texas with Cortinas instead."

She felt her eyes widen. Everyone was staring at her—including Adam now. She swallowed and forced herself to take a slow breath through her nose before venturing to speak. "When?"

"Tomorrow," Gavin said.

"And we're supposed to have the plant online when?"

It was Brad who answered this time. "Friday midnight."

Four days. Not even four days. With travel time, it was more like three and a half.

She considered her words carefully before speaking. "I'll need to do some research before I can say with any confidence whether—"

"Look, I'm briefing the board in an hour," Brad said, drumming his fingers on the tabletop. "I just need to know if this can be done or not."

Olivia tried again. "Sorry, that's what I was about to say. I'll need to know more before I can make that commitment. Can we wait a half day before talking to the board?"

"It's feasible," Adam said, speaking up for the first time. "I've done it this fast before."

Olivia shot a glare at him. "Yes, but we don't even know the characteristics of this plant, or what shape its gear is in. We need more information before we can—"

"Sure, and you can do that research on the plane," Gavin interrupted. "Cortinas is the one with the most experience here, and I trust his opinion. If he says we can do it, we can do it."

Of course. The rock star had just declared they could do it, which meant no one was going to listen to Olivia or her concerns. Why should they? She'd never done this before. Adam was the expert, and he was confident.

Brad looked pleased. "Exactly what I wanted to hear! Thank you all. Keep me posted on how things are progressing, Gavin." He stood, sweeping his phone and tablet off the table, and exited the conference room before anyone could say anything else.

"Great," Gavin said, looking relieved. "Glad that's settled. You two will fly out first thing tomorrow. That's not a problem, is it?"

"Nope," Adam said, and lifted a quizzical eyebrow at Olivia.

"Not a problem at all." She forced a smile, trying to project more confidence than she felt.

Gavin pushed his chair back and headed for the door. "Good luck, you two. You're gonna need it."

Olivia's guts churned as she watched him walk away. A commitment to the board of directors that she wasn't even sure she could meet, and daily reports to the boss that would be relayed to the CIO, if not higher—she'd wanted more responsibility and exposure, but this felt more like an ambush than an opportunity. Like she was being set up to fail.

"You okay there, Woerner? You're looking a little shell-shocked." Adam's expression was so smirky it made her insides burn. If her arms had been long enough, she'd have reached across the table and slapped it right off his face.

And then immediately be fired.

She breathed out through her nostrils for a count of three while she tried to come up with a retort that wouldn't be reportable to human resources. When that failed, she elected to take the high road, getting to her feet and walking out without a word.

If this was a preview of what the rest of the week would be like, she would need every ounce of patience she could muster just to keep herself from murdering him and hiding his body in a cow pasture.

Chapter Three

LAX on a weekday morning was a special kind of hell. LAX at any time was a hellscape, but apparently every business traveler in the greater Los Angeles metro area was flying on this particular Tuesday morning.

Olivia was glad she'd gotten there early. She always liked to get to the airport early to head off any unanticipated problems, like extra-long security lines or broken check-in computers—both of which had been in play this morning.

But she had successfully navigated the airport gauntlet with time to spare, and was through security and waiting at her gate forty-five minutes before boarding. She'd even had time to stock up on snacks and water in one of the airport shops.

Adam, on the other hand, was nowhere to be seen. Not that she was eager to spend time with him or awkwardly attempt to make small talk and pretend she could stand the sight of him. But as the minutes ticked toward their scheduled boarding time, Olivia grew increasingly worried.

She couldn't do any of this without him, and the schedule was already so tight they couldn't afford any delays. Once they got to Austin, they'd have to rent a car and drive another seventy miles to Fayette County, where the plant was located, before they could get started on the integration. If Adam missed this flight it would throw off everything. Even a few lost hours could mean the difference between success or failure with a schedule this tight.

And Olivia needed this assignment to be a success. It would bolster her application to the leadership program. Not to mention, if she botched her very first field assignment, she probably wouldn't be given a second one. She'd carry this failure with her for as long as she stayed on her current team.

That was why she was so pissed about having her concerns dismissed. No, they weren't even dismissed—she hadn't been allowed to voice them at all. You couldn't dismiss something until you'd actually heard it. She'd just been silenced.

Olivia had a bad feeling this assignment was doomed from the get-go, and she was pissed about it. It was fine for Adam. He'd done enough of these and pulled enough unlikely wins out of his ass that he was golden no matter what. One little failure amidst a long string of successes wouldn't tarnish his reputation. But if this went south, Olivia's official record would be zero for one.

Adam was the control in this experiment, so it couldn't possibly be his fault. She was the variable, so everyone would assume she couldn't carry her weight, that she wasn't up to the challenge. And there would go all her hopes of being a future leader, or getting any other plum assignments.

Five minutes to boarding now, and still no Adam. Their plane was at the gate, the previous flight's passengers had exited, and the cleaning crew was making their pass. All signs pointed to an on-time boarding and departure.

Olivia stared at her phone, wondering if she should try calling Adam. Was that what a future leader would do? Or would it make her seem like a Nervous Nellie?

Damn Adam for getting her into this situation. And for being late to the airport. But most of all damn him for making her doubt herself. She'd trusted her instincts before he'd come along and punctured her confidence. Now she was second-guessing everything.

Screw him; he was on his own. She wasn't his mother. If he'd overslept or broken down on his way to the airport, or whatever had happened, it was his problem. She was here on time, dammit.

"Hey, Woerner," Adam said, elbowing his way through the crowd beside her at exactly one minute to boarding. He was wearing faded jeans and a soft chambray shirt that made Olivia feel overdressed in her stretchy dress pants and blouse.

"Hey." She tried to offer him a smile, but it came out thin. "I was starting to wonder if you were going to make it." Dammit, now she sounded passive aggressive.

He shrugged as he glanced around the terminal. "They never start boarding on time." His eyes landed on her with a smug glint. "Let me guess: you got here seven hours ago, just to be safe."

"No." Only two, which was the amount recommended on the airport website. Seven hours was crazy. The earliest she'd ever arrived for a flight was four hours in advance—but in her defense it was an international flight at Christmastime.

"I wasn't going to miss the plane, if that's what you were nervous about."

"I wasn't nervous," Olivia lied, feeling her irritation rise.

He nodded like he didn't believe her. "I made it in plenty of time, so all that negative energy you expended fretting about it was wasted."

"I said I wasn't nervous."

"But you were though. I can see it on your face."

"You don't know anything about my face. Maybe I'm just annoyed about spending an entire week in your company."

Was that amusement that she detected in his expression? It couldn't be, because Adam didn't smile, *ever*, and he certainly wouldn't be smiling at *her*.

His eyes fell on her large black purse. "Are you sure that bag's going to fit under the seat in front of you?"

"Yes."

"It's practically bursting at the seams. What the hell's in there?"

"Just some essentials." Olivia's fingers tightened around the shoulder strap as she stared at the gate agent, telepathically willing her to start the boarding process. What she wouldn't give for Professor Xavier's mind control powers right now. She could get on the plane *and* make Adam stop talking. Forever.

"What kind of essentials?" Adam leaned closer like he was trying to look inside her bag.

"Essentials," she repeated through gritted teeth as she shifted her purse to her other shoulder, away from his nosy peeping. Why was he so interested in her goddamn purse, anyway? Why was he talking to her at all when he didn't have to? He never talked this much at work. "Just basic stuff like my laptop, phone charger, a bottle of water, some snacks for the plane, my knitting—"

His eyebrows shot up. "I'm sorry, your what?"

"Knitting."

"Are you an eighty-year-old grandmother?" That was definitely amusement on his face now—at her expense—and it made her teeth clench.

"Plenty of young people knit. It's a very popular hobby. Uma Thurman knits."

"Uma Thurman is old enough to be a grandmother. She may actually be a grandmother."

"She's not even fifty. Anyway, Demi Lovato knits. So does Cara Delevingne. Plenty of men knit too. Ryan Gosling knits, did you know that?"

Adam put his hands up in an exaggerated gesture of surrender. "Okay. Forget I said anything."

If only that were possible.

They'd been in each other's company for all of five minutes, and she was already exhausted. How was she going to survive an entire week of this? Interacting with Adam was burning through all her energy reserves.

"I notice they're not boarding yet," he pointed out in a self-congratulatory tone.

Christ on a Cheez-It, how had she ever found this smug asshole attractive? "Do you always have to be right about everything?" Olivia asked wearily.

"Do you?"

"Only when I am right."

He gazed at her, the corner of his mouth curving in what was definitely almost a smile. "Funny, I always thought you were nicer."

"I *am* nice."

"I'm not complaining. I like you better when you're not trying so hard to be nice."

She looked away, flustered that he'd sussed out her secret—that the sunny, friendly demeanor she adopted at work was just an act. Underneath it she was snarky and cynical and not nearly as nice as she pretended to be.

Adam glanced over at the gate, but when he saw that boarding still wasn't imminent, he returned his focus to Olivia. "Seriously though, why do you carry so much stuff with you?"

"In case I need it."

"Doesn't it get old, dragging that heavy bag everywhere you go? I've seen you lugging that thing around the office. I'm surprised you haven't developed a shoulder impingement."

"It's not that heavy. And I like to be prepared."

"For what?"

"Emergencies."

He raised an eyebrow. "What kind of emergencies do you expect to happen around the office?"

"That's the thing about emergencies: you never expect them. And then *boom*, you spill marinara on your shirt and wish you had a Shout wipe. Or the button pops off your pants and you need to sew it back on."

"So not really emergencies so much as minor inconveniences."

"Well, yeah, I'm not some crazy end-of-the-world prepper carrying around iodine tablets and gas masks."

"So you're just an over-planner, is what you're saying."

She felt her face redden, not from embarrassment, but irritation—not that anyone would be able to tell the difference by looking at her pink cheeks. "I don't think I'm an *over*-planner. I take an appropriate amount of precautions."

"I have literally never needed a sewing kit at the office in my life. It would be a ridiculous waste of energy to carry one around every day for years on the infinitesimal chance I might one day need one."

Honest to Christ, did this tool belt ever let up? The urge to punch him square in the dick was growing exponentially with every second she spent in his company.

"Well, I actually have needed a sewing kit," she replied, struggling to keep her voice level, "and I was glad I had it. And other people have needed one and I was glad to be able to offer one to them as well."

"So you're carrying this stuff around for other people who can't be bothered to carry it themselves?"

"No, I'm carrying it for myself. But it's nice to be able to help people occasionally."

"I think people should fend for themselves. If they don't care enough to carry something, you shouldn't be carrying it for them."

"If that's how you feel, don't come crying to me when we get stuck on the tarmac for hours with no food or water."

"That won't be a problem because I'm in first class, so I'll be served regardless."

"How did you swing that?" She knew for a fact the company would only pay for C-levels to fly first class on domestic flights.

She knew this because she'd reviewed the company policy thoroughly before booking her own travel.

"I upgraded with my miles."

Right. Of course he had. He spent almost half his time in the field, so he probably had millions of miles racked up. In fact, he probably had so many extra miles that he could have upgraded her too without even missing them.

The thought of him stretching out in first class, enjoying hot towels and a three-course meal while she was crammed into coach eating granola bars out of her purse, made Olivia unreasonably resentful. But she was also relieved to know there'd be a curtain between them for the next three hours. At least it would give her a brief respite from his sparkling conversation before they were stuck with each other for the entire rest of the week.

"Speaking of being in first class," Adam said. "I'd better go line up with the other one percent."

"What's your hurry? They never board on time, right?"

The gate agent was conferring with another gate agent now, and neither of them looked like they were about to start boarding.

Adam smirked. "Don't tell me you're going to miss my company, Woerner. We'll have plenty of quality time together over the next five days." They were staying through Sunday, so they could keep an eye on things after the changeover, just in case there were any problems.

"Be still my heart," Olivia muttered under her breath.

He lifted an eyebrow. "What was that?"

She was saved the trouble of answering by the announcement that their airplane was having mechanical issues and there would be a two-hour delay while they brought in a replacement.

"Two hours?" Adam said irritably as everyone around them let out a collective groan. "Where are they bringing the new plane from? Mars?"

Olivia's shoulders sagged in despair. "You know if they say two hours, it'll probably be more like three or four."

The crowd around the gate began to dissipate as their fellow travelers staked out seats or headed for one of the terminal's several bars and restaurants to pass the delay. Olivia gazed longingly toward a nearby Chili's, wondering if it was too early in the morning for a margarita, but Adam made a beeline for a pair of seats by the gate. She trailed behind him disconsolately.

"This is not good." He parked his roller suitcase in front of an empty chair, but didn't sit down, choosing instead to pace out his frustration. "We can't afford to waste half the day sitting around an airport."

Olivia sank into a chair and glared up at him. "If the time frame's that tight, why did you say we could do it?"

"Because it's totally possible, as long as nothing goes wrong."

"But something always goes wrong. Usually multiple somethings. You have to leave a buffer for unexpected problems to crop up."

He shook his head, still pacing. "It'll be fine, as long as we get started at the plant today. There's got to be another flight we can get on." He was already swiping through his phone to call the airline.

"To Austin?" she said. "Not likely."

It wasn't a major hub, and there was a lot of business traffic back and forth to LA, so any flights between the two cities had almost certainly been booked to capacity.

"I've got to try. It's better than sitting around doing nothing." He walked a few steps away as he put the phone to his ear. "You should call too," he threw over his shoulder at her. "Maybe you'll get through to someone before me."

Grudgingly, Olivia took out her phone and pulled up the number for the airline. While she waited on hold for an agent, she dug through her purse for a granola bar. She'd almost finished it by the time Adam got an airline representative on the phone. She could hear him talking in a clipped, irritable tone. After a minute of back and forth, he was put on hold again.

Olivia got out her earbuds and switched her phone to hands-free so she could knit while she waited on hold. She was knitting a shawl for Penny's birthday, which had seemed like a good idea at the time, but it meant she couldn't work on it around Penny unless she wanted to ruin the surprise. She was hoping to get a lot done on it during this trip—or a least during the travel legs of the trip. Once they actually got to the plant there wouldn't be a lot of down time.

As she knitted and waited on hold, Adam's representative came back on the line. Olivia could only hear his side of the conversation, but it didn't sound like it was going well. He grew increasingly terse, eventually hanging up with a muttered, "Thanks for nothing."

"That seemed to go well," Olivia commented without looking up from her knitting.

"Really? Because I didn't think it went well at all." His refusal to acknowledge sarcasm was one of the less appealing aspects of his personality.

"No luck, then?"

"We're stuck. The guy claimed the earliest flight he could get us on doesn't leave until four o'clock." He shoved his phone into the front pocket of his jeans, exposing a patch of flat stomach when he flipped up the hem of his shirt.

Olivia tried not to look, she really did, but he was flashing his torso right at her eye level, and even though her eyes remained on her knitting, she couldn't help catching a tantalizing glimpse of brown skin in her peripheral vision.

No, not tantalizing. She didn't like him anymore. His sexy muscled stomach wasn't the slightest bit tantalizing.

"You might as well hang up," Adam said. "They're just going to tell you the same thing."

Olivia was about to tell him that she still intended to try, thank you very much, when she finally got a representative on the line. Putting on her sweetest voice and letting a little of her native

Texas drawl seep through, she very politely explained their problem, addressing the customer service agent—who'd introduced himself as Lamar—by name and asking if there was anything at all he could do to help her out. After a few minutes of investigation, Lamar regretfully confirmed that there were no earlier flights to Austin he could get them on.

"What about a flight to Houston?" Olivia asked, and Adam's head snapped around.

"Now that, I might be able to swing," Lamar replied, and put her on hold again.

"Houston?" Adam said, frowning. "How far is that from Fayette County?"

"Maybe an hour or two farther than Austin, depending on the traffic getting out of the city. And Houston's a hub, so hopefully there'll be more flights going there."

Lamar came back on the line a few minutes later, and triumphantly reported that he could get them on a flight to Houston that was due to start boarding in just over an hour.

It was a tossup whether that would actually get them there faster than their current flight. If the new plane actually arrived when it was supposed to, it would be a wash. But if the new plane took longer than expected—and when didn't something like that take longer than expected?—it would save them time.

"Do it," Adam said, pulling out his phone again. "I'll call and change our rental car reservation."

"Do you want these two seats together?" Lamar asked.

"No," Olivia told him. "Definitely not."

Chapter Four

Once their amended travel plans had been secured, they grabbed their roller bags and set out for their new departure gate, which was at the opposite end of the terminal.

Olivia was feeling a bit smug about saving the day—not that Adam had acknowledged her victory in any way. A *thank you* might be nice, or a *good job,* but apparently that was too much to expect from Mr. Rock Star.

It felt like a just punishment that he would now be seated in steerage with the rest of the commoners instead of enjoying the luxury of first class. So much for all those miles he'd accumulated. He could eat off the snack tray and wait for the beverage cart to make its slow way down the aisle like a regular human for a change.

On the way to the gate, Olivia made Adam wait with her suitcase while she stopped off at the bathroom. His annoyed impatience at being asked to wait inspired her to take her sweet time about it. She washed her hands, refastened her hair into a fresh bun, and touched up her dark red lipstick—a shade appropriately named "Vendetta"—smiling to herself as she imagined his spittle-flecked rage.

"Thank you," she offered with an over-friendly smile when she finally emerged from the ladies' room, and Adam grunted irritably in response.

There were no free chairs at their new gate. In fact, there were no free chairs at any of the gates at that end of the terminal. The remains of a tropical depression that had come ashore in Louisiana seemed to be causing delays across a lot of the southern United States.

"I hope the bad weather doesn't affect us," Olivia said as she looked at all the travelers filling the terminal and camped on the floor along the walls.

"It'll be fine," Adam said, pointing at the monitor. "Our flight's still on time."

She bit down on the urge to knock on wood to ward off the bad luck his overconfidence might bring down on them. There didn't appear to be a single molecule of wood anywhere in the airport, so they were on their own with any malevolent spirits that might be eavesdropping.

They still had three-quarters of an hour left to wait, so they wandered around until they found an empty spot on the floor in front of a large picture window overlooking the tarmac. Olivia sat down in the narrow gap between a couple with a toddler and a group of college-aged kids. There was room for Adam to squeeze in next to her, but he chose instead to sit cross-legged in front of her with his back to the crowded gate area.

"This is fun," she said, leaning back against the glass and pulling her knees up to her chest. The toddler beside them waved a toy car at her, and she waved back.

Adam's lip curled in distaste as he looked around him. "You think this is fun?"

"Come on, who doesn't love sitting on dirty public carpets? I know I do. It's my favorite thing ever to do in dress pants."

His eyes narrowed at her. "You should have worn jeans."

"I was trying to make a good impression."

"On who?"

"I haven't got any idea," she admitted. "Definitely not you."

His gaze traveled from her short-sleeved white blouse to her sensible black dress loafers. He frowned slightly, as if he didn't like what he saw. "Did you bring any long-sleeved shirts? They're required at the plant. And boots, preferably steel-toed."

"Hey, you think that's something you might have mentioned before we were at the airport?" she shot back. He'd done this dozens of times before and knew it was her first time, yet hadn't thought to offer her even the most basic advice ahead of time.

He glanced away. "I didn't think of it."

"Clearly."

"Did you? Bring clothes to wear to the plant?"

"Yes, as a matter of fact. I asked Gavin about it."

"Good." Adam was still frowning. Actually, it was more like a scowl. He kept glancing around him too, and shifting position like he couldn't stay still. She'd never known him to look this obviously uncomfortable before.

The toddler next to them threw her toy car, and when it bounced off Adam's thigh he flinched like he'd been struck with a brick instead of a tiny piece of plastic.

"I'm so sorry," the child's mother said as she leaned over to retrieve the toy.

The smile Adam offered her in response was as taut as a bowstring. "Don't worry about it."

"What's wrong with you?" Olivia asked him. "You're acting weird."

"I don't like crowds."

"This is nothing. You should try going to Comic-Con. One hundred thirty thousand people squeezed into a city block for four days."

His scowl deepened. "That sounds like my worst nightmare."

"It's an adventure, that's for sure."

The toddler let out a high-pitched wail and threw herself to the floor. Apparently her parents had confiscated the offending toy. As her cries grew in volume and intensity, Adam's expression grew more pained.

"We're so sorry," the toddler's father said as he attempted to quiet the screaming child. "She's way past her nap time."

"It's fine," Olivia told him. "We're all pretty cranky."

"I'm going to get some food," Adam said, pushing himself to his feet.

"Bring me back something," Olivia called after him, and he raised his hand in acknowledgement. "Since you didn't ask," she muttered at his retreating back.

When Adam returned ten minutes later with a fast food bag and a soft drink, the toddler had fallen asleep in her dad's lap, and Olivia had managed to knit two more rows of Penny's shawl.

"What'd you bring me?" she asked as Adam sat back down in front of her.

"Here." He reached into the bag and withdrew a much smaller bag that he handed to her.

She set down her knitting and stared at the smiling cartoon robot on the outside of the bag. "A kid's meal? You got me a kid's meal?"

"You're tiny," he said with a shrug as he unwrapped a juicy double-cheeseburger. "I thought a regular-sized meal would be too much."

"Thanks," she gritted out.

He crammed a huge bite of delicious-looking burger into his mouth. "You're welcome."

"Where's my drink?"

"There's milk in the bag."

She blinked at him in disbelief. "Milk? Am I five?"

"Did you know that between the ages of twenty and eighty, women lose one-third of their bone mineral density?"

"So you were just looking out for my bone health, is that it? And not being a cheapskate?"

He ignored her. "Our flight's still on time, according to the board. Thirty minutes to boarding." He had a habit of changing the subject when he didn't like the way the conversation was going.

"Let's hope it stays that way," she said, unwrapping her tiny hamburger. It was barely larger than a makeup compact, and she polished off the whole thing in three bites. There was also a tiny bag containing twelve whole french fries, and underneath that— "Oh! A toy!" she exclaimed in genuine delight.

It was a tiny wind-up robot. According to the bag her kid's meal came in, there were five different robots you could collect, each with a slightly different expression on its molded plastic face. Hers looked vaguely grumpy and disapproving.

"I'm going to name it Adam," she declared, setting it on the floor after she'd twisted the little lever in his back. "Because he's so much fun to wind up."

"Har har," Adam said sourly.

Tiny Adam toddled across the floor until he ran into Big Adam's leg and fell over onto his back. Olivia snickered as his legs kicked helplessly in the air like an overturned turtle. "He's so cute! I love him."

She reached over to rescue Tiny Adam from the floor, and the back of her hand brushed against Big Adam's knee. An unexpected shiver traveled up her arm at the contact, and she jerked her hand away.

"You know," Adam said as she wound the robot for another go, "I could make a comment about how much you seem to enjoy twisting my crank, but that would be inappropriate on a business trip with a coworker."

"You're right, that would be inappropriate." She set Tiny Adam on the floor again, and he marched off across the carpet. "I could also make a comment about how cute your teensy weensy little lever is, but that would also be inappropriate."

When she lifted her eyes to Adam's, she was surprised to find him smiling. She wasn't sure she'd ever seen a genuine smile on his face before. He only ever seemed to offer a distracted sort of half-smile around the office—and only when it was absolutely required to satisfy the minimum demands of politeness. This smile looked sincere and spontaneous, and for one shining moment, it relaxed all the muscles of his face, giving his handsome, Instagram-perfect visage an even more appealing, boyish gleam.

Adam seemed almost as surprised by it as she was, and he quickly steeled his expression again as he reached out to save Tiny Adam, who'd keeled over after a collision with his shoe.

"Here." He extended his arm and placed the toy robot in Olivia's hand.

Another shiver went up her arm as his fingers brushed her palm.

Stop it. You do not like Adam Cortinas. Not anymore.

"So you've been to Comic-Con?" he said, and for once Olivia was grateful for his subject-changing tactics.

She nodded as she tucked Tiny Adam into her purse for safekeeping. He would definitely be getting a place of honor on her desk next week when she got back to the office. "I go every year."

"Why?"

"Because I like it. I usually go to Dragon-Con too, although I couldn't last year because my sister got married over Labor Day."

"What do you like about it?"

She considered him for a moment before answering. In her experience, people who questioned her about her con-going fell into one of two camps: either they knew nothing about it and thought it made her a weirdo loser, or they were self-appointed gatekeepers challenging her nerd cred. She couldn't even count the number of times she'd been quizzed on her knowledge of geek trivia by some guy who couldn't handle the fact that a woman might genuinely share some of the same pop culture interests.

If she had to lay money on it, she'd bet Adam fell into the

former camp. He seemed way too good-looking—and too boring—to be a nerd.

She braced herself for the inevitable judgment and disdain. "I like looking at all the booths and the presentations for upcoming movies and TV shows. And some of the smaller panels are really good, like with comic artists and writers. Plus, I'm a cosplayer, so I get to show off my latest costume creation."

He paused with a fry halfway to his mouth. "*You* dress up in costume?"

And there it was.

He was staring at her like she'd suddenly sprouted a second set of eyebrows, and she helped herself to one of his fries as a reward for pegging him accurately. "Yes."

Instead of objecting to her fry theft, he pushed them closer to her. "And you walk around in public like that?" He sounded more surprised than anything. She assumed the judgment would come after he'd gotten over the shock.

"Not like all the time or anything. I only do it at cons, when I'm surrounded by other people in costume too. That's sort of the point of going, to be around people who share your interests."

"What kind of costumes do you wear?" The way his eyes traveled up and down her body, she could only assume he was trying to imagine her in some sort of super skimpy, sexy outfit.

She pointed a fry at him accusingly. "Not the sort you're thinking of, gutter brain."

"How do you know what I'm thinking?"

"Because you've got that same lecherous look all guys get when they hear I'm a cosplayer and their dirty minds immediately start picturing a slave Leia gold bikini."

"I was actually thinking more along the lines of chain mail and swords. Or maybe Daenerys Targaryen. You could pull that off without a wig."

Okay, fine, so he watched *Game of Thrones*. So did everyone with HBO. It didn't make him a geek. "Everybody does Daenerys," she said. "I like to be a little more creative. My specialty is mashups and twists on existing characters."

"Like what?" He seemed genuinely interested rather than scornful.

"A few years ago I went as a female Fourth Doctor from *Doctor Who*—before there actually was a female Doctor."

"That's the one with the scarf, right?"

"Yeah," she said, impressed that he knew which Doctor wore the scarf. Could it be—was Adam Cortinas actually a nerd?

Dammit, that was going to make it harder to hate him.

He nodded at the knitting she'd set aside. "Did you knit the scarf yourself?"

She grimaced at the memory. "I did. It was my very first knitting project. Damned thing took me forever."

"I feel like most people would start out with a pot holder or something simple."

"Not me. I started with a twenty-five-foot scarf. I do not recommend it."

It was so strange to be talking to him like this. To have him actually seem interested in what she had to say. Usually, when she talked to him, his face was a mask of boredom and impatience. Like he was waiting for her to finish and go away again.

"What other costumes have you made?"

She described her steampunk Miss Marple costume from last year, and the post-apocalyptic Ruth Bader Ginsberg costume she'd made the year before that, and he seemed almost—impressed? Was that possible?

"So you sew all the clothes and everything yourself from scratch?" He peeled the lid off his soft drink and tipped some ice into his mouth.

"Mostly." She dug through her purse for a napkin, because he hadn't brought any with their food. "If I can repurpose an existing garment I will, but usually it's easier to just make it myself."

"What are you wearing this year?"

"It's a mashup of Rosie the Riveter and Ash from *Evil Dead*." She'd been working on it for three months, which was why she was so behind on Penny's birthday present.

"Holy shit," Adam said. "That's really cool."

Olivia had always been a glutton for praise. Growing up as the unexceptional middle child between two overachievers had left her a little recognition-starved, so she couldn't help glowing at Adam's approval.

She reached for her knitting in an attempt to hide the color in her cheeks, unable to believe he'd just paid her a compliment—on her super nerdy hobby, no less. Who was this guy and what had he done with the Adam Cortinas she knew and disliked?

"You done?" he asked, waving at what was left of his fries.

She nodded, and he gathered up their trash and carried it to the nearest garbage can. "Scoot over," he said when he came back.

Olivia shifted to make room for him, and he squeezed in next to her, leaning his back against the window as he stretched his legs out in front of him. He had long legs, almost a foot longer than hers, and thick, muscular thighs that pulled the denim of his jeans taut.

One of his muscular thighs was touching her leg. His hip was pressed against her too, and his arm, and his shoulder. He'd left as much space as possible between him and the woman next to him, choosing to cozy up against Olivia rather than a random stranger.

She wasn't sure if she should be flattered, but she was definitely having a hard time concentrating on her knitting with Adam's body heat soaking into her and his shirt rubbing against the bare skin of her arm.

He'd pulled out his phone to read his texts, and she couldn't help peeking at it. He seemed to get a lot of texts from women. In addition to the work names she recognized, he had texts from a Michelle, and a Vanessa, and also an Angela. He opened the most recent text from Angela, which was an invitation to dinner on

Friday, and replied to let her know he'd be out of town but maybe they could do it next weekend.

"See anything interesting?" he asked, shooting Olivia a sideways glance as he typed.

"Sorry," she said. "It's hard not to look when you're holding your phone right in front of me like that. Who's Angela?"

"My sister."

"Ah."

"Why? Did you think she was my girlfriend?"

"I didn't think anything."

She was in no way relieved to find out that Angela was his sister, because she had no interest whatsoever in Adam's love life, aside from whatever mild entertainment it might provide while they killed time at the airport. This weird feeling she was having was merely relief that she hadn't accidentally read anything too personal.

Yeah, sure.

"Should we talk about our plan for when we get to the plant?" Olivia asked, adopting Adam's tactic of changing the subject.

He shoved his phone back in his pocket, which in the tight space required him to do a sort of twisting hip thrust that resulted in his head basically resting on her shoulder for a second. She tried not to react as his hair brushed her neck and her senses filled with the heavenly scent of his hair product. It was spicy and masculine, with a hint of cedar—or was it sandalwood? Whatever it was, it made her mouth puddle with drool.

"What plan?" His breath puffed warmly on her shoulder before he straightened. "We get there, we assess the situation, and we deal with whatever we find."

She cleared her throat as she tried to suppress a shiver. "Do you know how much network bandwidth is available at the site?"

"Nope."

"Do we have all the cabling we'll need to connect the RTUs?"

"I had everything drop-shipped yesterday."

"What if we get there and find out their equipment is so old it won't integrate with our systems?"

"Like I said, we'll figure it out when we get there. There's no point worrying about it now, when we can't do anything about it." He leaned his head back against the window and closed his eyes. "You need to relax."

Olivia ground her molars together. She didn't like being told to relax. Not only was it patronizing and presumptuous, but it wasn't like she was equipped with a magical Zen switch she could flip to turn off all her worries and chill out. She'd relax when she damn well had a reason to relax, and not because someone said she should.

How the hell was Adam so relaxed under the circumstances? His discomfort at the crowded airport seemed to have dissipated, along with his momentary stress over their delayed travel plans. How did he do that? Just let things go, and embrace the unknown future without a care?

Olivia couldn't help feeling a little envious. It was exhausting always thinking ahead and trying to prepare for every outcome and surprise that might lie around the corner. Why did people like him get to relax while she was putting in all the advance work to help things run smoothly?

He was so relaxed, in fact, that he might actually have dropped off to sleep—sitting on the floor of a crowded airport, with only fifteen minutes until their boarding time.

How was that even possible? He'd been talking just a minute ago, and now his breathing had slowed and his shoulders were sagging and his lips were slightly parted.

Seriously?

She gave his arm an exploratory nudge and his head snapped up like he'd been jolted with electricity.

"Were you *asleep*?" Olivia asked in amazement.

He rubbed a hand over his face. "Maybe. Why?"

"We should probably go stand by the gate."

"We've still got fifteen minutes, and we're in the last boarding group."

"Which means most of the overhead bins will be full by the time we get on board. We need to be the first in our boarding group if we want any chance of stowing our bags."

"We can always just gate check."

"It takes forever to get your bags when you gate check, and we've already lost enough time today, don't you think?"

"Fine." He pushed himself begrudgingly to his feet and held out a hand to help her off the floor.

She accepted his hand as begrudgingly as he'd stood up, levering herself upright and letting go of him as quickly as possible—but not so quickly she failed to appreciate the rough warmth of his skin.

They started toward their gate, but when they passed a restroom she stopped and shoved her roller bag at him. "I want to use the bathroom one more time before we board."

His mouth pursed in irritation. "You know they have bathrooms on the plane, right?"

"I hate using airplane bathrooms. They're tiny, and between the people with bad aim and the periodic turbulence, I'm pretty sure every single surface has been spattered with urine. It'd be one thing if I didn't have to sit down—"

"Okay, Jesus. Just go." He took her roller bag and moved over against the wall to wait out of the way.

If he wasn't so annoyed by it, she wouldn't enjoy making him wait half so much. She was almost tempted to make him wait again while she stopped off to buy more airplane snacks, but since she could already see people lining up at the gate, she decided to forgo further Adam tormenting.

They lined up with the other three hundred people flying to Houston with them. Adam began to grow tense again as the impatient crowd filled in behind and around them. His neck muscles stood out taut as bowstrings, and his mouth pressed into a thin line as his eyes flicked around him.

Olivia wasn't uneasy in crowds like Adam clearly was, but she always struggled a bit because of her size. People tended to overlook her and try to usurp her space by using their size advantage to crowd her out of the way. She was used to it though, so she'd learned to defend herself with the tools she had at hand: her big purse, her elbows, and even the judicious application of her shoe heel when necessary.

The large man standing next to her at the gate was doing that thing where he kept bumping into her as he talked to the woman he was traveling with, oblivious both to Olivia standing there and her attempts to make her presence known by nudging him back. She was on the verge of employing her signature move, which involved turning sharply to look at something and "accidentally" letting her heavy purse slam into the offender at full force, when Adam's hand wrapped around her arm.

He shifted her away from the shoving guy and edged over to take her place. Only there wasn't a lot of room to maneuver in the crowd, which meant he basically had to press the front of his body against her back and do a sort of sliding shimmy to get past.

The move clearly wasn't intended to be sexual, but the sensations it inspired in Olivia definitely were. She couldn't help it—he was basically dirty dancing up against her, and she swallowed a lump in her throat as her ass glided across his thighs.

Once he was standing next to the big guy, who wasn't really all that big after all, Adam casually hip-checked him, giving him a dose of his own medicine. The man took a stumbling step away, opening up more space which Adam immediately moved to fill.

Olivia snorted in amusement, and Adam looked pleased with himself. "Better?"

"Yes, thank you. But I could have handled him."

"Okay."

"I'm used to crowds. I can take care of myself."

"I'm sure you can." There was amusement in his voice, but it was the good kind of amusement. Warm amusement. Fond sounding, almost.

But that was impossible, because Adam Cortinas was not fond of her. He didn't even like her enough to give her a simple fucking reference.

Except the way he was looking at her said otherwise. His eyes were soft and flecked with gold at the center that glittered at her like he was pleased. All the tautness she'd noticed a moment ago had melted away, and his head was tilted slightly to one side. As he continued to gaze at her, he bit down on his lower lip, and—Jesus jumping Christ on a pogo stick—that sexy lip bite was too fucking much to handle.

"Why aren't they boarding yet?" Olivia wondered, turning away to peer at the gate—which was a futile exercise, given her height and the comparative heights of the people around them, but at least it allowed her to look at something other than Adam's lips.

"They never board on time, remember?"

Her hand squeezed the handle of her roller bag. "I'm just worried this flight is going to be delayed too, and then it'll turn out we would have been better off sticking with the first one."

"It's done now. There's no point second-guessing the decision. Relax."

And just like that, her hackles were up again. "Can you quit telling me to relax?"

"I'm just saying, worrying about problems before they happen won't accomplish anything."

"Actually, worrying about problems before they happen is how you head them off before they become problems."

"It's also how you stress yourself into high blood pressure."

"My blood pressure is fine."

"If you say so."

She opened her mouth to reply, but stopped when a voice came on the PA system to announce pre-boarding for their flight to Houston.

Adam looked smug. "See, they've started boarding. Everything's going to be fine."

"Don't jinx it!" she hissed.

He made a scoffing sound. When she continued to glare at him, he tilted his head at her, narrowing his eyes. "Wait. Are you serious?"

"Yes. You'll bring down the wrath of the whatever with that kind of cockiness."

He looked disconcerted. "You don't actually believe that."

"I believe it's not worth taking the chance."

"I thought you were more rational than that. Aren't you an electrical engineer?"

"An education in science doesn't preclude the belief that there might be forces in the universe outside our understanding. In fact, it's far more rational to accept that we can't know everything and leave yourself open to possibility."

"The realm of the possible is not infinite." He put his hand on her shoulder to edge her out of the path of a passenger in a wheelchair being pushed through the mob of people. The crowd was like a living, breathing thing swelling toward the gate, but Adam stood his ground like a pylon in the surge, making a safe little bubble to shelter her from the pushing and shoving around them. "Whether we understand it or not, there is a mundane, scientific explanation for everything, and it does not involve jinxes, woo-woo, or not stepping on a crack to avoid breaking your mother's back."

Olivia shrugged, enjoying how much her position seemed to bother him. "You live your life your way, and I'll live my way. But keep your fate-tempting to yourself."

"There's no such thing as fate. The universe is ruled by cause and effect."

"Exactly. And by acting too cocky you can bring a bad outcome down on yourself." She wasn't so superstitious that she really believed that—it was more a habit than anything—but it obviously rankled him, and she was having too much fun to let it go.

"That's not cause and effect." His voice rose with his dismay. "You know that, right? Please tell me you know that."

She shifted closer to him as the first general boarding group was called, sending a ripple effect through the crowd. "It could be. You don't know everything about how it works. We're only just barely beginning to understand chaotic complex systems and their sensitivity to initial conditions. For all we know, superstitions are based on an innate understanding of the laws of the universe we've yet to explain scientifically."

She could tell she'd scored a point, because he crossed his arms and glared in the direction of the gate. "In the meantime, I'll stick to believing in things that can be scientifically tested and proven."

"Are you saying you don't have faith in anything but science? There's nothing silly or romantic or fantastical you believe just because it makes you happy to believe it?"

His chin lifted, and he sniffed as if she'd suggested he try adding dog turds to his salad. "I believe in observable, measurable, and repeatable phenomena. Not fantasies and children's stories."

"That's sad."

He looked affronted. "It's not sad."

"It is. The reason humankind invented religion is because it's comforting to believe in something bigger than your own understanding."

His eyes flashed in triumph. "You just admitted that it's all invented." If she didn't know better, she'd think he was enjoying himself.

"So what if it is? That doesn't make it any less powerful."

"It literally does."

"I mean emotionally powerful. Psychologically. Life isn't an experiment, it's an experience. By refusing to believe in anything that can't be measured by empirical evidence, you're closing yourself off to wonder and the comfort of belief."

His eyes moved over her face in surprise, like he was reassessing what he saw there. "I would not have guessed you were this religious."

"I'm not. You don't have to believe in religion. You can put your faith in anything you want, so long as it gives you hope and makes the world a little more wondrous."

"There's more than enough wonder in science." His gaze dropped to her mouth for a second before skating away. "I don't need more than that."

"Everyone needs more wonder in their lives."

"You can really just believe in stuff? Just like that? Things you know aren't real."

Was she crazy or was that a hint of envy she detected in his expression?

"Millions of children believe in Santa," she said. "His image is everywhere you look for two months out of the year, and every Christmas Eve presents appear under the tree from him. So is he real or not?"

"He's not real. Obviously."

"But he is. He might just be a story, but stories have power. He inspires people and brings joy and hope and excitement into children's lives, and that's very real."

"You're saying you believe in Santa Claus?" He was smiling at her now.

"I'm saying he's a force that exerts influence on objects in the universe, so whether or not he's a literal living person who delivers the toys himself is beside the point."

"No, it's not. The aim of science is to accurately describe the world around us, so determining whether he's an actual living organism or simply a folktale that's been co-opted by capitalism as a mascot for the marketing juggernaut of the Christmas season is precisely the point."

She pursed her lips at him. "You're a real buzzkill, you know that?"

His smile turned wry. "So I've been told."

"Santa Claus is real if you believe he's real," she said stubbornly.

"So you do believe in Santa Claus?" There was that warm amusement in his voice again.

"Maybe I do, a little, because it makes me happy to believe he could exist, along with fairies and Bigfoot and narwhals."

"Narwhals *are* real."

"Shut up."

"I'm serious. Did you not know that?"

Her eyes widened. "I thought they were made up like unicorns."

He shook his head, huffing an amused breath. "They're very real."

"I literally thought they were from a Lewis Carroll poem."

"You're thinking of the Jabberwock."

She smiled, impressed he knew which poem she was talking about. "And the frumious Bandersnatch."

"Isn't that the guy who played Dr. Strange?" Adam deadpanned, looking pleased when Olivia laughed. "But see?" He jostled her shoulder with his. "Narwhals exist in the world and you didn't even know. There's still plenty of wonder in science. Leave the make-believe for fiction."

"Make-believe is fun. You should try it sometime." She didn't mean it to sound dirty. Honestly she didn't. But somehow it came out dirty-sounding anyway.

He shook his head at her again, smiling in a way that seemed to shimmer in the air between them. "You're nuts, Woerner."

The disembodied voice over the PA called out their boarding group, and their portion of the crowd surged forward like a herd of starving cattle. Adam rested his hand in the small of her back to fend off any rude, pushy folks who might try to shove her out of the way. Olivia wanted to feel resentful, but somehow she couldn't muster the will to mind.

When she finally showed the gate agent her boarding pass and took her first step onto the jetway, she felt a powerful sense of relief.

They'd made it onto the plane. Maybe things really were going to be fine now.

Not that she'd dare say that out loud.

Chapter Five

"I can get it," Olivia insisted when Adam tried to help hoist her carry-on into the overhead bin.

He let go of her bag and watched while she stood on her tiptoes and gave a little hop, trying to shove the bag into place. "You sure about that?" he asked with that smirky smile that made her blood boil.

She hated that because she was short, she didn't have the leverage to maneuver her bag into the overhead like everyone else. She was strong enough to lift it, she just wasn't tall enough to give it the shove it needed to slide into place. It was always a problem for her when she traveled, but she'd be damned if she'd let Adam think she couldn't do it herself.

With another vigorous hop, she managed to tip the bag into the overhead, and did a fist pump of victory. "Ha! Suck it, overhead compartment!"

"Well done, Woerner." Adam shook his head in amusement as he moved down the aisle toward his seat, which was closer to the back of the plane.

"This is me," Olivia said apologetically to the two people already sitting in her row, and they stood up to let her slide into her window seat. She had no idea how Lamar had managed to get her a window seat at the last minute, but he was a goddamn hero for doing it.

The woman sitting next to her was an older lady who smelled pleasantly of lavender. She smiled at Olivia, but made no move to strike up a conversation, which was perfect. Peace and quiet.

Olivia took out her knitting and crammed her purse under the seat in front of her before settling in to relax and enjoy the flight. It would be nice to have a few hours of solitude. Just her and her knitting and the relaxing white noise of the engines. No one aggravating her or arguing with her or filling her with all these confusing, conflicting feelings.

Sometimes it was hard to remember she disliked Adam. He'd say all these annoying things that pushed her buttons, then turn around and do something considerate or say something that sounded like a compliment. She needed a break from him just to get her head on straight.

"Excuse me," she heard Adam say, and snapped her head around.

He'd tapped the woman next to Olivia on the shoulder. "I don't suppose you'd mind trading with me so I could sit next to my girlfriend? I'm only four rows back." He gifted the woman with a smile that could have melted the Snow Miser's heart. There was more warmth in that smile than Olivia had known Adam was capable of, and it struck something deep in her chest, like a gong that reverberated through her whole body and left her fingertips tingling.

The woman next to her was ensorcelled by it. "Oh! Of course," she tittered. And was she actually blushing? *Good Christ.*

When the man sitting on the aisle unfastened his seat belt to get up and allow them to trade, Olivia started to panic.

"It's okay," she told the woman next to her. "You don't have to move. Really."

"It's no trouble," the woman said as she gathered up her bag.

"I wouldn't want to come between young lovers." She gave Olivia a wink as she slid out of her seat.

Ew.

"Thank you," Adam said, giving the woman's arm a squeeze as she moved past him, and her blush turned a shade deeper.

Double ew.

"Why did you do that?" Olivia hissed as he dropped into the seat beside her.

His face was guileless when he looked at her. "Because I wanted to sit by you."

She didn't know how to take that, so she picked up her knitting and looked at it instead of at him. Except her hands didn't seem to work right. An odd sort of ache had formed in her chest and traveled all the way down to the tips of her fingers, which were tingling with pins and needles and refusing to obey her command to start knitting. It was like she suddenly couldn't remember how. She'd lost the muscle memory and her fingers were stiff and ungainly, like they'd never held needles before. She was forced to settle for counting the stiches in her current row in order to look busy.

Pull it together.

This was just a regular business trip and they were just two regular coworkers. Why should she be uncomfortable sitting next to Adam?

"Are you uncomfortable sitting next to me?" he asked.

Fuck me dead. She was usually better at hiding her feelings. How was Adam seeing so many things she didn't want him to see? More importantly—why was he looking at her at all?

He was *really* looking at her too. Like, so hard it was impossible to pretend otherwise. Those piercing eyes of his were focused on her face like she was a puzzle he was trying to solve.

"I'm not uncomfortable," she said.

"That's a lie."

"How would you know?"

"Because it's obvious. Your kinesics are an open book."

"My what?"

"Body language. Your cheek is twitching, you keep reaching up to touch the suprasternal notch at the base of your throat, and that's the third time you've tried to count that row of stitches and had to start over."

Maybe she'd never been good at hiding her feelings. Maybe she'd only thought she was good at it because most people didn't look at her closely. When they looked at her at all, they only tended to see what was on the surface. But not Adam, for some reason. It was unsettling how much he saw.

Olivia's fingers tightened on her knitting needles. "I'm uncomfortable because I'm squeezed into a tiny seat in a flying tin can that smells like portable toilets and fast food farts, okay?"

"That's not it," he said. "I mean, it does smell like farts in here, but that's not why you're uncomfortable."

"You don't know as much about me as you think you do."

Except he did. Somehow, he seemed to know *everything* about her, just by looking at her.

He really needed to stop looking at her, or he'd figure out the secret she didn't want him to know: that she'd *liked* him, and he'd crushed more than just her ego last week. He'd crushed her heart as well.

"Why won't you just admit it?" he persisted.

"Because it's not true. Can you drop it, please?"

"Fine." He faced forward and fastened his seat belt.

They'd started preparing for takeoff, thank god. The sooner they got off the ground, the sooner Olivia would be released from this metal prison. They were only a few hours into this cursed trip, and she already felt like one of the characters in *No Exit*, condemned to spend eternity being tortured by her companion in the afterlife. *Hell is other people*, indeed.

As they taxied to the runway, she couldn't help noticing that Adam was staring straight ahead. He wasn't reading his phone or a tablet like nearly everyone else on the plane. He wasn't doing anything.

Who did that? Just sat there staring at nothing instead of reading?

His hands were clenched on the armrests, and she wondered if maybe he was a bad flyer as well as being uncomfortable in crowds. He better not get airsick on her. She snuck a glance at his face. His color looked okay, but he seemed tense, like he was bracing himself for something terrible.

"You all right?" she asked. "You're not scared of flying, are you?"

He shook his head slightly. "I just don't like takeoffs and landings. I'll be fine once we get in the air."

"Okay." She went back to her knitting. But as the plane picked up speed in preparation for takeoff, she threw another glance his way, just to make sure he wasn't going to ralph. He still had the same look of determined resignation, so she figured she was probably safe.

To be honest, she wasn't a huge fan of takeoffs and landings either. The g-force was unpleasant, and the bumpiness made it impossible to focus on anything without triggering a headache. She laid her knitting in her lap and closed her eyes as the wheels left the ground and the plane hurtled itself into the sky.

The sensation was an odd mix of exhilarating and terrifying with a side order of uncomfortable jouncing and jolting. Sort of like riding a rollercoaster, but without the spectacular views and the feel of the wind in your face.

Adam probably didn't like rollercoasters any more than he liked flying.

Gradually, the plane leveled off and the unpleasant sensation passed. Adam seemed to relax as they gained altitude, his fingers uncurling from the armrest and his shoulders loosening, until it was like he'd never been tense at all.

Olivia picked up her knitting again, and by the time the flight attendants began moving around the cabin, Adam was so chill she could almost believe she'd imagined the whole thing. He'd never been nervous at all. What a ridiculous idea, that someone as cool and confident as Adam could be afraid of flying.

And yet, she remembered it. It had happened.

Now that he wasn't a ball of tension anymore, his broad shoulders had spread out, bleeding over the invisible barrier into her seat. The top of his arm was pressed against the top of her arm, and her skin felt warm where it touched him through his shirt. His warmth sank into her and traveled straight to her chest. It made her body feel tense but also somehow like syrup. Viscous and slow-moving. Warm, oozing, and entirely too sweet.

And now she could feel his eyes on her again. He was looking at her in that too-perceptive way he had. It was almost like a physical touch. Like a finger stroking over her cheek. It was practically a caress. The tiny hairs on the surface of her skin were bristling where his eyes bored into her, and she was too hot inside her shirt. Her bra felt like it was strangling her, like the straps were too tight, abrading her skin and digging into it all at once.

The tension was unbearable. He was about to say something. She could feel it building in the air between them. And whatever it was, she was certain she wasn't going to like it.

"What are you thinking about?" he asked.

"Nothing." The word came out too quickly and too loud. Instead of easy, breezy and nonchalant like she'd intended, she sounded defensive.

"Why is your first instinct always to lie?"

"It's not." More defensiveness. Why was she always so defensive around him? She didn't think of herself as a defensive person in general. But something about him made her dig in and start fortifying her walls.

"You were thinking about *something*. People are always thinking about something. So it's a lie to say you're thinking about nothing."

The knitting needles clacked as she channeled her irritation into them. "Maybe it's none of your business what I'm thinking about."

"So why not say that instead of lying?"

"Because it's rude." She recited the shawl pattern in her head like a meditation mantra as her fingers formed the stitches. *Knit three, knit two together, yarn over.*

"Lying's rude too. Do you think it was rude of me to ask what you were thinking?"

"Maybe a little." *Knit three, knit two together, yarn over.*

"You really can't stop equivocating, can you?"

"Yes, it was rude to ask me that," she snapped, and the man sitting on the other side of Adam glanced their way.

"So if I started the rudeness, you should be able to be rude back."

"The world doesn't work that way." Olivia reached up and raised the window shade. The view outside was an icebox gray haze. Too bad she wasn't in an exit row, so she could hurl herself into oblivion.

"Sure it does," Adam insisted.

"No, it doesn't." She couldn't believe she had to explain this to him. But then look who she was talking to. No one would ever dare be rude to Adam Cortinas—or point out his own rudeness. They were too busy throwing roses at his feet. "If everyone escalated every time they were annoyed or inconvenienced by someone else's behavior, no one would ever get anything done and society would break down. The world works because people compromise and forgive. The ones who don't are the gremlins in the machinery, they just don't realize it because they're only thinking of themselves."

"So according to you, we should all just let people take advantage and walk all over us for the sake of compromise and pretending to get along."

Olivia unclenched her jaw and blew out a breath. *Knit three, knit two together, yarn over.* "Not always. Just sometimes. When it benefits everyone."

"Like when one of the traders wants a generator configuration that you know won't work, and you don't say anything because you don't want to rock the boat? Is that the kind of compromise that benefits everyone? Or is that just you being afraid to stand up to the trade desk?"

His words struck her like an electric shock, bringing belated realization. She turned on him with an accusing look. "Is *that* why you wouldn't give me a reference? Because of Tulelake?"

"That mistake cost the company hundreds of thousands of dollars."

"You think I didn't try to warn them?"

"You should have tried harder. You should have taken a stand."

"Yeah, like Cassandra."

His forehead scrunched in confusion. "Cassandra in accounting?"

"Cassandra from *The Odyssey* who was cursed to utter prophecies no one believed."

"I'm familiar with the mythology, but—"

"You heard me in that meeting with Gavin and Brad, and how much good it did when I raised my concerns about the timeline for this integration. I was immediately overruled in favor of you. That's what it's like being a woman in business, every day. Being talked over and ignored, having your mistakes put under a microscope while your ideas and accomplishments are credited to someone else."

"I'm not saying sexism in the workplace doesn't exist—"

"Gee, thanks for not denying my lived experience." Her voice had risen again, and the man beside Adam looked like he was regretting his seatmates.

Adam, on the other hand, actually seemed to be enjoying himself. His eyes were bright and he had a self-satisfied look that made Olivia's molars grind together. "I'm just saying nothing will ever change if you don't stand up for yourself. You need to be more assertive, not less."

"Don't feed me that *Lean In* bullshit," she spat. "It's not that simple to be more assertive when you're a woman. Maybe *you* can get away with acting like a jerk, but if I tried that crap I'd be labeled a 'problem' and suffer repercussions."

"I didn't say it was simple, just that it was something you need to do. You can't just give up and go along to get along."

"Why not? Why can't I do that?" Her stupid window seat was making her feel trapped. Her only means of escape from this conversation was to climb over Adam's and a complete stranger's legs.

"Because it's wrong. It perpetuates a broken system and allows incompetence to rise to the top."

"I didn't break the system," she said through clenched teeth. "Why should I have to take all the risks to fix it?" Her jaw was aching from all the clenching.

"Because you actually care about doing a good job."

"Stop acting like you know me. You don't know anything about me or what I care about." She unsnapped her seat belt and stood, setting her knitting on her seat. "I need to use the bathroom. Get up."

Adam and his neighbor stepped out into the aisle, and Olivia made her way to the bathroom at the back of the plane. She really did hate airplane bathrooms, but she needed some space and some quiet. Just for a minute. She needed to breathe in an Adam-free zone—even if it was gross toilet air.

She glared at her bright pink cheeks in the water-spotted bathroom mirror. It was the curse of her complexion. Even the slightest rush of blood to her face announced itself like a flashing neon sign. No wonder Adam thought she was an open book.

Her cheeks went even redder at the thought of Adam reading her so easily. Or was it the mere thought of Adam that made her face hot? Of Adam looking at her and really seeing her—which was what she'd wanted for so long.

But no more. She didn't want Adam's attention.

Did she?

Ugh. How could she be simultaneously so attracted to *and* so infuriated by someone? It boggled reason.

Her only hope of getting through this week with any sort of dignity whatsoever was to convince him all her red-faced blushing was anger rather than...all the other things he made her feel. Unwelcome, inappropriate things. Things she absolutely did not want to be feeling about Adam Cortinas.

She could do this. She had excellent social skills. She was a calm, collected person, capable of having benign conversations with a coworker. He didn't need to know there was anything extraordinary about their interactions—or her reactions to them. She could pretend to be cool and normal.

She'd have to, if she was going to survive the next five days.

When Olivia finally went back to her seat, she found Adam examining her knitting. "Don't touch that!" she exclaimed in alarm.

He withdrew the hand that was caressing a corner of Penny's shawl and moved so Olivia could get back to her seat. "I was just looking."

She directed an apologetic look at the gentleman in the aisle seat as she stepped past him. "You were touching," she said to Adam. "If you hold it wrong, the stitches will drop off the needles."

"I wasn't holding it. I was just poking it."

"Don't do that either." She cradled the half-knit shawl like a newborn baby and sat back down in her seat.

"See how good you are at being assertive?" Adam said.

She hated herself for the involuntary thrill she felt at his approval, even though she knew he was mocking her. "I'm not talking about this with you anymore."

"What are you so afraid of?"

That you'll guess why the blood keeps rushing to my face. That I'll lose control and punch you in your smug, handsome face. That you can see all the flaws I try so hard to hide.

There were so many things she could say, but she didn't say any of them, because that would be handing the nuclear codes to an enemy agent. Self-assured destruction.

"I'm not afraid of anything," was what she said. "I'm just tired of this conversation. Why don't we talk about your failings instead?"

Adam's gaze was sharp and penetrating. "When people don't want to talk about something, it usually means they're afraid of revealing some truth about themselves they'd prefer stayed hidden."

How did he keep doing that? Was he telepathic?

She stroked her thumb over the stitches on her needle. "And sometimes it means you're on their last nerve and they want you to listen to them asking you to *drop it*." She meant to sound tough, but there was a tremor in her voice that made her sound pathetic instead.

"You're right. I'm sorry."

"What?" Her ears had to be deceiving her. Adam Cortinas could not possibly have just said the words *you're right* and *I'm sorry*. She'd expected him to pounce at the first sign of weakness, not lay down his sword.

"I was doing exactly what you were complaining about: talking over you without listening because I thought I knew better." His dark eyebrows drew together, forming a triplet of creases above the bridge of his perfectly straight nose. He was being serious. He was actually disturbed.

She lifted her chin in vindication. "Yes, you were."

"I apologize."

"Apology accepted."

"I was just trying to help."

She'd heard that excuse too many times to let it go by. "Until you've spent your entire life navigating misogyny, maybe don't criticize how I choose to do it."

"Fair enough."

She wasn't used to hearing him agree with her and didn't know how to respond to it. "I'm going to review the site's operating manuals, if that's okay with you." Maybe if she was studying up on the equipment they'd be working with in a few hours he'd stop trying to talk to her.

"Knock yourself out."

She traded her knitting for her laptop, and pulled up one of the manuals she'd downloaded yesterday. It was boring and technical and had way more information than she needed for a simple integration with their market systems, but it made her feel a little better. Like she was actually doing something to prepare.

She could sense Adam reading over her shoulder, but at least he was being blessedly quiet. Even if he was breathing on her. Each exhalation warmed the side of her neck and stirred the strands of hair that had escaped from her bun.

Which meant his lips must be very close to her. Nearly touching her, in fact. If she turned her head and moved it just a few tiny inches, those sulky, tantalizing lips would be perfectly positioned to brush against hers.

Now that she'd had the thought, it was impossible to think about anything else. Impossible not to imagine actually doing it. How would he taste? Salty, probably, from the fries they'd shared in the airport. And sweet, from the Coke he'd been sipping.

Salty and sweet happened to be her favorite combination of flavors—like the sea salt chocolate chip cookies Penny made. Olivia's mouth was watering just thinking about it.

And the longer she thought about it, the stronger the impulse became to do something about it. Even though she knew it would be a Very Bad Thing.

You don't just randomly kiss your coworkers on an airplane when they're reading a generator operating manual over your shoulder. Especially not a coworker you could barely even stand, and who, more importantly, couldn't stand you back.

And yet.

It would be so easy.

Just a little taste. Just—

Was that a snore?

Oh good Christ.

He'd fallen asleep again. How did he keep doing that? Not that she could blame him. This manual was about to put her to sleep too. If she hadn't been so busy fantasizing about the taste of Adam's lips, she might be the one snoring right now.

Annoyingly, he even had a cute snore. It wasn't a loud, ugly, snorting snore. His was a soft, gentle snore. More like a long, deep breath. It was sort of relaxing to listen to. Which was fortunate, because he was doing it right next to her ear.

At least now she had the peace and quiet she'd been hoping for.

Olivia settled in to study the operating manual while Adam dozed beside her. When the flight attendant came down the aisle offering pretzels, she helped herself to Adam's as well as her own. She also availed herself of his complimentary beverage, ordering him a diet Coke which she drank for herself.

By then, his head had drifted its way down onto her shoulder. If he was going to use her as a pillow, she felt entitled to his beverage.

She probably ought to move him off her or nudge him awake, but she couldn't bring herself to do it. For once today, he wasn't bothering her. If she woke him up, he'd almost definitely start to annoy her again.

Also, he smelled fantastic. His hair smelled much better than the air in the plane, and every breath she inhaled through her nose was like a little hit of pleasure.

So she let him continue to nap on her shoulder, with his hair nestled against her neck and his breath warming her arm.

It was really quite pleasant.

Until the plane tried to fall out of the sky.

Chapter Six

At first it was just a bit of shaking. Nothing too bad, but enough to rouse Adam from his snooze.

His head popped up, and he stared around in sleepy confusion. Olivia was about to tease him about his catnap when the plane took a sudden, terrifying dive.

They leveled off again quickly—thank all the gods and Beyoncé—but not before Olivia's stomach tried to leap into her throat. The airplane continued to shudder and pitch, sending cups and pretzels and other assorted items sliding off tray tables.

Okay, so they'd hit some turbulence. It was buffeting them around pretty good, but they'd be fine. Turbulence was normal.

That was what Olivia tried to tell herself as they lurched through the air thirty thousand feet above the ground. The fasten seat belt light dinged on belatedly, and the flight attendant who'd been moving through the cabin collecting trash scurried back up the aisle.

A moment later, the pilot came on the intercom. "As you can probably tell, folks, we've hit a spot of turbulence. Looks like there's some bad weather outside Houston, so we're gonna try to go around that and get you to your destination as smoothly as possible. In the meantime, I've turned on the fasten seat belt sign, and I ask that you remain in your seats for your own safety."

Olivia tried to find his words reassuring, but his soothing pilot's drawl had sounded a bit harried. It didn't help that almost immediately after the announcement, the plane did another one of those frightening drops.

This one lasted even longer than the last. It felt like it lasted ten years, although logically Olivia knew it was probably only a second or two.

Adam's hand clamped onto hers, and she wanted to tell him that she didn't need comforting, that she was fine, but she couldn't actually say the words on account of her stomach being lodged in her throat again. And okay, maybe she curled her fingers around his and squeezed, and maybe she felt slightly better when he squeezed back so hard it was almost painful.

She had a moment to wonder if she was going to die holding Adam's hand—followed by the surprising thought that it wouldn't be the worst way to go if her number was up. Then the plane leveled off again, and it didn't feel quite so much like they were plummeting to their imminent, fiery deaths.

But Adam continued to hold her hand, and she continued to let him.

She felt the plane tilt, not like it was out of control, but like it was changing course. They'd turned away from the bad weather. There was still quite a bit of turbulence, but it felt like maybe it was easing up. After another minute or so passed without any more awful dives, Olivia relaxed enough to think about the fact that Adam's hand was on her thigh.

That was where her hand had been when he'd reached for it. So not only were they holding hands, but they were doing it in her lap. The moment she became conscious of that fact, she felt a surge of warmth between her legs.

She chose to blame the adrenaline rush. Didn't they say near-death experiences made people horny? Something about reaffirming life in the face of death?

Fortunately, she doubted there was any blood left in her face to cause a visible blush, so at least she was spared that humiliation for once in her life.

Good thing too, because now Adam wasn't just holding on to her hand—in her *lap*—he was also moving his thumb over her knuckles. It felt like—yep, he was definitely stroking. His thumb wasn't simply shifting position benignly. That was a deliberate back-and-forth caress, and it sent another surge of warmth shuddering through her.

It was probably just self-comforting behavior on his part. He probably didn't even realize he was doing it. He'd been nervous during takeoff, so he must be pretty freaked out right now.

She risked a glance at him for the first time since the turbulence had started. His eyes were wide and nearly black, and his Latino complexion had lost most of its color, leaving his face a sallow taupe.

But his expression softened as his gaze met hers, and his fingers tightened ever-so-slightly around her hand. "You okay?"

She swallowed and nodded. "Yeah. You?"

He attempted a smile that only managed to curve one side of his mouth. "I did not find that enjoyable."

"No, me neither."

The turbulence was almost completely gone now, except for an occasional mild shudder, but his thumb was still stroking over her knuckles. She should probably pull her hand away from his, but she couldn't seem to do it. She liked it too much.

"Hopefully we're through the worst of it," he said.

"Hopefully."

He looked down at their clasped hands and another asymmetrical smile curved his mouth. "I can probably let go of you now."

"Okay."

He loosened his fingers and shifted his hand into his own lap.

The spot on her thigh where his hand had been resting felt warmer than the rest of her leg. Her fingers felt warm too, and they were tingling where they had touched his. A phantom sensation of pressure lingered. If she closed her eyes, it would almost feel like he was still holding her hand.

There was a crackle of static as the pilot came back on the intercom. "Hey, folks. You've probably noticed we've moved out of the turbulence. That's because we're no longer headed toward Houston Bush Intercontinental, which has been put on a ground stop due to bad weather. We've been directed to land at DFW instead. We should have you on the ground in Dallas in about forty minutes, and once you're there, the gate agents will help you make arrangements to complete the rest of your journey. We apologize for the inconvenience, but sometimes Mother Nature has her own ideas."

There were a few groans and grumbles around the cabin, but most people were too grateful to have made it out of the turbulence alive to complain too much.

"Dallas," Adam said hollowly. "We're going to Dallas."

That was two hundred miles north of where they needed to be, which meant two extra hours of driving they couldn't afford.

THERE WERE no cars available for rent. Their rental car reservation was for Houston, and all the cars at the Dallas airport were either rented out already or reserved.

"Are you kidding me?" Adam said to the rental car agent. "What are we supposed to do? Just live here?"

The agent's smile turned hard and glassy. "You could try one of the other rental car desks, sir, but I can promise you they don't have any cars available either."

Olivia put her hand on Adam's arm and pushed him aside. "I'm sorry," she said to the agent in her sweetest voice, letting her

Texas accent out again. "You'll have to forgive us. We just got off the scariest flight of our lives, and we're both a little shaken up still."

The agent's expression softened. "Weather's pretty bad down south, I heard."

Olivia nodded, squinting to read the agent's name off his tag. "I swear, Glen, for a minute I thought we were all about to meet our maker. But we made it." She offered him a watery smile. "Now we just have to get ourselves to Fayette County. It's about seventy miles outside Austin? I don't suppose there's anything you can do? We're desperate."

"I wish I could, but there's hundreds of people stranded here in pretty much the same boat. We rented out our last car three hours ago." He sounded genuinely sorry.

"You've got other locations around the city though, right? Is there any chance one of them has a car available?"

"Possibly." He gave her a smile and a nod. "Let me see what I can do."

"Thank you so much!" When Olivia turned back to Adam, he was watching her with an odd look on his face. "What?"

"You're good at that."

"What?"

"Getting people to like you."

"It's called being nice. You should try it sometime."

He shook his head slightly. "I'm not as good at it as you are."

"You just need practice, that's all. It's not like it's an innate talent."

"Maybe for some people. Others seem able to do it unconsciously, like they rolled a natural twenty for their charisma score."

She blinked at him. "Did you just say 'natural twenty'?"

"It's a D&D term."

"I know what it is. Do you play D&D?"

"I used to." His eyes narrowed. "Do you?"

"I also used to play." Mostly in college. She hadn't been part of an active group in years. "And for the record, I wasn't blessed with a high charisma score. I actually have to work at it, which is what most people do."

He shrugged. "I guess I prefer to stick to things I'm good at."

"So you're afraid of failure. Or is it hard work?"

She could tell she'd scored a point from the way he bristled. "Neither."

"But you never try to learn new skills because you won't be good at them at first?"

"I've found you a car!" the agent announced as Adam opened his mouth to reply.

Olivia pasted on her brightest smile before turning back to the counter. "That's amazing! Thank you so much!"

"The closest one I could find is up at our Farmers Branch location, about twenty minutes away."

"That's okay," Olivia told him. "We can get a cab or something."

"I switched your original reservation over, so they're holding a car in your name."

"Thank you so much! You're a real lifesaver!" She threw a pointed glare at Adam.

"Yes, thank you," he said to Glen, dredging up a smile. "We really appreciate it."

"Have a good day!" Olivia chirped and offered Glen a wave goodbye. "See?" she told Adam as they walked toward the taxi line. "You are capable of being friendly."

BETWEEN THE WAIT in the airport taxi line and rush hour traffic, it took them more like forty-five minutes to get to the Farmers Branch rental car office. But they made it, and there was in fact a car waiting for them, just like Glen had promised.

"It's not much of a car, is it?" Adam observed as he opened the hatchback trunk of the Honda Fit they'd been assigned.

It was pretty small, Olivia agreed. And it looked like it had seen better days. But it was theirs, at least.

"It's a car," she said as she hefted her suitcase into the back. "It'll do the job."

"Will it? I'm afraid the hamsters will crap out on the open highway."

Olivia stared at him with an expression of shock. "Oh my god. Did you just make a joke?"

"I do actually have a sense of humor," he said as he slammed the hatch closed.

"My data doesn't support that thesis."

"Seriously though, what if Barbie decides she wants her car back?" he deadpanned, and Olivia's stomach did a giddy flip-flop. He was even hotter when he was being funny, which was really unfair.

She lifted a hand to shield her eyes from the glare of the Texas summer sun, but really it was to shield them from Adam's face. "Barbie drives a Corvette. She wouldn't be caught dead in this."

"Smart woman."

"Want me to drive?"

His hands clenched around the keys like she might try to take them from him. "I can do it."

"It's my home state, you know. I'm used to the highways here." It wasn't that she wanted to drive—she didn't, actually—it was the fact that he didn't want to let her that rankled.

"Highways are highways."

"Who's the control freak now?" she muttered under her breath.

"What?" Adam asked, shooting her a narrow glance.

She gave him her fakest of fake smiles. "Nothing."

They got in the car, and he plugged the address of their hotel into his phone's GPS and let it direct them out of town. Unfortunately, the rental car place was on the north side of the city and they needed to go south, which meant driving through the most congested part of Dallas smack in the middle of rush hour.

The summer sun burned hot and low in the west, casting a blinding glare off every windshield and bit of chrome on the sea of cars around them. To the south, where they would eventually be headed once they got past the mass of humanity fleeing the city center, a shelf of gray clouds hovered in the sky. It looked like there might be rain in their future.

At least Adam was a good driver. He didn't tailgate or change lanes erratically, and he paid attention to the other cars, anticipating their moves and adjusting accordingly.

If only this traffic would ease up a little. Olivia had expected a logjam heading out of town, but the current standstill seemed extreme even for rush hour.

"There must be an accident or something ahead," Olivia said.

Adam's thumb tapped impatiently on the steering wheel as they crept forward a few feet, only to come to another halt. "The GPS would tell me if there was. This is probably just normal rush hour traffic."

"Sometimes the GPS lags. I think we should get onto Loop 12 instead."

He scowled as a car forced its way in front of them. "This is the most direct route."

"Unless there's an accident or blocked lanes from construction or something. I've been to Dallas a few times before. I can direct you around this mess."

"So can the GPS, which it would do if it was necessary." His lips pursed stubbornly, and she tried not to think about how sexy they looked.

"Accident two miles ahead," the robot voice piped up cheerfully. *"Rerouting."*

Olivia snickered as the GPS directed them to take the fork for Loop 12, just like she'd suggested.

Adam threw her an exasperated look. "Laugh it up, Woerner."

"I told you we should go around."

"Yes, and I told you the GPS would let me know if it was the best route. Which it did. So we were both right."

As she took out her knitting, Olivia wondered if it was going to be like this all week, and what that would mean for the work they had to do together. Was he going to fight her on every little thing? Was she going to fight him back?

They'd never butted heads like this when they'd crossed paths before. Not that they'd collaborated all *that* much or had much reason to come into conflict. But on the occasions when they'd interacted in the past, things had always gone much more smoothly.

Probably because Olivia had never pressed her opinions before. She'd always just gone along with whatever he'd suggested. It was easier that way. He was Adam the rock star, so she'd told herself he knew best, even when she had her own ideas. She had let him take the lead and agreed to all his suggestions so he'd like her.

Which was exactly what he'd accused her of doing.

Well, no more. She hoped he was ready to reap what he'd sowed, because she was done rolling over for him.

The traffic was still pretty backed up on Loop 12, but at least it was moving at a steady ten-mile-an-hour clip, which was a distinct improvement. Olivia watched the minutes tick by with a growing sense of fatalism. Their original flight would have landed them in Austin at three, with only a one-hour drive to the plant, allowing them to start work around four or five. But now, thanks to their various calamities, it was coming up on seven, and they still had three hours of driving ahead of them.

"Should we stop for dinner somewhere?" she suggested once they'd cleared the Dallas city limits. "I'm hungry."

"I don't think we can spare the time for a sit-down meal," Adam said.

She set her knitting down to massage her hands, which had

started to ache. "Agreed, but I'm going to need a pit stop and some food unless you want me to turn into Hungry Hulk."

"Fine." He put his signal on to take the next exit off the highway.

"Not here," Olivia said. "Keep going."

"There's a truck stop just ahead."

"Yes, but there's someplace way better two miles up."

"How do you know that?"

"Because I saw a billboard for it." More like five billboards on their way out of the city, but she wouldn't expect him to appreciate what the giant yellow signs with the beaver cartoon meant. "Just trust me."

Chapter Seven

"Did you bring me to a mall?" Adam asked as they cruised through the sprawling parking lot.

"Nope," Olivia said. "Just a roadside convenience store." More like the best roadside convenience store in the world, but she'd let Adam figure that out on his own once he was inside.

He parked the car a couple rows away from the side entrance at one end of the long building, and Olivia led him inside. As soon as they stepped through the automatic glass doors, his feet stuttered to a stop as he gaped at the massive store around them. "What is this place?"

"This is Buc-ee's."

"But...what is it?"

"It's roadside heaven. It has everything you could possibly need on a road trip: coolers, fishing gear, inner tubes, cowboy hats, all kinds of food, plus a whole bunch of other stuff. But most importantly, it has the cleanest public bathrooms in America. Come on."

She gave his arm a tug and led him past the T-shirts, travel mugs, and other assorted souvenirs adorned with the store's beaver mascot. Past the barbecue smokers, the camping supplies, and the decorative signs, both religious and humorous. Past the bakery, the sandwich counter, and the jerky counter—yes, there was a whole counter just for jerky, which came in a dozen different flavors—and finally to the bathrooms that were located in the middle of the store.

A steady stream of customers flowed through the doorway leading to the bathrooms, alongside another steady stream of people coming out again. "I'll meet you back out here in a minute," Olivia told Adam before heading toward the ladies' room.

The miracle of the Buc-ee's bathrooms—aside from their cleanliness in the face of so much traffic—was that there were so many toilets there was never a wait. There had to be at least forty stalls in this one, all of them separated by thick floor-to-ceiling dividers for maximum privacy and monitored by dedicated cleaning staff who kept the place spotless and well-stocked twenty-four hours a day.

No matter how busy Buc-ee's got, you never had a long wait for a register or a bathroom, although getting up and down the aisles through the crush of shoppers could be murder during peak times on the weekend. Fortunately, it wasn't too crowded on a Tuesday night, and when Olivia came out of the bathroom, she quickly spotted Adam over by the wall of fountain drinks.

"Look at them all," he said with a shell-shocked expression as he waved his arm at the eighty soda fountains plus coffee, tea, and hot chocolate dispensers. "This is insane. There are so many to choose from, I'm paralyzed by choice."

She gave him an encouraging pat on the shoulder. "Okay, well, I'm gonna go grab some food. Meet back up at the registers where we came in when you've got everything you need?"

"Sure. Yep."

She left him gazing in wonderment at the selection of fountain drinks, and went on her own quest for something that would pass for dinner.

Ten minutes later, Olivia carried her carefully curated selection of road trip snacks to the register, where Adam was already waiting for her with a plastic bag and a ginormous soft drink cup.

She shook her head in disappointment as he unwrapped a protein bar. "That's what you got? A protein bar and a Coke?"

He lifted up the plastic bag. "No, I have a second protein bar and a Monster Energy for later. And this"—he shook his cup at her—"is a Dr. Pepper Icee." He grinned, looking happier than she'd ever seen him before.

Who would have thought Adam Cortinas's stone-cold heart could be melted by a frozen Dr. Pepper?

But that was nothing compared to what happened next.

Adam's lips closed around the straw and he sucked, making a sexy pucker as his cheeks caved pornographically.

And then his face…

When the sweet drink hit his mouth, his face contorted into an expression of unadulterated bliss. His eyes rolled heavenward as his lids fluttered closed, and he tilted his head back, his shoulders sagging bonelessly as he let out a long sigh of pleasure. He was basically making his orgasm face right there in the middle of Buc-ee's.

It was a lot.

Olivia turned to the college-aged cashier, and caught her watching Adam in wide-eyed astonishment. She and Olivia shared a moment of silent communication which, if it had involved actual words, would probably translate as something to the effect of: *Oh my god! Did you just see that guy's O face too, and was it not the hottest thing ever?*

Olivia cleared her throat as the cashier began ringing up her items. "They have barbecue, you know," she threw over her shoulder. "Texas barbecue."

"I can't eat barbecue while I drive," Adam said.

She considered pointing out that he could let her drive for a while, but decided it was useless. He didn't seem inclined to give up control of the driver's seat, and she didn't actually want to drive anyway. "Okay, but is that enough food for you? There's probably not going to be much open by the time we check into the hotel tonight, so this might be all the food you'll get until morning."

"I'll be fine. Pay for your stuff so we can get back on the road."

Olivia handed her credit card to the smiling cashier. "Oh! Hang on! I need this too," she said, seizing a bag off the endcap and adding it to the pile.

Adam's eyebrows shot up as he read the package. "Beaver Nuggets?"

"Don't mock my Beaver Nuggets," Olivia said. "They're delicious."

His lips pressed together like he was restraining himself from making an inappropriate comment. "If you say so."

"Just wait. You'll see. They're crazy addictive."

"I'm sure they are." His eyes were shining with suppressed humor, and she couldn't help smiling back.

The cashier bagged up Olivia's items, and they carried their spoils out to the car. Compared to the air-conditioned store, the air outside felt like a hot, sweaty gym sock that had been peeled off a runner's foot. There were some things Olivia missed about Texas, but the humid summers were definitely not one of them.

"I'm almost sad we don't need gas," Adam said as they drove past the massive row of pumps on their way out of the parking lot.

"Told you this place was better than that grungy truck stop two miles back."

"You were right. I'm glad I trusted you."

Olivia felt her cheeks heat. It was the second time he'd admitted she was right, and it gave her all kinds of feelings she didn't want to think about.

"How about some music?" she asked, casting about for a distraction. They'd had the radio off before so they could hear the

GPS directions, but the remainder of their route was fairly straightforward.

"Okay, but the driver has veto authority."

"Fine."

She pressed the power button and country music blared out of the speakers at them.

"No," Adam said immediately.

"Cool your jets. I wasn't stopping there." She hit the seek button, moving through the stations until she found one playing an old Nirvana song that took her back to elementary school. "How about this?"

"Acceptable."

Olivia settled back in her seat and dug into the sausage and cheese kolaches she'd bought for herself while Adam sucked on his Icee. Fortunately, there was no repeat of the O-face incident in the close confines of the car.

She was on her last kolache when he finally took notice of her food. "What is that?" he asked, throwing a curious look her way.

"It's a kolache."

"A what?"

"It's a Tex-Czech pastry. Sausage wrapped in sweet dough."

"Like a pig in a blanket?"

"Sort of. They make sweet ones too, with fruit and cream cheese."

"Smells good."

She'd already eaten half, but she held out what was left of the kolache in her hand. "You want to try?" She didn't know how Adam felt about eating something her mouth had been on, but she figured she ought to at least offer, out of politeness.

He glanced at her half-gnawed sausage kolache, then back at the road, seeming to think about it before holding out his hand. "Yeah, okay."

As she passed him the rest of the kolache, she wondered if he was going to make *that* face again. The one he'd made over the Icee.

She wasn't sure what she would do if he did.

She watched him closely as he bit into the soft dough. He didn't close his eyes this time or throw his head back, which was probably a good thing since he was driving. But that blissed-out expression came over his face again and he broke into a grin.

"That's fucking delicious," he said.

"I know."

"Now I'm sad I didn't get myself some of those." He offered her the remaining nub of kolache.

"You can finish it," she said. "There's probably somewhere near the motel we can get them. They're sort of a staple around here."

"Cool." He popped the last bite in his mouth, and she handed him a napkin to wipe the sausage grease off his fingers. "Thanks." He threw a quick, self-conscious smile at her. "And thanks for sharing."

"You're welcome," she said as she dug her knitting back out of her bag. "Thank you for driving."

She wasn't sure why she'd been so annoyed about him driving earlier. She didn't enjoy highway driving, especially at night, and this way she'd be able to get more knitting done—at least until it got too dark to see. So why had it bothered her?

It was getting harder to remember that she wasn't supposed to like him. In fact, it was starting to feel like maybe she *did* like him despite everything. Even when she was butting heads with him over stupid things, she sort of...enjoyed it? He seemed genuinely interested in her opinions, even when he didn't agree with them.

The more time they spent together, the less abrasive his bluntness seemed, and the more she realized that behind it lay a sweetness he seemed reluctant to let anyone see.

He was like her mirror opposite in that way. She had always made a show of pretending to be sweet around the people she worked with to hide the fact she was actually sarcastic and sharp-tongued underneath. But Adam hid all his sweetness behind a prickly exterior that seemed designed to keep people at arm's length.

She wondered why he felt the need to do that. What was he trying to protect himself from? Why wouldn't he want to be liked?

"Hey, listen," he said, shifting in the driver's seat a little.

"Yeah?" Her fingers stilled on her knitting needles as she looked over at him.

"About earlier, on the plane..."

She bit down on her lip, uncertain which part of earlier on the plane he was referring to. The part when they'd held hands? When his thumb had caressed her knuckles long after the plane had stopped tossing them around? That part?

"I think I offended you, when I suggested you should be more assertive."

Oh. *That* part of earlier on the plane. The part where she'd gotten so upset she'd had to flee to the bathroom.

She lowered her eyes to her knitting again and tried to make her voice sound light and casual. "I wasn't offended." More like outraged, resentful, and mortally wounded, but admitting that would be opening the door to talking about it some more, which was the absolute last thing she wanted.

"You seemed offended."

"Well I wasn't," she replied flatly, hoping he'd get the message and drop it. She thought they'd put this subject behind them. Why did he have to go and bring it up again? And just when she was starting to feel more comfortable around him.

"You sound offended again now."

Yeah, okay, his bluntness was definitely still a pain in her ass. But honesty had worked to get through to him last time, so maybe if she told him how she actually felt he'd be satisfied enough to leave the subject alone.

"Because I don't want to talk about this," she said. "No one likes to be criticized or have their past mistakes thrown in their face."

"I'm just trying to help."

"No, you're spitting in my face and telling me it's moisturizer."

When he glanced at her, he looked surprised. "That is really not what I was doing. Feedback helps you improve. It's not personal."

"It *feels* personal."

"But it's not," he insisted, as if feelings were irrelevant. Like she was getting emotional about nothing and ought to be able to just get over it.

"I can't change how I feel," she snapped. "But I guess you'd have to have feelings in the first place to understand that."

He ignored the insult—or maybe he didn't even consider it an insult. Maybe he was impervious to the concept of insults, because to him it was all just feedback and honesty. "I don't mind when people give me constructive criticism," he said. "It helps me learn and improve myself."

"Okay, then how's this for constructive criticism: your bluntness is off-putting, your failure to listen when people attempt to set boundaries is rude, and your over-literal obsession with honesty is frankly kind of weird."

As soon as the words were out of her mouth, she regretted them. Yes, he'd sort of asked for it, but she'd gone too far. Surely he hadn't wanted that much honesty?

This was exactly why she worked so hard at pretending to be nice. Because she wasn't a very nice person when she let her real personality peek through.

Adam nodded slowly, like he was taking her words in, and Olivia braced herself for his reaction. When it came, it wasn't at all what she expected.

"You're right. Those are things I'll try to work on in the future." He said it mildly, without a trace of resentment. She might as well have told him his shoe was untied for all the emotion it seemed to have provoked.

"Seriously?" She stared at him in disbelief. "That's it? That's your only reaction?" He really was a robot.

The look he threw her way was utterly guileless. "Yes."

"You're not offended? Or hurt? Or the slightest bit upset?"

"No." His shoulder lifted in a small shrug. "Everything you said was true—from your perspective at least. It wasn't said with malice, so why should I be upset?"

Guilt stabbed through her. "There was maybe a little malice."

"No there wasn't. You're not a malicious person." There was that guilelessness again. She didn't understand how he could be so abrasive one second and so utterly sincere the next.

"You don't know me well enough to know that."

"I know you well enough to know you'd never hurt someone on purpose."

She shook her head at how wrong he was. He had this idea that she was some meek, sweet little thing, and she needed to disabuse him of it for both their sakes. "I thought it would hurt you when I said those things, but I did it anyway."

"I explicitly told you it wouldn't."

"But I didn't believe you. Part of me wanted to hurt you, because you'd hurt me."

"Telling someone the truth isn't hurting them."

"Sometimes it is."

"I don't accept that," he said with a vehemence that surprised her.

"You've never been hurt by the truth?"

"Not as much as I've been hurt by lies." There was something in his voice when he said it—a rawness, as if she'd touched on a wound that wasn't quite healed.

She wanted more than anything to know what had happened to leave him so sensitive on the subject of lies. Who had hurt him? But he didn't seem like the type to open up about himself, and Olivia wasn't enough of an asshole to prod a scar that was so obviously painful.

She kept all her questions to herself. "Sometimes it's kinder to say nothing than to tell someone what you really think about them."

He frowned and shook his head. "I think it's more comfortable, but comfort isn't necessarily kindness. If you're withholding information that could help someone improve their life, is that really kindness? Or is it just contributing to a miserable status quo?"

"But who are you to judge whether or not someone's miserable or their life needs improving? When some catcalling cheesedick on a street corner tells me I should smile more it makes me want to punch him into the sun, because who the fuck is he to weigh in on me or my life? Whether or not he thinks it's true, it doesn't give him the right to force his opinions on me." It was possible she had strong feelings on this particular subject.

The corner of Adam's mouth twitched in suppressed amusement. "Okay, but I'm not just some street corner cheesedick, am I? We have an established professional relationship. And you invited my opinion by asking for a reference. I'm sorry if you didn't like what I had to say, but it's unfair to expect me to lie just because you've put me on the spot."

As much as she hated to admit it, she had to concede the point. "You're right. I brought it on myself by asking you for a reference. But I didn't ask for you to keep bringing it up over and over again. Because that feels like you're throwing my failures in my face for sport."

His forehead furrowed with deep creases, as if he were genuinely distressed she'd think that about him. "I really didn't mean it that way. I was just trying to offer constructive criticism. I thought I was helping."

She believed him, but she needed to make him understand that it wasn't that simple for her. "It's hard for me to hear constructive criticism when I'm not prepared for it. It's too upsetting to be helpful."

"I don't understand that. Because you're really smart, and you're obviously ambitious, so I'd think you'd want to improve."

His words sent a warm rush shooting through her, and she turned her face to the window to hide her smile. *He thinks I'm smart*.

But her smile faded as another question loomed in her mind, casting a shadow over the compliment he'd just paid. She turned to him again, knowing she was inviting more pain by asking it aloud. "If you think I'm so smart, why wouldn't you give me a reference?"

His eyes slid over to her, betraying a satisfying hint of guilt before returning to the road. He shifted in his seat again. "I told you why."

"Are you applying to the leadership program too?" It would be easier if that was really why he'd refused. Because he didn't want the competition. She would prefer that to the alternative: that he really didn't respect her enough to give her a reference.

He let out a light snort as he checked the driver's side mirror. "No."

"Why not? With your track record, you'd be a shoe-in." It didn't make sense that he wasn't applying.

His hand tightened on the steering wheel. "I don't have the people skills for management."

She couldn't help the laugh that escaped. "No shit."

His head swiveled her way, and his mouth curved in one of his almost-smiles. "It's just not something that interests me. I'd rather keep my head down and do my own work."

"I guess I can understand that." She could see the appeal in it, but couldn't help wanting more for herself. The thought of being stuck in the same job forever made her brain feel itchy.

Adam's job was more exciting than hers, between the travel and the constant supply of new challenges and situations—not to mention the adrenaline rush of pulling off a miracle in the face of a looming deadline—and she could see how that might be enough for him.

Olivia's job was slightly less exciting. Even if Gavin started handing off more off-site integrations to her, she didn't actually love unexpected crises and flying blind into a strange situation under a tight deadline. It seemed to be Adam's forte, but Olivia was a planner who preferred structure and having multiple contingency plans ready at hand.

Plus, she actually liked working with people. Even when she didn't necessarily like the people, she derived some enjoyment from solving the puzzle of them. More than that, she felt like she was pretty good at it.

"So you think I'm smart, just not good enough at my job to be a manager. Is that it?" She was doing it to herself now, refusing to let it go. But she couldn't seem to stop.

Weirdly, it didn't hurt as much as before. She could think about it and talk about it without that sour feeling in the pit of her stomach that felt like it was trying to crawl into her throat and choke her. It was a duller sort of discomfort now, like a half-healed scar. She could poke at it gently without too much pain, as long as she was careful not to press too hard.

"I'm sorry if I hurt your feelings," Adam said.

"You did," she admitted, which felt like a big step. "But I'll get over it. I accept that you're entitled to your opinion, and I did put you on the spot by asking."

"I really didn't mean to upset you."

"I know."

She hadn't quite solved the puzzle of Adam Cortinas yet, but a picture was starting to take shape. She felt like she knew him well enough by now to believe there was no malice behind his matter-of-fact criticisms. Which was exactly what he'd just said about her.

"So we're okay?" he asked uncertainly.

"Yeah. We're okay. I don't agree with you, but you're right about one thing: I'm not good at taking feedback."

He glanced over at her, but wisely didn't say anything. Maybe he actually was learning.

Olivia looked down at her lap and squeezed her hands until the knuckles cracked. "Have you ever heard of Rejection Sensitive Dysphoria?"

"No."

"It's associated with ADHD. Basically it means you can have an extreme emotional reaction to even the perception of being rejected or criticized."

She didn't usually talk about her ADHD, which hadn't been diagnosed until she was in college. Before that, Olivia had just thought *everyone* felt anxious all the time and had trouble making decisions and executing them—that it was normal to feel that way. She'd always been a good student—not as good as her sister, but good enough—so no one had ever thought to have her tested for ADHD until the stress of college had sent her into a tailspin that had almost forced her to drop out.

Adam glanced at her. "Extreme, meaning…?"

"Mood swings, depression, sometimes rage. It varies from person to person, but with me it usually manifests as anxiety."

"So you're extra sensitive?" The way he said it made her sound like some sort of wimp or fragile snowflake who just needed to develop a thicker skin. As if it was that easy to overcome a chemical imbalance in your brain.

"It's more than just that," she said, wanting him to understand. "Simple tasks that most people wouldn't think twice about, like texting a friend, can seem insurmountable, because RSD makes you fear rejection even when it's unlikely or completely benign."

"Everyone feels that though, to some extent. I know I do."

"But what I'm saying is I feel it more than is normal. And it's not just something I can decide to get over, because it's neurological and genetic. The messages my brain is sending me are worse than the messages your brain sends you."

She could tell from his expression that he still didn't really get it, so she tried an analogy her therapist had used. "It's like—let's say we both want to ask someone out on a date. That's pretty scary no matter who you are, right?"

He humored her with a nod, even though she doubted he'd ever in his life been scared to ask anyone on a date.

"So for the purposes of this metaphor," she explained, "in order to work up the courage to do it, you have to walk across the room, fill up a bucket, and carry it back to where you were."

"What are we filling the bucket with?"

"It doesn't matter. Anything. It's just how we fill our imaginary courage reserves. It's like a fuel tank."

"Okay."

"And filling your courage tank takes a certain amount of energy, but it's manageable, so you go ahead and do it, so you can overcome your fear and ask the girl out—or maybe for you it's a dude. I don't know. Whatever." She felt the need to tack that last part on, because she didn't want to seem like she was making assumptions about his sexuality. It was only a little because she was fishing for information about him.

"It'd be a girl," he offered matter-of-factly.

"Okay, fine," she said, like she couldn't care less. "Anyway. If I want to do the same thing, because of my ADHD and Rejection Sensitive Dysphoria, instead of just walking across the room to fill up my bucket like you did, I've got to walk two miles down the road. It's still possible, but it's a *lot* farther, and uses a lot more energy, and when I get back, I'm going to be a lot more tired than you were. So maybe I still do it, if I can convince myself the thing is important enough—or maybe I decide it's too much trouble and it's not worth all that walking and making myself so tired. Does that make sense?"

His forehead furrowed as if he were working on a really difficult calculus problem. "Yeah. I never really thought about it that way before, but I think I get it."

"It's not that it's impossible, it's just a lot harder. And because it's so hard, you become hypervigilant about avoiding situations that could result in rejection. It can seem like social phobia, because it's this paralyzing terror you're going to humiliate yourself. You try to cope by being so perfect you're above criticism—which is impossible, of course—or else you just give up and don't ever take risks."

Adam was quiet for a moment, digesting everything she'd said. "So when you asked me for that reference, that was really hard for you, because you have this extreme fear of being rejected...which was exactly what happened."

She looked down at the abandoned knitting in her lap. "Pretty much, yeah."

"Jesus, Olivia. I had no idea." He sounded pained.

She swallowed, unable to look at him. "I'm not trying to make you feel bad." Her fingers plucked at a corner of Penny's shawl as she spoke. "You couldn't have known, and you didn't do anything wrong. I'm just trying to explain why I didn't want to talk about it anymore, and why I get so tense whenever you start in on me with your constructive criticisms."

"I'm sorry. I get it now, and I'll try to be more sensitive."

"Thank you. I appreciate that."

They both fell silent. For a minute, the only sounds inside the car were road noise and the incongruously upbeat No Doubt song on the radio.

"So did you like totally hate my guts after that?" Adam asked. "You must have."

Olivia looked at him. Even in profile, she could see the worry etched in his features. He actually cared what she thought of him. "Hate's a strong word. Let's just say you weren't exactly my favorite person."

"And now?" His eyes darted sideways, but he didn't let himself look all the way at her.

"You're slowly making your way back up the chart."

The corner of his mouth tugged into a smile. "Yeah?"

"Yeah," she said. "Top 100, even. With a bullet."

Chapter Eight

They lost the classic rock station a half hour later, and Olivia found another one playing eighties pop hits. There wasn't much to look at on this particular stretch of Highway 77. A lot of pastures. Some cows. The occasional gas station. And a spectacular Texas sunset splashed across the sky to their right.

She watched the colors change through the passenger window, knitting until her hands began to ache again, and gave up when she finally lost the light.

"Beaver Nuggets!" she exclaimed in happy surprise when she leaned over to put her knitting away. She'd forgotten she had them.

"What?" They'd both been quiet for a while, so Adam seemed startled when she suddenly spoke up.

"I just remembered I bought Beaver Nuggets at Buc-ee's."

"Right." He ran his hand over the side of his face, like he was trying to wake himself up. "So what are they?"

"They're like sweet Cheetos. But a thousand times better."

"Sounds gross."

"Just you wait. You'll see."

He threw her a disbelieving look. "You don't actually think I'm going to put something called a Beaver Nugget in my mouth?"

She grinned as she tore the bag open, breathing in the buttery caramel flavor. "Hey, it's your loss if you don't want to try them. More for me." She popped one in her mouth and crunched down on the crispy sweetness, letting out a moan of happiness. "Damn. So good."

Adam's eyebrows lifted in interest, but he continued to look skeptical. "Uh huh."

Olivia helped herself to another one. And another. They really were addictive. The more you ate, the better they tasted.

"Are you going to keep doing that?" he asked.

"Doing what?"

"Moaning like that. It's unsettling."

"You'd be moaning with me if you tried one."

His knuckles whitened on the steering wheel as he pressed his lips together. It was hard to tell in the failing light, but she thought his cheeks might be slightly pink.

"Fine." He stuck out his hand. "Give me one."

Olivia placed a sugar-coated corn puff in his palm and watched closely as he ate it. He was staring straight ahead, which left her free to admire the slight pout of his lips and the manly slope of his jaw as he sampled the Beaver Nugget.

There was no pleasure-face this time. Instead, he shrugged slightly as he chewed. "It's really sweet."

"Yeah." Her eyes remained laser-sighted on his throat as he swallowed.

He licked his lips and wrinkled his nose. "*Too* sweet."

"Says the guy who just drank forty ounces of frozen corn syrup." She forced herself to stop ogling him and faced forward in her seat, reaching into the bag for more Beaver Nuggets.

"I don't get it," he said. "It's just a caramel-flavored Cheeto."

"I know! Isn't it amazing?"

"I mean…it's fine."

"It's more than fine. It's like a nugget of pure crunchy happiness."

His lip curled in distaste. "I think it's the word nugget that's putting me off."

"What's wrong with the word nugget?"

"It makes me think of turds."

"Do chicken nuggets make you think of turds?"

"No, they make me think of pink slime and snotty toddlers, which isn't appetizing either."

"I'm pretty sure the name is supposed to be funny."

He glanced over at her and raised a mocking eyebrow. "Is it funny, or is it just gross?"

"Why can't it be both?" she asked, popping another nugget in her mouth.

"It's a food named after toilet humor."

"It could also be referring to the beaver's testicles," she pointed out. "You know, his nuggets."

Adam shook his head, but he looked more amused than disgusted. "Yes, I get it. But is that better?"

"I guess it depends if you think a genitals joke is better than a poop joke."

"Either way, it seems inappropriate to associate it with food sold at what is otherwise a family-friendly shopping experience."

"The inappropriateness is what makes it funny."

"Does it though?" he asked, cutting a wry look her way.

"They're delicious, so I don't really care what they're named. Plus, it's fun to say Beaver Nuggets. Try it."

He shook his head. "No."

"Come on."

"Why would I do that?" He was trying not to smile, which just made her press him more.

"Because it's fun. Say it."

He pressed his lips together and shook his head again, like he couldn't believe they were having this conversation. Olivia couldn't believe it either.

And then he just went and said it: "Beaver Nuggets."

She burst out laughing, and the sound of it filled up the car, drowning out the radio and making the night seem a little less dark outside.

Adam looked over at her, grinning, and stuck out his hand. "Give me some more of those."

"Told you they were addictive." As she poured some out into his palm, she felt a little giddy, like her head was a helium balloon. She didn't know if it was the sugar, the long day, or something else altogether.

"They're okay," he said as he shoved a handful into his mouth. He looked a little giddy himself.

"You love them." She said it with a playful lilt, the way a little kid would tease someone about a crush just before singing about them sitting in a tree, K-I-S-S-I-N-G.

But even spoken in a childish tone, the word *love* felt too large for the confined space they were sharing. It expanded as soon as it hit the air, like a popcorn maker gone out of control, filling up the tiny car and making it feel even smaller.

When Adam looked at her again, the smile on his face seemed to catch, suspended for a moment in time. Their eyes met, and something in them set Olivia's stomach spinning.

She turned to stare out the passenger side window even though it was too dark to see much of anything beyond the glass. Swallowing, she pressed a hand to her cheek. Her skin radiated heat like a sunburn, even though the air conditioner vent was blowing right on her.

She was enjoying this too much. Enjoying *Adam* too much. Everything felt different between them, and the sea change had happened so fast she didn't know how to deal with it.

It had begun to rain a little, and the drops pattered a soft rhythm on the roof of the car. Adam flicked on the wipers, and they made a groaning sound as they scraped over the dusty windshield.

His hand bumped against Olivia's leg. "More nuggets, please."

She dug into the bag and passed him another handful. An old Wham song was playing on the radio, and he tapped his thumb on the steering wheel in time with the beat as he chewed.

"Adam?"

"Hmmm?" he answered through a mouthful of corn puffs.

"Tell me the truth. Do you think we're going to be able to finish this integration by Saturday?"

He shifted in his seat, rolling his shoulders to loosen them up. "We'll have to work a little smarter is all. Put in a few long nights. It's doable."

"Is it?"

He glanced over at her, then back at the road. "Yes." His fingers tightened on the wheel. "We should make it to the hotel by ten. So we check in, get a good night's sleep, and start bright and early in the morning. It's not like we would have gotten all that much done today even if we'd arrived on time, so at most we've only missed a few productive hours. We can make it up later in the week if we have to."

He sounded so sure of himself. She envied him his ability to be so confident in the face of the unknown.

"Hey, maybe we'll get there and it'll turn out to be a simple job," he said. "Maybe their systems will be up-to-date and compliant."

"You really think that's likely?" she asked.

"I think it's possible, and it's not worth worrying about it until we're actually there."

"Right."

He glanced at her again, and his eyes seemed to soften. "Trust me, it's going to be fine. I've done dozens of these integrations."

"And of all of those, how many times have you missed the deadline?"

"Only once."

"So it does happen sometimes."

"Rarely."

"But if the first and only time I'm given the assignment we fail, you know they're going to blame me, right?"

He shook his head, frowning at the rainy highway ahead of them. "That's not true. You can't control the airlines, or the fact that the lawyers dragged their feet for weeks, or the condition of the plant's systems when we get there."

She wondered if he was really that naive, or if he was just trying to make her feel better. But then she remembered he wouldn't do that. He'd never lie just to make someone feel better.

"It doesn't matter whether it's actually my fault," she said. "Someone's always got to take the blame, and you can bet it's not going to be legal or the C-levels who overcommitted to the board. Maybe they won't come right out and say it, but it'll be implied that I wasn't up to the task. It'll be a black mark against me. A reason not to give me more responsibility in the future."

The rain was falling even harder now, and Adam's frown deepened as he increased the speed of the windshield wipers. "Listen, I won't let them do that, okay?"

"You can't control who they blame."

"Sure I can, if I say it was my fault. I'll take the blame if I have to."

She blinked at him. "You wouldn't do that."

"Why not?"

"Because. Why would you?" Why would anyone do something like that for her? Especially him.

He shrugged, like it was nothing to throw himself on his sword for her sake. "I'm the one with more experience here, and I'm the one who committed us to this timeline—over your objections. Therefore, it's my responsibility, and I'll make sure they know that."

A lump formed in her throat. "Adam—"

"Look, it's not going to hurt me any. One missed deadline after all the wins I've pulled off for them isn't going to matter."

"Still."

"Still what?"

"Not many people would do that."

"Sure they would."

"No. I can't think of many who would." Something squeezed around her heart, like a big warm hand had reached into her chest. "You *are* nice."

He didn't look at her, but she could see his mouth turn up at the corner. "Shut up."

"Okay, maybe not *that* nice."

THE RAIN WENT from moderate to torrential in the space of a few seconds. It was like they'd driven headfirst into Niagara Falls.

Olivia had been living in LA for so long, she'd almost forgotten what real storms were like.

"This is insane," Adam said as he leaned forward, struggling to see through the downpour. The windshield wipers couldn't keep up, and the visibility was only a few feet in front of the car. "I've never seen anything like this before."

"Storms out here aren't like in LA. When it rains, things can get apocalyptic fast."

"No shit. Jesus."

Olivia squirmed in her seat as a ball of anxiety settled in the pit of her stomach. Her feet pressed against the floorboards. "Be careful. The roads can get slick when water starts to collect on them."

"I understand how physics works."

"You should decrease your speed to reduce the risk of hydroplaning. And leave extra space between us and the car ahead."

"I don't need you to womansplain driving to me right now."

Her fist clenched around the handle on the door. "Womansplaining would imply you have more knowledge of driving in rainy conditions than me, but since I grew up here and you've already admitted you've never driven in anything like this before, I am simply *explaining* it to you."

"Whatever you're doing, it's making me nervous."

"Sorry."

Adam's hands tightened on the wheel and he decreased his speed. "I should have let you drive. I didn't realize we'd be heading into a typhoon."

Olivia bit down on the impulse to point out that a typhoons occurred in a specific region of the Pacific Ocean and were therefore unrelated to the tropical depression currently dumping rain on them in central Texas. Now wasn't the time to give in to her knee-jerk impulse to push his buttons.

"You're doing great," she told him instead. "I'm only side-seat driving because I'm nervous too. To be honest, I hate driving in the rain."

"Really?"

"You get caught in a few blinding rainstorms on the highway, and you start to develop a complex."

"I'll bet." He almost had to shout to be heard over the sound of the rain battering the car. It was impossible to see the lines on the road. The only way to know they were in their lane was to follow the taillights of the car in front of them.

Adam's arms and neck were bowstring taut. His fists gripped the steering wheel at ten and two like a driving school student. But he was doing everything right. Going slow, but not so slow they were likely to get plowed into from behind. Keeping plenty of distance between them and the car ahead, but not so much they lost sight of where their lane was. Every once in a while he'd veer a little too close to the shoulder and the friction paint on the road would hum, but he always course corrected smoothly, without jerking on the wheel.

After fifteen minutes that felt more like an hour, the rain started to let up a little. They could see the lines on the road again, and the windshield wipers were able to keep up with the raindrops pelting the front window.

Just as Olivia started to relax, there was a sound like a small explosion, and the car lurched sideways. She recognized the flat squeal of rubber dragging across asphalt as her insides rearranged themselves.

They'd blown a tire.

All the breath left her lungs as Adam wrenched on the wheel to keep them from careening across the highway, and she felt the remaining tires start to hydroplane on the wet road.

They were going to spin out. She was going to die sitting next to Adam today after all—not on the plane, but in a shitty rental car in the middle of nowhere.

Only they didn't die this time either.

Miraculously, Adam managed to wrestle the car back under control and steer them safely onto the right shoulder of the road. As soon as the car rolled to a stop, Olivia sucked in a long, shuddering breath and let it out again with an involuntary whimper. Her fingers had practically embedded themselves in the plastic door handle, she was squeezing it so hard.

"Are you okay?" Adam asked, slapping on the hazards and the interior car lights as he swung his head to look at her.

She gave him a weak nod. There was so much adrenaline spiking through her system, she wasn't sure she could speak yet.

"Olivia?"

Rain pelted the windshield and rattled on the roof of the car as Adam twisted in his seat to face her. His fingers touched her cheek, hesitating for a second before turning her face to his.

Those beautiful dark eyes stared into hers like they were staring right into her soul.

Her lips parted, but no sound came out. If she couldn't speak before, she definitely couldn't do it now with those eyes on her.

"You're okay." He said it like he was willing it to be true. His thumb moved over her cheek in the softest of caresses. "We're fine. We made it."

She managed another nod, and he took his hand away.

He leaned back in his seat and rubbed his palms on his thighs as he blew out a long breath. "That was terrifying."

"Are *you* okay?" she asked, finding her voice finally. The blood was still pumping in her ears, making her voice sound oddly distant, and her stomach was tied in about a million knots.

He nodded. "Yeah." He kept on nodding, like he was trying to convince himself.

She reached across the console and squeezed his hand. "You did great. You saved us."

He swiveled his head to look at her, and gave her hand a squeeze back. "Not too bad for a rain novice, huh?"

She smiled at him. "Not bad at all."

His forehead creased in a frown. "You sure you're okay?"

"I did not expect to have two near-death experiences today, but other than feeling like a character in a *Final Destination* movie, I'm fine."

"I'm not sure either of them really count as near-death."

There was the Adam she knew. If he was arguing with her, he must be fine.

He plucked his phone out of the console. "I'm calling Triple A."

Olivia looked out the window at the rain-sodden night. It had to have been twenty miles since they'd passed their last town, and it hadn't been much of a town. "It's going to take forever to get a wrecker out here in this weather."

"I know, but what choice do we have?"

"We could change the tire ourselves."

He stared at her like she'd just suggested they rob a bank. "In the dark, on the side of the highway? In the rain?"

"It's fine," she said with more confidence than she felt. "The rain's letting up and the visibility's better already. Just pull up a little more, so we're on a straightaway instead of a curve." The easier they were to see, the less the chances of someone hitting them from behind.

Adam pulled the car up, slowly and carefully. He cut the engine and turned to look at Olivia uncertainly. "Maybe we should just wait for Triple A. They can do it for us and then neither of us has to mess with it."

"Are you afraid of getting your hands dirty?"

He looked embarrassed. "I've never changed a tire before. Have you?"

"Sure." Her dad had forced her to learn how to do it when she'd gotten her license. It had been a while, and she'd never had to do it on the side of a highway before—at night, in the rain—but she ought to be able to manage it. Especially with Adam lending his strength to turn the lug wrench, which was the part that gave her the most trouble. "I'll teach you. Come on. Get out on my side of the car. It's safer."

She got out and ran around to the back of the car while Adam slid out from behind the steering wheel and clambered over the passenger seat. Despite her optimistic declaration about the weather a minute ago, it was starting to rain harder again, and she was thoroughly drenched by the time she got the hatch open.

But it was just a little rain, right? If she could get this tire changed, they'd be back on the road in a few minutes. As opposed to waiting for a wrecker, which could put them hours more behind their already fucked schedule.

Adam met her at the back of the car, and they both huddled under the rear hatch while they flipped the back seat down and shoved their bags out of the way so they could lift up the bottom panel of the cargo area where the spare tire was stowed.

Or was supposed to be stowed.

"There's no spare," Olivia said, staring at the empty tire-shaped space.

"Nope," Adam agreed.

"I can't change the tire if we don't have a spare." There also wasn't a jack or a lug wrench, so even if there had been a spare, they still would have been screwed.

"Can I call Triple A now?" Adam asked.

"Yep."

He slammed the hatch shut and they ran back around to the passenger side in what was ramping up to another torrential downpour. By the time Adam had crawled across her seat and fit his large frame behind the wheel, Olivia was soaked through to the skin.

She did her best to wipe the excess water off her face and arms while Adam called AAA. Without a towel it was pretty much a fool's errand. Why, oh why had she worn a white shirt today? Now that it was wet it was semi-transparent, and her beige lace bra was showing through. Also, she was freezing, despite the fact that it was eighty-five degrees outside.

She toed her shoes off and pulled her knees up to her chest, wrapping her arms around them for warmth. Which mostly just succeeded in squeezing her wet clothes against her body, making her even colder.

"You want the good news first, or the bad news?" Adam asked when he got off the phone.

"Good news," she said. "I can't take any more bad news."

"They should be able to get a wrecker here in an hour."

She hugged herself tighter. "That's the good news?"

"The only garage in the area is closed for the night, so the wrecker's going to drop us off at a nearby motel."

She groaned and banged her forehead against her knees. "We're so fucked."

"Yeah, that about sums it up."

"I'm starting to feel like we're on a D&D quest instead of a business trip, and there's an evil dungeon master who keeps throwing obstacles into our path."

It took her a moment to realize Adam was laughing. It sounded strange and dusty, like he hadn't used it in a long time. Even he looked surprised by it, like he wasn't used to the sound of his own laugh. Maybe it was that rare of an occurrence, like an eclipse or a leap year. Or even rarer, like a comet that only came around once every century.

He reached up to wipe his eyes. "If I meet that dungeon master, I'm definitely going to beat the shit out of him."

"Have you ever been on a trip that went this bad?" Olivia asked.

"No. This is definitely the worst trip I've ever had." He laughed again, but this time it sounded shaky, with maybe a slight tinge of hysteria. "Congratulations, you're witnessing history."

"Lucky me."

He dragged a hand through his wet hair. "It could be worse, I guess."

"How?"

"I could be here with Gavin instead of you."

Olivia's stomach flipped over. Was he actually enjoying her company? She would write it off as a dig at Gavin, except for Adam's eyes. They'd gone soft again, and there was something in them she'd never seen before. It hinted at possibilities she wasn't prepared to think about or acknowledge.

Before she could formulate any sort of response, Adam twisted around and lowered his seat back to rummage around in his suitcase. "Here," he said, tossing her a heather gray hoodie.

She accepted it gratefully, using it to dry off her face and arms before putting it on and letting the softness encircle her in its warm embrace. A pleasant scent enveloped her: laundry detergent, something that smelled a little like leather, and whatever it was that Adam used in his hair.

"Better?" he asked as he dried his head with a black T-shirt.

"Yes. Thank you." She pulled the hoodie tight around her, resisting the urge to bury her face in it and huff it like glue.

When he'd finished drying off, he twisted back around in his seat with a tired-sounding sigh. "I guess I should probably turn the ignition off." He'd cut the engine earlier, but left the ignition on so they'd have light inside the car.

"Why?" She didn't want to lose the little bit of light they had, or the radio for that matter. It was one thing to be stuck in this tiny car together, but to be sitting here in the dark without even music as a distraction was an alarming prospect.

His hand was already halfway to the dash, and it paused in midair as he gave her a questioning look. "So we don't run the battery down?"

"Triple A is already coming," she pointed out. "If the battery dies, I'm pretty sure they'll be able to give us a jump."

"I guess." He sounded unconvinced.

"I'd rather have the light on so we're easy to see."

His expression shifted to alarm. "Do you think we're in danger here?"

"From flash flooding?" she asked, because flash flooding was always a danger with this kind of rain.

His eyes widened. "Oh my god, are we in danger from flash flooding?"

"Probably not here."

"*Probably not here?*" he repeated, sounding panicky.

She tried to reassure him. "I mean, it seems like we're on decently high ground. And I don't remember crossing any bridges recently, so we're probably fine." Her voice rose a little at the end, making it sound more like a question than a statement.

Adam sucked in a shaky breath. "Okay, I was actually worried about the danger from a car hitting us from behind, but now I'm afraid we're going to be swept away in a flash flood, so thank you for that."

"You're welcome," Olivia said. "If it's any consolation, I'm now worried we're going to be hit from behind, so I guess we're even."

"Terrific."

An eighteen-wheeler blew past them on the highway, making their car rock and the windows rattle.

"It's probably fine," she said. "On both counts."

"Yeah. I'm sure it is." Adam leaned back in his seat and she watched his chest rise and fall as he tried to make himself relax. It was just like at the airport, when the crowd had made him nervous. Or on the plane, when he'd been anxious about takeoff.

The urge to take his hand was so strong her fingers actually twitched. She shoved them under her leg instead. "Where would we even go if we decided to go somewhere safer?"

"No idea."

"There's nothing around here. I mean nothing."

"True."

"Like, maybe if we happened to set out in the right direction, I guess we might stumble across a barn or an old shed or something eventually, but I don't know how that would be any better."

It sounded too much like the setup of a fanfic or erotic novel. Two people stranded in the middle of nowhere take shelter from the elements in a rustic barn and end up huddling together for warmth until their repressed urges take over and then…

She couldn't think about what happened after that.

Or repressed urges.

Or huddling.

Not when they were sitting in a car with the windows fogging up. Against her will, Olivia's mind traveled back to the last time she'd been inside a fogged-up car with a member of the opposite sex. It had been way back in high school, with Bobby Barger. Olivia's face heated at the memory, and she was grateful Adam wasn't looking at her.

"How would Triple A even find us if we were off hiding in

some ramshackle barn?" he mused as he peered out the window at the inky darkness.

Olivia's mouth was dry, and when she spoke the words came out in a hoarse whisper. "They wouldn't."

He nodded. "We're better off staying here in the car."

"It's the safest thing to do." She uncapped her water bottle and took a long drink.

"Definitely."

"Yep." Her thumbnail scraped at the label on the bottle. "We'll just…stay here."

They both fell silent as they stared straight ahead at the rain battering the windshield. Tiffany's "I Think We're Alone Now" came on the radio, and it felt way too pointed, like some higher power was looking down on them and laughing, but Olivia couldn't make herself reach for the radio to change it. The air in the car felt too heavy, like it was pressing down on her. Pinning her to her seat. Her wet clothes clung to her skin like adhesive tape under Adam's hoodie as his scent twined around her.

He cleared his throat, and she tensed.

"Are there any more Beaver Nuggets?"

Chapter Nine

It only took the wrecker forty-five minutes to get to them. Good thing, because Olivia's phone was running low on battery by then. When she'd gotten tired of reading her social media accounts, she'd resorted to playing Candy Crush, which she'd forgotten she still had on her phone.

The rain had stopped, thank god. Olivia was halfway to being dry after their earlier soaking, and she didn't relish the idea of getting drenched again.

There was a small cargo space in the cab of the tow truck, behind the seats. It was just big enough to fit their suitcases. The tow truck only had two seats, but the console lifted up to provide an uncomfortable-looking platform for a third person to sit.

As the smallest, Olivia assumed the middle seat would fall to her, and she resigned herself to spending the drive pressed up against their wrecker driver, Wes. But Adam stopped her when she tried to climb into the cab ahead of him, and took the uncomfortable middle seat for himself.

She felt guilty as she watched him try to fold his long legs into the cramped space under the dash, but also grateful. Wes seemed perfectly nice, albeit in a part-time motorcycle gang member sort of way, but as a rule, Olivia didn't love being pressed up against strange men in tight quarters.

It was chivalrous of Adam to take the hit for her. More than chivalrous. It showed a greater degree of empathy and concern for her comfort than she'd known he was capable of.

Once he'd gotten himself settled in the middle seat, Olivia climbed in and fastened her seat belt, trying very hard not to touch Adam's butt in the process. Which turned out to be completely impossible, since her seat belt was basically *under* his butt.

"Sorry," she said, flinching like she'd been shocked when the back of her hand grazed his haunch.

"Here, let me help."

Adam wrapped his hand around hers and guided her seat belt into the latch wedged between them.

Dirty thoughts flitted through her mind as the two pieces clicked together. Never mind that they were in a tow truck that smelled like Funyuns and motor oil, while a guy in dirty coveralls winched up their poor Honda Fit behind them. Suddenly she was thinking about seat belt latches as a metaphor for male and female sexual organs, and how Adam's hand was so big it completely covered hers, and what that might say about the size of other parts of his anatomy.

It was a relief when Wes finally climbed in the truck, distracting her from her dirty train of thought. Wes was in no way a small man, and his presence made things even more cramped. Adam was forced to lean toward Olivia in order to give Wes room to work the gearshift.

Adam was tilted at almost a twenty-degree angle, his shoulder crushed up against hers and their heads practically touching. It probably would have been easier and more comfortable for both of them if he'd just put his arm around her, but no way in fresh hell was she going to suggest it.

Country music poured out of the speakers when Wes started

up the engine, and she saw Adam wince. Without thinking, she put her hand on his thigh to give him a sympathetic pat.

In her defense, his leg was pressed up against her leg, and her hand had already been resting on her own thigh, only a couple inches from his, so it wasn't like it had far to go.

Adam's gaze slid over to her, his brows slightly raised in amusement, and she snatched her hand back in embarrassment.

After that, Olivia kept her hands clasped in her lap like a prim schoolgirl for the remainder of the ride.

Wes dropped them off at the nearest motel, which was just down the road from the auto shop where he was taking their car. When the garage opened in the morning, they'd be able to walk there to pick up their car after the tire had been replaced.

The Budget Motel was a dreary-looking place sandwiched between an RV park and a medical supply store. It reminded Olivia a little too much of the Bates Motel for her comfort. The parking lot was poorly lit and mostly empty except for a few eighteen-wheelers and pickup trucks.

The inside of the motel wasn't much more reassuring. The walls were covered in fake wood paneling, the carpet was stained, and the ceiling was discolored from old water damage.

"How many rooms?" the desk attendant asked. He couldn't be much older than twenty-five, but he had wispy, thinning hair and a leathery look about him, like bacon that had been left in the skillet too long.

"Two," she and Adam both answered at once.

The attendant's eyes shifted to Olivia, lingering on her for an uncomfortably long time before returning to his computer screen. Everything about him looked vaguely greasy. Greasy scalp, greasy beard, greasy clothes. He looked as if he'd smell like the inside of a deep fryer if you got close enough to smell him—which she planned to avoid at all costs.

She crossed her arms over her chest and shuffled closer to Adam, suddenly reminded of an old episode of *Criminal Minds* where the creepy hotel proprietor had let himself into female guests' rooms in the middle of the night as they slept. "Preferably adjoining rooms," she added. "If you have them."

Adam gave her an odd look but said nothing.

The attendant finished checking them in and gave them their keys, his eyes slithering over Olivia once more as he slid the plastic cards across the counter. Adam held the door for her as they exited the lobby, and she felt his hand lightly brush the small of her back as she stepped past him.

She wondered if he'd sensed her unease or noticed the attendant leering at her. Had he been trying to comfort her or warn the other guy off?

The rooms they'd been given were side by side, on the front of the building facing the highway. There was indeed a connecting door between them Olivia discovered after she bid Adam goodnight and let herself inside.

The single queen bed was shrouded in a hideous polyester spread that matched the hideous orange carpet. She could hear the sound of a TV coming through the wall from the room beyond hers, and the window rattled every time a truck blew past on the highway outside. Despite all that, it looked decently clean, although she wouldn't want to go over the place with a black light.

She engaged both the deadbolt and the safety latch on her door before stripping out of her still-damp clothes and washing her face. While she was digging through her suitcase for dry pajamas, there was a knock on the door.

Panic clogged her throat for a second before she realized it had come from the adjoining door to Adam's room and not the outer door.

"Hang on," she called out, hurrying to pull on a black T-shirt and pair of pajama pants before opening the door.

Adam had changed too, into gray sweatpants and a plain white undershirt that was so thin she could actually see his chest hair through it. The dark hair grew in two small tufts around his nipples, and in a thin trail down the middle of his abdomen. Was it her imagination, or was that the contours of an actual six-pack beneath the fabric? She'd thought only actors and bodybuilders had six-packs, yet here was one in the flesh, and almost close enough to touch.

"You look different," Adam said.

Olivia dragged her eyes away from his torso and reached up to touch her face. "I took off my makeup."

"I almost didn't recognize you."

She didn't know whether to be insulted or flattered. "Thanks?"

"No, I mean..." He shook his head, grimacing. "I like your face without makeup."

"Oh." She was so stunned all she could do was blink as he shifted from one foot to the other.

"I'm starving," he admitted sheepishly. "I don't suppose you have any food in your Bag of Holding you'd be willing to share?"

"Sure," she said, grateful for something to focus on other than the fact that he'd just said he liked her face. "Come in." She left the door open and crossed to the table where she'd set her purse down.

Adam padded into the room behind her. "You can say it if you want."

Her fingers stilled inside her purse. "Say what?"

"You were right. I should have bought more food at the truck stop."

She let out the breath she'd been holding and went back to laying out the food in her purse. "Can I get you to repeat that so I can document it for the record? 'Adam Cortinas officially concedes that Olivia Woerner was right.'"

He let out a low, husky laugh as he surveyed the selection of granola bars, nuts, chips, cookies, and beef jerky she'd arrayed on the table. "Sure, if I can take a picture to document this bag-lady food stash. Were you seriously carrying all that in your purse?"

"Yes." She'd bought snacks to last the whole week, in case there wasn't an opportunity to replenish her supply after they started working.

"Why are you like this?" he asked as he chose a granola bar.

"I just am. This is the personality I was born with."

He shook his head as he tore open the wrapper. "There has to be a reason you are the person you are. Something in your past that informed your hoarder tendencies."

"No there doesn't. Some of us just came from the factory broken."

"I don't think you're broken."

Once again, she found herself flummoxed because he'd said something nice to her. She chose the path of least resistance by ignoring it completely. "Not everyone has some deep, dark personal tragedy lurking in their past that molded them."

He stopped chewing for a second. "Must be nice."

Her eyebrows raised, along with her curiosity. "Do you have a tragedy in your past?"

"No," he answered way too fast.

"Now who's lying? You know what I think? I think it's easy for you to tell the truth when it's about someone else, but it's another matter when it's your feelings on the chopping block."

She could tell she'd scored a point, because his face looked like a door that had been slammed shut. But instead of feeling smug she felt bad. Whatever painful experience had made him into the person he was today obviously wasn't something he wanted to talk about.

"Never mind," she said. "I didn't mean to push."

"Yes you did."

She lifted her eyes to his. "No, and that's the truth. I wouldn't have brought it up if I'd realized there was really something there. It wasn't my intention to make you uncomfortable."

He nodded, seeming to accept this. "I'm not uncomfortable."

"Okay." She was certain he was lying again.

"I'm not. I'm..." He trailed off, frowning.

"What?"

"I don't know what I am."

"That's okay too."

He shoved the last bite of granola bar in his mouth and carried the wadded-up wrapper over to the trash. "It's not really a tragedy. Not like you're thinking. No one died."

"Okay," she said simply. She gestured at the table. "You want something else?"

He selected another granola bar, shrugging as he unwrapped it. "It was just your standard-issue, run-of-the-mill heartbreak. The kind of thing that happens to people every day."

The tautness in his expression caused a surge of protective feeling in her chest. "There's nothing run-of-the-mill about having your heart broken."

"No, I guess not." He bit into his granola bar and swallowed with a grimace.

She sat down on the foot of the bed but didn't say anything. She wouldn't push him to talk about something that was obviously painful. If he wanted to tell her more, it was up to him.

He walked over to the window and pushed aside the blackout liner to peer into the darkness. "It's raining again."

"It rains a lot here this time of year. Except when it doesn't. It's always either flooding or a drought."

They both fell silent.

"I had a girlfriend," he volunteered finally, still staring out the window. "A serious one. We worked together at my last job and dated for almost two years. I was going to propose." He fell silent again, although that clearly wasn't the end of the story.

"What happened?" Olivia asked when he didn't say anything more.

He turned around, but kept his eyes on the floor. "I found out she was sleeping with my best friend."

"Motherfucker."

He was so startled by her language he almost smiled. "Yeah, that's one word for it."

"I'm sorry," she said. "That sucks."

"Yeah, it really does." He sat down heavily on the bed beside her. His weight dipped the mattress, tipping her toward him so their shoulders touched.

Instead of scooting away, he stared at the remains of the granola bar in his hand, almost but not quite leaning against her. "It's one thing to be betrayed by the person you think is the love of your life. It happens, you know?"

Olivia didn't know, not firsthand, but she nodded sympathetically.

"But Jeff and I had been best friends since our freshman year of college," Adam went on. "I'd told him I was going to propose to Hailey. Shit, we'd even talked about what kind of fucking ring I should buy her. And the whole time he was banging her behind my back." His eyes met Olivia's. "Can you believe that?"

"No. I can't even imagine. What a festering shitbag."

She'd never loved anyone enough to get married, but she had a best friend. It was unthinkable that Penny could ever do something like that to her. If she did—Olivia didn't even know what she'd do.

"I lost both my best friends in one fell swoop," Adam said. "And I had to change jobs, because I couldn't go to work every day and face her. It was almost like I lost my whole life." His face looked vacant, like he'd gone wandering through dusty memories and gotten lost.

Olivia wanted to take his hand, but instead she pushed herself off the bed. "This calls for chocolate."

He dropped back into the present with a jolt, giving her a questioning look. "You had chocolate in your bag this whole time and you weren't going to offer me any?"

"It's for emergencies," she said as she dug into her purse.

"What, like late night motel confessionals?"

She tore open a bag of mini peanut butter cups with her teeth. "Exactly like that. I always carry emergency chocolate with me."

He smiled. "Just like Remus Lupin."

Sitting back down on the bed, she passed him the open bag of candy. "Hey, you never know when you're gonna run into a Dementor."

He popped a peanut butter cup into his mouth and drew in a sharp breath through his nose. "I never told anyone all of that before."

She blinked at him. "Seriously?"

"I told people we broke up, obviously. But I never told anyone why. I guess some of our friends must have put it together after, but I don't see any of them anymore."

"Why not?"

"Because they were Jeff and Hailey's friends too."

"You don't think they'd be on your side?"

"It's not about sides," he said, shaking his head. "They reminded me too much of what I'd lost—of the life I thought I had that was all a lie. I didn't want to see them anymore. I didn't want to see anyone." Two spots of color bloomed on his cheeks. He was embarrassed.

"So you just cut everyone out of your life?" Olivia asked, starting to understand why he was so detached and standoffish at work. He'd been so damaged by this one betrayal that he'd turned himself into a hermit.

"Not everyone. I still see my family."

"But you didn't tell them what happened?"

He stared at the floor, miserable. "Not all of it. I was… ashamed, I guess. I felt like a fool, and I didn't want my family to see me that way. It's easier if people think things just didn't work out. Irreconcilable differences or whatever."

She couldn't imagine what it must be like to keep all that betrayal bottled up inside. To hide it from the people you cared about the most, and push everyone else away. Isolating himself like that meant he'd never had a chance to work through it and lance the poison in the wound.

He looked so broken, she wanted to say something to repay the trust he'd shown by confiding in her. But everything she could think to say sounded trite and hollow. So instead she laid her head on his shoulder, hoping he would understand what she meant, but couldn't find the words to express.

When he didn't seem to mind that, she worked up the courage to take his hand. She pressed her soft palm against his rough one and twined their fingers together. His hand was warm and hers was cold, she realized when she felt his body heat soaking into her skin. It traveled up her arm and radiated through her whole body before settling in her chest.

They sat there together, holding hands in silence. Keeping each other company and giving each other space at the same time. Olivia didn't even know how much time they spent that way before Adam cleared his throat with a sound like a rusty chainsaw.

She lifted her head and her eyes met his.

Oh man, those eyes.

She was in no way prepared to stare directly into those eyes of his. Especially the way they were looking at her now, deeper and darker than she'd ever seen.

For a moment Olivia was paralyzed, unable to look away even though looking was almost more than she could stand.

"We've got a lot of work to do tomorrow," Adam said.

It took her incapacitated brain a second to register the meaning behind his words.

His hand slipped out of hers and he stood up. "We should get an early start in the morning. Like, crack of dawn early."

Jesus everloving Christ, did he think she was coming on to him? Was that how it had seemed? Because that was *not* how she'd meant it.

Not that she was disinterested, necessarily.

To be honest, she was having trouble parsing how she felt

about him. It seemed to change from moment to moment. One second she wanted to sock him in his annoying, sexy mouth, and the next she was imagining what it would be like to kiss him. It was starting to give her whiplash, all this pinging from one extreme to the other.

And now she'd accidentally given him the impression she was coming on to him, when she was just trying to be a friend.

Fine. Whatever. She couldn't be held responsible for his misapprehensions.

"Do we know what time the auto shop opens?" she asked, trying to play it cool as he backed away from her.

"Seven, I think."

"Okay," she nodded. "I'll be ready."

"Well, goodnight. And thanks for—" He waved his hand at the snacks on the table, but she suspected he was talking about more than just the food.

"Anytime," she told him, hoping he knew what she meant.

When he got to the doorway he paused and half turned back. "You want to get some breakfast while we wait for the car?"

"Sure. Sounds great."

Adam stepped into his room and started to close the door.

"Do you mind leaving the door open a little?" she called out.

His eyebrows drew together in confused surprise. "Why?"

"This'll sound dumb, but that guy at the desk creeped me out the way he stared at me when we asked for separate rooms. I just —I'd feel better if the door were cracked a little. Just in case—you know—so you'd be able to hear if anything..."

Adam's face went all hard and protective, like she'd inadvertently engaged some sort of alpha male *Terminator* mode. "You think he's going to try to come into your room or something?"

"No, not really. I'm just being paranoid, probably."

"Did you do the extra latch on the door?" He walked over to her door and double-checked all the locks. Then he went to the window and checked that too. "I'll make sure my room's secure too, just in case."

"I know it's weird that I'm worried about it."

"It's not weird," he assured her.

What was weird was that she trusted Adam so much without really knowing him. If you'd told her yesterday that tonight she'd be asking him to leave the door between their rooms open, she'd have called you a raging nutbar.

What was she doing trusting him this much? Giving him access to her room while she slept? That wasn't something you did on a regular business trip with a regular coworker.

But she did trust him. Because of the way he'd held her hand on the airplane during the turbulence, and the hesitant way he'd touched her face in the car after their flat tire, checking to see if she was okay. How he'd taken the middle seat in the wrecker, and made sure her door was secure just now, without mocking her or making her feel stupid for being frightened of a motel desk clerk.

Her gut told her she was safer with the door between them open than with it closed.

"Is a few inches all right?" Adam asked, moving back to the doorway.

"Yeah, that's great. Thanks."

"Just scream or something if you need me."

"You better believe it."

His mouth twisted into a smile. "Goodnight, Olivia."

"Night."

When he was gone, she went into the bathroom to brush her teeth. By the time she came out, the light was already off in Adam's room. She tried not to look at the crack in the door as she padded across the room, or think about him lying there just a few feet away as she turned out her own light and crawled into bed.

It was a long time before she fell asleep.

Chapter Ten

Olivia's alarm woke her at six thirty in the morning. Adam's room was still dark and quiet, so she slipped out of bed to shower.

She dressed for a day working at the plant: long-sleeved plaid shirt over a white tank top, comfortable jeans, and a pair of battered Doc Martens she'd had since college. When she came out of the bathroom, the light was on in Adam's room, and she could hear him talking on the phone to someone. Rather than eavesdrop, she dug her makeup bag out of her suitcase and went back into the bathroom, leaving the door open to let the steam out.

A few minutes later, there was a rap on the door between their rooms. "Hey," Adam called out.

"Morning," Olivia said, leaning out of the bathroom.

He was still wearing the sweatpants and T-shirt from last night, and his hair was all sleep-mussed and unbearably attractive. It was so unfair that he could roll out of bed looking like a snack, when she looked like the Bride of Frankenstein's homely cousin before she'd brushed her hair and put on makeup.

"I just talked to the guy at the auto shop. Car will be ready in an hour." He was typing on his phone as he spoke. "I'm updating Gavin and Brad on the situation. Anything you want me to add?"

Olivia chewed on her thumbnail. "Make it sound even worse than it is. Be sure they know we could have died when that tire blew on the highway last night."

He nodded without looking up. "Don't worry. I've got your back."

The funny thing was, she believed him. What a difference twenty-four hours could make.

Adam finished what he was typing and reached up to scratch his head. "Anyway, we've got plenty of time if you want to walk somewhere for breakfast."

"Sounds good."

He hooked a thumb over his shoulder. "Lemme just shower and get dressed."

When Adam was ready, they set out for the Whataburger just down the highway. It was only a five-minute walk, but it was already as hot as the asscrack of hell outside. Two minutes after stepping out the door, Olivia took off her plaid shirt and tied it around her waist. She looked like a background extra from an old episode of *My So-Called Life* and she didn't care.

Adam had changed into a faded denim shirt, Dickies work pants, and well-worn Wolverine boots, and he fit right in with the truckers and blue-collar workers grabbing breakfast at the Whataburger. The coffee tasted like it had been made in the iced tea urn, but Olivia's honey butter chicken biscuits were as delicious as she remembered.

Adam's lip curled as he unwrapped one of the tacos he'd ordered. "There's American cheese on these."

"It's a burger place, not a taco truck." She pushed one of her chicken biscuits over to him and claimed a taco. "Trade me. I like their tacos."

Things felt different between them this morning. After everything they'd lived through yesterday, topped off by Adam's late night motel room confession about his ex, it was impossible to look at him the same way she had before.

They were…maybe not quite friends, exactly, but somewhere on the way to becoming friends. Now that she understood him a little better, she felt a new sort of affection for him and all his odd ways.

"This chicken biscuit is fucking delicious." Adam was making The Face again. He ought to come with a warning label. *Caution: may erupt into spontaneous orgasm face while eating.*

"It's the honey butter," Olivia said, shamelessly enjoying the view.

He took another bite and let out a happy sigh. "Goddamn." His tongue shot out to lick the honey off his lips, and her eyes nearly bugged out of her head. "From now on, I'm ordering whatever you order everywhere we go."

She gulped down the rest of her tea-flavored coffee to cover her smile.

Their car was ready a half hour later. There was a different clerk in the lobby today, an older woman with long acrylic nails who chewed gum with her mouth open while she checked them out, and looked like she might be the mother of the creepy guy from last night. This place really was the Bates Motel. They were probably lucky to get out alive.

The auto shop was just a little farther down the road than the Whataburger, but there were no sidewalks and the wheels on Olivia's carry-on bag were useless on the gravelly shoulder. As soon as Adam noticed her struggling to carry her suitcase, he took it out of her hands.

"I can do it," she protested half-heartedly.

He tossed her a wry look over his shoulder. "I know you can, but it's faster if I carry both of them."

For once, she didn't argue with him.

Tejano music blared out of the open garage bays at Miguel's Auto Shop. A couple of pick-up trucks and a Tahoe were jacked up on the hydraulic lifts. Their tiny blue Honda Fit sat out front by itself looking like the runt of the litter. Adam talked to one of the mechanics in Spanish and paid for their shiny new tire with his corporate AmEx.

"Do you want me to drive?" Olivia offered, hoping he'd say no.

"Do you *want* to drive?" he asked her.

"Not really. But after all that driving you did yesterday, I figured you could use a break."

"I'm okay." He shrugged. "I got us this far, right?"

It was only two hours to the plant from here. They were so close Olivia could practically taste it. Soon they'd be able to assess the plant's systems and get started on the integration. They'd know if it was going to be possible to meet their deadline.

Halfway there, it started raining again, and Olivia abandoned her knitting to clench the door handle. Her mother always called it the Jesus Handle, as in *oh Jesus, oh Jesus, we're gonna die*, which was exactly what happened to be going through Olivia's head.

"It's gonna be okay," Adam said, throwing a concerned glance at her. "I had the mechanic check all the tires to make sure they were sound. We're in good shape."

Fortunately for both of them, the rain confined itself to a steady sprinkle that eased up after a half hour. Twenty minutes later, they got their first glimpse of the Walhalla Power Plant in the distance.

It squatted in the middle of a wide valley like a fairy-tale castle in a steampunk dystopia. The plant was some fifteen miles east of the tiny town it had been named after, built in the nineteen eighties beside a giant man-made reservoir. Adam turned off the highway at a sign that read *Plant Traffic*, and onto a narrow two-lane road.

Only as they drew near did Olivia truly appreciate the massive size of the plant. She'd thought it was close when they turned off the highway, but it turned out to be nearly two miles away. It was far larger than any castle she'd seen on her one trip to Europe, and far uglier, with great gouts of steam belching out of its stacks.

They pulled up to the gate, and Olivia squinted up at the behemoth structure while Adam rolled down his window. There was no guard shack or human being in sight, just a badge reader and automated chain-link gate.

"Let's hope the network guys remembered to give us access," Adam said as he dug his company ID out of his wallet.

"What happens if they didn't?" Olivia asked, chewing on her thumbnail. She hadn't been a nail-biter since middle school, but this trip was taking its toll on her self-control *and* her fingernails.

"Then we sit here until we can get someone on the phone to come out and let us in."

Fortunately, the network guys had come through, because the gate slid open with a rusty screech when Adam swiped his badge.

There were only eight or so cars in the crushed gravel parking lot, and he parked beside them, in front of a low cinder-block building that resembled a construction site office. There was safety signage everywhere, including one directing visitors to check in at the control shack, and another warning them to wear hard hats at all times.

Olivia didn't have a hard hat. When she got out of the car, she untied her shirt from around her waist and pulled it on over her arms. Long sleeves and long pants, that was what Gavin had said.

While she was doing that, Adam went around to the back of the car and dug into his suitcase, coming out with his laptop bag and a hard hat. When he put the hard hat on, he looked like Mr. July in a sexy construction worker calendar.

"Do I need one of those?" she asked, trying not to ogle him too much.

"They'll have extras inside you can use." He slammed the hatch closed and locked the car. "Come on, let's go find the plant manager."

He turned out to be a big bear of a guy named Kurt, whose

office was inside the control shack. He was built like a mountain made of muscle. His biceps were the size of honey-baked hams under the long sleeves of his blue work shirt, and he had to be at least six foot four. He made Adam look small, and Olivia feel positively Lilliputian.

"We were starting to worry you two weren't gonna make it." Despite his intimidating size, Kurt had a warm, friendly smile that got warmer as he shook Olivia's hand in his huge bear paw.

Adam's eyes seemed to narrow as he watched them. "We had a few setbacks on the road."

"All that matters is you're here now, safe and sound," Kurt replied with Zen-like congeniality. He gestured at the empty room around them. "You can set up at any desk you like."

The control shack was simple and spartan, dominated by an open area filled with desks and monitors displaying status messages and stats on the various parts of the plant. There was a break room area off to one side with a vending machine and a Bunn-o-matic coffee maker that looked like it dated from the eighties, and next to that a single unisex bathroom.

Across the room was the building's only office, belonging to their new friend Kurt. It was separated from the main space by windows affording a view of everything. Next to that was an open door leading to a utility closet containing all the networking equipment.

"You let me know if there's anything I can do for you while you're here." Kurt's bluff, hospitable smile settled on Olivia again.

"She needs a head and eye protection," Adam said, scowling like he'd tasted something bitter. "It's her first time at a plant."

Olivia pinned him with a sharp look of displeasure as Kurt headed into his office. They'd only just gotten here and the last thing they needed was to alienate the perfectly nice plant manager.

Adam's sour expression melted into bemusement as he mouthed a silent *What?*

Be nice, she mouthed back. Honestly, how did he do this on his own all the time?

"I got you covered," Kurt said as he emerged from his office and presented Olivia with a hard hat and safety goggles. "Make sure you wear these anytime you leave this building."

"Got it, thanks." She tried the hard hat on for size. It swamped her whole head, tilting forward into her eyes.

Kurt reached up to adjust it for her, grinning as he tipped it back out of her face. "Works better if you can actually see. There's a strap inside you can adjust."

"Don't suppose these come in child-sized?" she asked, tightening it to the smallest size.

"'Fraid not," Kurt said as she tried it on again. It was a little loose, but workable. He gave her an approving nod. "I think it suits you just fine."

Adam was looking annoyed again. "We should get to work. We've got a lot to do and not a lot of time to do it in." He'd already claimed a desk and unpacked his laptop.

Olivia followed suit, choosing the desk directly behind his. A cool calm settled over her as she sat down and logged into the VPN. She might be a nervous wreck before a job started, but once she had a concrete task in front of her, everything clicked into place and her focus was absolute.

The RTU at the plant turned out to be over twenty years old. In fact, Kurt told them proudly, it had been installed by his father when he'd been plant manager.

The outputs weren't compatible with their newer system, but Adam had already shipped a brand-new RTU to the plant, which was waiting for them in Kurt's office. While he went out to install it, Olivia went over the site's run book, familiarizing herself with the standard operations and procedures for stopping, starting, and debugging the plant's systems.

They spent the rest of the day making sure the new RTU was picking up data from all the sensors, eating out of the vending machine, and drinking pot after pot of scorched coffee from the ancient Bunn-o-matic. From time to time, one of the workmen on shift would come into the control shack for a bathroom or coffee break, or to shoot the shit with Kurt, but mostly it was quiet, and they were able to work uninterrupted.

Hours after Kurt had bid them goodnight and been replaced by the swing shift manager, Adam spun his chair around and tapped Olivia on the shoulder.

She'd been concentrating so hard on the telemetry data on her screen, she started at the unexpected touch. Adam smiled in response, and the fluorescent lights overhead seemed to glow brighter. It was the first time he'd smiled since they'd gotten here, and the sight of it was like laying eyes on an old friend after a years-long absence.

"We should take a break." He stifled a yawn, his shoulders slumping with fatigue. "We've been at it for hours."

"What time is it?" she asked, stretching her arms toward the ceiling until her vertebrae popped. She'd been hunched over her computer so long her body had tried to fuse itself into the shape of a question mark.

Adam glanced at the watch on his wrist. It was one of those big round ones with lots of tiny dials set into the face. With his shirtsleeves pushed up, it emphasized how muscular his forearms were. "Nearly seven. We need to check into our hotel before they give our rooms away."

"Yeah, okay." She put her laptop to sleep and shoved it and the power cord into her purse. No way was she letting it out of her sight, even for a second.

"I'm thinking we'll grab some dinner while we're out and then come back here to work for a few more hours." Adam already had his laptop packed up, and he lifted his messenger bag onto his shoulder, grabbing his hard hat as he headed for the door.

It was raining when they stepped out of the control shack, and the two of them blinked at the masked glow of the late-day sun like a couple of mole rats emerging from the bowels of the earth.

"How long's it been doing that?" Olivia asked, pulling her borrowed hard hat down to shield her face from the rain.

Adam shrugged as he started for the car. "No idea." He unlocked it and held her door open for her.

He drove them back down the two-lane road until it met up with the highway again, and turned toward their motel. It was a fifteen minute drive from the plant, past a couple farming towns too small for even a post office, much less a hotel or restaurant, and over a river that wound back and forth across the highway a few times.

They were staying at the Quality Inn, which was positively luxurious compared to their accommodations the night before. It had been recently renovated, and the lobby featured shiny new tile, a pair of faux-leather couches, and a cluster of high-top cafe tables alongside a granite bar where a continental breakfast was served each morning, according to the motel manager who checked them in.

Their rooms were at opposite ends of one wing of the long, low motel. Olivia's was closest to the lobby, and before Adam left her at her door they made a plan to meet back up in five minutes and walk over to the diner across the parking lot for dinner.

It was just enough time to drag her bag into her room, wash up a little, and reform her frizzy hair into a fresh bun.

The rain had ramped up into a proper downpour by then, so she grabbed her umbrella on the way out the door. Adam didn't have one, so they huddled under hers together as they splashed across the parking lot.

The diner reminded Olivia of what IHOPs were like when she was little, before the corporate facelift: sticky and a little grungy, but homey in an old-fashioned, Formica-covered sort of way. The menu was of the unpretentious, stick-to-your ribs variety that was becoming harder to find in Los Angeles. Sure, she could practically feel her cholesterol rising just sitting in the vinyl booth, but it was reassuring to know there were still restaurants in America that didn't serve quinoa or kale.

They both ordered coffee to fuel them through the second half of their late night at the plant. She was feeling more hopeful now that they'd actually gotten started. The situation wasn't nearly as bad as she'd feared—in fact, it felt pretty manageable. They had two full days before their deadline, and barring any unforeseen catastrophes, they might actually be able to make it.

Olivia ordered chicken-fried steak from a middle-aged waitress who called her "honey," and Adam followed through on his earlier pledge by getting the same thing.

There was a TV on the wall behind Olivia, and he frowned as he stared past her. "That looks pretty bad."

She swung around to look at the screen. It was tuned to a local Austin station which had interrupted programming for a weather report. The radar image showed all of central Texas blotted with stripes of red, yellow, and green.

"That must be the storm that kept us from landing in Houston," she said. "Looks like it's headed our way."

"More like right on top of us," Adam said, gazing out the window. The downpour had turned into a full-scale deluge, and the parking lot was filling up with water.

"We might have to wait it out," she said. "At least until this band passes."

The waitress brought their food, and they dug in with the enthusiasm of people who'd been eating out of a vending machine all day. The chicken-fried steak was as big as a hubcap, and Olivia only made it a third of the way through before throwing in the towel.

She watched Adam thoughtfully as he piled a mound of mashed potatoes on his fork. He was three-quarters of the way through his chicken-fried steak and still going strong. How did he eat like that and still have a flat stomach? He must spend every second of his free time in the gym.

"Where did you grow up?" It occurred to her that she knew next to nothing about him, aside from last night's revelation about his ex-girlfriend—and even that had been light on the details.

He'd mentioned having to change jobs, but he hadn't said where he'd worked before. For all Olivia knew he'd fled from another city entirely. Not that she could blame him. The whole situation sounded like an absolute nightmare. It was no wonder he'd wound up so prickly and closed off—and so obsessed with truthfulness.

"Riverside." He gulped down the last of his coffee and poured another cup from the carafe. By Olivia's count it was his eighth cup of the day. On top of all the Cokes he'd gotten from the vending machine, his blood had to be at least fifty percent caffeine at this point. "What about you? You said you're from around here somewhere?"

"Houston."

"So you're a city mouse, not a country mouse."

Her lips pursed in irritation. "I'm not signing off on your mouse metaphor."

"I've noticed you seem sensitive about your size."

"Remember yesterday, when you told me I should point out when you're being rude?"

He blinked at her over a forkful of steak. "I'm being rude again?"

"If you suspect I'm sensitive about something, maybe just don't bring it up."

"Fair enough," he said. "What brought you to Los Angeles?"

"College. I transferred to Cal State LA after my freshman year at UT."

"Why'd you transfer?"

She leaned back in the booth, cradling her coffee mug in both hands. There were a lot of reasons—culture, weather, generalized boredom—but one had motivated her above all others. "Mostly, I wanted to be farther away from my family."

"What's wrong with your family?" he asked. "Or are you sensitive about that too?"

"No, I brought it up, so it's fair game." She shrugged and glanced out the window. The rain was still coming down in buckets. "Nothing's wrong with them. I just wanted to forge my own path, preferably in another state."

"What path did they want for you?"

"Not much of one, to be honest. I was always in the shadow of my siblings. My older brother was this star football player until he blew out his knee a few years ago. And my little sister was an annoyingly perfect straight-A student who ended up at Harvard Law. I couldn't compete with either of them."

"You didn't get straight A's?" Adam asked, cocking an eyebrow as he forked the last bite of chicken-fried steak into his mouth.

Olivia snorted. "I had a solid A-minus average. In any other family I'd have been considered a great student, but not with Emily around."

He pushed his empty plate away. "Do you resent her? Or them?"

"Not excessively so." Mostly, she tried not to think about them at all. "Do you get along with your sister?" She assumed so, since she'd invited him to dinner.

"Sisters," he corrected with an emphasis on the *s*. "I have three of them—all older."

"Wow." So he'd grown up in a house full of women. That helped explain some things—like his incongruously chivalrous tendencies and considerate streak.

"We get along okay," he said with a one-shouldered shrug. "My family's pretty close. Too close, sometimes."

"But you didn't tell them what happened with your ex."

He stiffened, his eyes skating away. "No."

"And I can see you'd rather not talk about it, so I'll drop it."

He threw her a grateful look. "Should we get dessert?" he asked, turning to catch the waitress's attention.

"Might as well." Olivia's eyes went to the window again. Outside, the parking lot looked like a lake, and the rain was still pouring down. "Doesn't look like we're going anywhere anytime soon."

They ordered hot fudge brownie sundaes and took their time eating them. The storm still hadn't abated when the waitress came to clear their empty dishes away a half hour later. "Hope you folks weren't planning on going anywhere tonight."

"We've actually gotta get back to work," Adam told her as he dug his wallet out of his back pocket.

"Where you work at?" she asked.

"The Walhalla plant down the highway."

The waitress clucked sympathetically. "Not tonight you don't. Remember that river you drove over on your way here? It's out of its banks. Highway's completely flooded out west of here."

"But we have to get back," Olivia said as panic rose in her throat.

The waitress nodded at the window. "You see any cars out there getting through?"

They turned to look. The highway that had featured a steady stream of traffic an hour ago was now dead quiet. Not a single pair of headlights shone through the rain.

They were stranded.

Chapter Eleven

"How long before the road's drivable again?" Adam asked the waitress. His fingers drummed the Formica tabletop like a court stenographer jacked up on speed—or eight cups of coffee and four cans of Coke.

The waitress shrugged. "Rain's gotta stop first. After that, maybe a few hours? Assuming the bridge doesn't take any damage in the flooding. Last year an RV got swept into it and took out a couple of the pilings."

"There's got to be another way around," Olivia reasoned. "An alternate route to get to the plant so the workers can get back and forth."

"Oh, sure. You can get to it from Rutersville."

"Where's that?" Adam asked.

"Another five miles down the highway, on the other side of the river that's out of its banks."

"So we can't go that way either," Olivia said.

"Not right now you can't. 'Fraid you're stuck here for the time being. But don't worry, hon. The water always goes back down eventually." The waitress swept Adam's credit card off the table and carried it away with their dirty dishes.

"Fuck," Adam said, rubbing his forehead with the heel of his hand. "Fuck, fuck, fuck."

"Maybe we're almost through the worst of the storm and it'll stop raining soon?" Olivia pulled out her phone to check the weather, but the cellular signal was crap and she couldn't get her weather app to load.

"Or maybe not." Adam pointed to the TV behind her.

It was showing another weather bulletin. The radar was pretty much solid red all around them, with more rain bands headed their way from the southeast. The crawl at the bottom of the screen announced a flash flood warning *and* a severe thunderstorm warning in effect until six the following morning.

"What now?" Olivia asked numbly. She shouldn't be surprised, the way the rest of this trip had gone. They really were cursed.

Adam shrugged helplessly as he stared at the flooded parking lot. "I guess we wade back to our rooms, get a good night's sleep, and wait for it to stop raining."

Even with Olivia's umbrella, the dash back to their rooms left them both soaked to the skin. Adam left her at the door of her room, and she went into the bathroom to strip out of her wet clothes and dry off.

She changed into pajamas and crawled into bed with her laptop, but the hotel Wi-Fi wasn't working. Not surprising, she supposed, given the strength of the storm. The wind had increased in the last hour, and thunder rumbled ominously in the distance. Her phone still didn't have a signal either, and when she tried to turn on the TV she found the cable was out too.

There was nothing to do but try to get some sleep and hope things would be better in the morning.

SOMEONE WAS POUNDING on Olivia's door.

She wasn't sure how long it had been going on, because it was hard to hear over the storm raging outside. The wind had picked up considerably since she'd fallen asleep, and the roar of it was punctuated by a deafening crash of thunder.

She grabbed her phone off the nightstand to check the time and saw that it was after midnight. When she tried to turn on her lamp, she discovered the power was out.

The pounding on her door resumed with renewed vigor, joined this time by Adam shouting, "Olivia! Wake up and open the fucking door!"

She used her phone to light her way to the door and fumbled open the locks.

Adam stood outside in the rain, barefoot, in nothing but the work pants he'd been wearing earlier. "Were you asleep?" he asked incredulously. "How the hell can you sleep through this shitstorm?" The parking lot lights were out behind him, as were the diner's lights and the lighted sign for the motel.

A flash of lightning sliced through the sky, illuminating the rain blowing nearly sideways outside. Olivia stepped back so he could come in out of the elements, which was when she noticed he had his suitcase with him. "What's going on? Why do you have all your stuff with you?"

He ran a hand through his hair and droplets of water flew everywhere. Several of them hit Olivia's arm, leaving pinpricks of cold on her skin. "A tree limb got blown down and punctured the roof. Water started coming through the ceiling of my room."

She went to get him a towel. "Shit. Is your laptop okay?" Priorities were priorities. Clothes could be replaced, but they needed both their laptops in working order tomorrow.

"Yeah, the leak was in the bathroom, so most of my stuff is okay."

"That's a relief." She handed him a bath towel and pointed her phone's light at the floor, trying not to watch as he dried off his bare torso. "Not that it's good your room sprang a leak, but it's good it wasn't like over the bed or something."

Adam grunted as he ran the towel over his head, leaving his hair sticking up in spikes. Another crash of thunder rattled the window, and Olivia wondered how she had managed to sleep through all this racket. She must have been dead exhausted.

"Yeah, that's the good news," Adam said grimly as he draped the towel around his neck like an athlete in a locker room. "They don't have any empty rooms because of all the people stranded by the storm."

"Oh." Olivia was suddenly, acutely aware of the fact that she wasn't wearing a bra and Adam was shirtless and soaking wet in her motel room—that was now *their* motel room, if she was correctly interpreting the situation.

"So I need to share with you." Adam's eyes drifted to the king-size bed behind her.

Olivia swallowed down a wave of nervous panic. "Of course," she told him, forcing nonchalance into her voice. "Of course you can." It was an emergency, and in an emergency you had to make do. Even if it meant sharing a bed with a gorgeous coworker you were totally obsessed with who didn't like you back.

Poor Adam was the one getting the shit end of this stick. If he'd suspected how she felt about him, he must be feeling mega uncomfortable right about now—even more uncomfortable than she was.

But what choice did they have? She supposed she could offer to sleep on the floor—or in the car maybe. But she couldn't imagine him allowing her to do either. If she even suggested it, he'd probably insist on being the one to do it. And she couldn't let him do that. It would be unfair to let him be so uncomfortable, just because she was having inappropriate feelings about him.

She could do this. It was a big bed. This would be fine.

Belatedly, she realized they'd been staring at each other without speaking for a weirdly long time, and her nervousness multiplied, filling her stomach with a small swarm of bees.

Adam seemed to become aware of the awkwardness at the

same moment she did and turned abruptly away, dragging his suitcase into the far corner of the room. Using his phone as a light, he bent to unzip it and rummaged around inside. "I'm gonna go change into dry pants, if that's okay."

"Sure. Totally." She waved him toward the bathroom door. "Make yourself at home. You can just shove my stuff aside if it's in your way." As the words left her lips, she suddenly remembered all the wet clothes she'd left hanging in the bathroom to dry. Both her bra and her underwear were hanging from the shower rod, right at eye level.

Adam disappeared into the bathroom, and Olivia waited for the inevitable wisecrack about her display of intimate apparel, but it never came. He was either too polite to comment on her underthings or too tired.

She tried not to imagine him on the other side of the bathroom door, confronted by her lingerie as he unfastened his pants and pushed them down his narrow hips, peeling the wet cotton off his legs, leaving him in nothing but his underwear.

Assuming he even wore underwear.

Olivia shook her head to chase away that particular thought spiral and shined her phone's light on the rumpled bed. She leaned over to smooth out the sheets on the far side and fluff Adam's pillow before getting in and turning off her phone, plunging the room into total darkness. She'd been sleeping smack dab in the middle of the bed before, but now she lay so close to the edge of the mattress that her arm kept trying to slide off and flop toward the floor.

Adam emerged from the bathroom a moment later, his phone's light casting a blue glow around the room. He paused for a second before padding over to the nightstand on the empty side of the bed. His phone went dark, and she heard him set it on the nightstand. The bed shook as he lay down beside her and arranged the sheets, trying to get comfortable.

"I'm sorry about this," he said, as if the storm and the leak and their current situation were somehow his fault. "Pretty sure the last thing you wanted was to end up sleeping with me."

It took all of Olivia's willpower not to laugh out loud. "It's fine," she said, struggling to keep the strain out of her voice as sleazy thoughts filled her brain.

"I promise I'll keep my hands to myself." There was a hint of humor in his tone, as if the idea of wanting to touch her was hilarious.

Her libido deflated like a punctured balloon. "Great."

"And you do the same." He was joking, but the warning went straight to the pit of her stomach.

She attempted to play along. "Right. I'll try not to feel you up in your sleep."

There was a long beat of silence before he said, "Every time I think this week can't get any worse..."

She let out a thin laugh. "Just imagine if Gavin were here instead of me."

The bed vibrated with Adam's laughter, and Olivia wished she could see him. She loved the way he looked when he laughed, and it happened so rarely.

"I wonder what Karen in human resources would say about this," he said.

"I think she'd probably have a stroke." Olivia felt like *she* was having a stroke. She was pretty sure she could smell burnt toast. Or maybe it was just ozone from the lightning outside.

"I don't think there's anything in the HR manual for situations like this."

"No, probably not. Although maybe there should be. We should raise it with Karen when we get back to the office."

Lightning flashed outside, momentarily casting a glow across the ceiling, and Olivia braced herself for the inevitable crash of thunder to follow. When it came a second later, it was as loud as an explosion, and she felt Adam flinch beside her.

"I really don't like storms," he said in a tight voice.

"I used to love them when I was a kid. Of course, when you're a kid they're not as much of an inconvenience as they are when you're an adult and you actually have responsibilities and stuff." Like needing to get back to work.

Every hour that it continued to rain, it became less likely the roads would be clear by morning. With the power out they couldn't even log in remotely, and who knew how long it would take to restore service. There were probably a lot of downed trees and downed wires, which would take time to fix, and the utility crews wouldn't even be able to start until the flooding receded enough to let the trucks through.

"Did you ever see the original *Poltergeist?*" Adam asked, interrupting her anxiety spiral.

"Yeah." Olivia's friend Esther was a horror movie nut and had dragged her to a revival showing a couple years ago. It had been cheesy as hell, but still scared the living shit out of her.

"My sisters used to babysit me, and they let me watch it when I was way too young. You know that scene where the kid is in bed listening to the storm and counting the seconds between the lightning and the thunder to track the storm's approach?"

"Oh yeah, and then the tree outside—"

"Yeah," Adam interrupted tightly. "It basically scarred me for life."

"How old were you?"

"Like eight or something."

"That is *way* too young for that movie."

"Tell me about it."

There was another flash of lightning and they both fell silent, counting in their heads. *One, one thousand…two, one thousand…* This time the thunder wasn't quite as deafening.

"The storm's moving away," Olivia said, stifling a yawn.

"Thank god."

"We're so fucked." She wasn't talking about the storm anymore. "This whole project is a disaster."

"It'll be fine."

She turned her head toward him, but it was too dark to see anything. "How can you say that?"

The mattress squeaked as he rolled onto his side. "Because it will be, one way or another." He sounded a lot closer, now that he was facing her, but she knew there was still a good two feet of empty mattress between them. No-man's-land, where none dare to tread. "No one's going to die or lose their job if we miss a deadline because events beyond our control conspired against us."

"Speak for yourself."

"You're not going to lose your job." His tone was gently chiding.

"Maybe not, but it sure isn't going to help me get ahead."

"I told you I wouldn't let them blame you for any of this and I meant it." His voice was feather-soft. A hushed promise made in bed late at night.

Olivia reached up to rub her tired eyes. "Thank you."

"It really is going to be okay."

She could almost believe him. Outside, the storm howled and raged, overturning all their best-laid plans, but lying there next to Adam in the dark, she felt strangely secure. Maybe his confidence was contagious.

Another flash of lightning glowed through the curtains, momentarily lighting up his face. Their eyes met just before the room plunged into darkness again.

One, one thousand…two, one thousand…three, one thousand… As she silently counted the seconds between the lightning and thunder, she knew Adam was doing the same. *Four, one thousand…five, one thousand…*

Sometime between six and seven, she fell asleep.

OLIVIA CAME SLOWLY awake to the ghostly gray light of a new

day leaking through the blinds. The storm had died down, but she could hear a steady rain still falling outside, which meant the roads probably weren't even close to being clear yet.

She didn't want to get up, because she was too warm and cozy in bed.

Mostly on account of the warm body spooning with her.

Adam's arm was draped over her waist. His breath warmed the back of her neck, his chest was pressed against her back—and she was pretty sure that was his morning wood she could feel on her ass cheek.

It had been an embarrassingly long time since Olivia had woken up in the arms of a man. She'd forgotten how nice it was. Heat rolled off his bare chest, soaking into her skin through the thin fabric of her T-shirt. The pressure of his body against hers was intensely comforting, like a weighted blanket, but instead of a blanket it was a half-naked man in her bed.

She tried not to move, so she could enjoy the sensation a little longer. The scent of his skin enveloped her like a dream. He smelled like sunshine and fresh air. Zesty and sweet, with just a hint of spice. They should create a Yankee Candle based on him, because Mountain Lodge had nothing on Adam Cortinas.

Any second now, he would wake and realize what he was doing, and it would be all over. He'd spring away from her, mortified, and try to pretend he wasn't grossed out and appalled.

Which was exactly what happened.

He must have sensed a change in her breathing, or maybe her muscles had tensed from trying so hard to stay still. Whatever it was that alerted him, she felt him stiffen behind her, and he rolled away with apologies spilling out of his mouth.

"It's okay," she said, refusing to look at him as she swung her feet over the edge of the bed. "Don't worry about it."

"Can we just pretend that didn't happen?" His voice was agonized, and it hurt more than she expected it to.

"Already forgotten," she assured him and fled to the bathroom, exhaling in relief as she shut the door between them.

Unfortunately, she'd left her phone by the bed and the power was still out, which meant it was pitch black in the windowless bathroom except for a faint strip of light leaking under the door. She had to feel her way to the toilet and then feel her way to the sink to wash her hands.

When she came out of the bathroom, Adam was sitting on the edge of the bed rubbing his face. His skin looked ashen when he glanced her way, but maybe it was just the wan gray light coming through the blinds he'd thrown open.

The rain was still coming down at a steady rate outside, but at least the wind and lightning seemed to have abated. It was definitely past dawn, but how long past was impossible to tell under the low ceiling of pea-soup clouds blotting out the sun.

Adam got up and shuffled past her without a word, clutching his phone as he disappeared into the bathroom. When the door clicked shut, Olivia went to get her own phone and check the time.

It was almost eight and her battery was at ninety percent. Hopefully it would last until the power came back on—and hopefully that would be soon. If she let herself think about all the work waiting for them that wasn't getting done, she might actually throw up.

Her phone showed one whole bar of reception, up from zero last night, and when Adam came back out of the bathroom smelling of toothpaste she was attempting to download her email.

"Do you have a signal?" he asked. "Because I've still got nothing."

He wasn't wearing a shirt, which she'd known from their bout of inadvertent morning cuddling, but this was the first time she'd seen his bare chest in the light.

He was all taut muscle and smooth skin. Broad shoulders narrowed to a flat stomach framed by two perfect hipbones. Square pectorals stacked above the ridges of his abs like building blocks, with a narrow trail of dark hair running down the midline to his navel and below.

Of course she'd known he had a good body before—it had been obvious from the way his clothes clung to him—but there was something much too real and too raw about seeing him exposed like this in the feeble daylight coming through the window.

He didn't seem to know what to do with his hands, which kept running over his forearms in a way that made him seem vulnerable and unsure of himself. When he lifted his eyes to her face, she saw that same vulnerability in them, and it made her want to hug him.

But she was pretty certain that was the exact opposite of what he wanted, so she looked back down at the phone in her hand, which was struggling to display the images in a sale email from...

Adam and Eve.

There was a photo of a bright pink vibrator on her phone.

And now Adam was coming closer like he was going to peer at the screen.

Holy shit. Delete.

Her panicked thumb missed the trash button twice before finally hitting the mark and making the accursed photo disappear —just as Adam drew close enough to see what she was looking at.

"More like half a signal," she answered in a voice that sounded like it had been squeezed out of a dying frog. "So far I've downloaded two whole emails, both of them junk."

He paced to the window and gazed out at the rain. "I hate being cut off from information like this. How the hell are we supposed to know what's going on?"

"We go find some other people, that's how." She got up and went to her suitcase. "Lemme put on some clothes on and we'll try the lobby."

Other people would be good. Other people would provide a buffer between them, and more importantly, a distraction from the memory of Adam's erection pressed against her ass.

Chapter Twelve

Olivia remembered to take her phone into the bathroom with her this time, so she could actually see to brush her teeth and do something with her hair.

When she came back out a few minutes later, Adam had pulled on a T-shirt, to her simultaneous disappointment and relief. But mostly relief. It was a hell of a lot easier to deny her attraction to him when he wasn't flaunting his beautiful bare chest in front of her.

Unfortunately, he was still wearing his heather gray sweatpants, which were a lot to take. They clung to his hips and other assorted parts of him—parts that had recently been snuggled up against her, Olivia's unhelpful brain reminded her—in an almost indecent way that did not leave as much to the imagination as she would have liked under the current circumstances.

Not that any clothes would be able to fully mask his attractiveness. The man would probably look sexy in a garbage bag.

But not *as* sexy.

So that's what she imagined on the wet walk to the lobby—Adam wearing a garbage bag instead of those stupidly hot sweatpants of his. It almost sort of helped a little.

There were a bunch of other motel guests gathered in the lobby, listening to a local news station on an old battery-operated radio like the one Olivia's dad kept for hurricanes.

"Morning, you two!" Linda, the motel manager who'd checked them in last night, greeted them with a raised hand and a wiggle of her nicotine-stained fingers. Her smile grew wider, a hint of mischief bleeding into it as her gaze flicked from Adam to Olivia and back to Adam again. "You poor thing. Did you manage to get any sleep at all last night?"

"Yeah, some," he mumbled, staring at the floor.

Was Olivia imagining it, or was he *blushing*?

Linda waved at the coffee bar where the promised continental breakfast had been set up. "I'm afraid the power outage has made for slim pickings today. There's instant coffee and hot water—thank heaven for gas stoves. No pastry delivery today, but we've got cereal and yogurt and fruit. And bread and bagels, but of course the toaster doesn't work."

"Thank you," Olivia said, already dumping a packet of instant Folgers into a styrofoam cup. "This is great."

"What's the word on the storm?" Adam asked, grabbing a couple yogurts and a banana.

"Highway's still shut down and they've extended all the warnings until two," Linda said. "Sounds like there's another band headed our way."

Adam set his food on an empty cafe table and looked at his phone. "Still no signal. What about you?" he asked Olivia.

She joined him with her coffee and a yogurt, and pulled her phone out of her purse. "Still just the one."

"See if you can send Gavin a text to let him know what's going on."

While Adam went to make himself an instant coffee, Olivia composed a text to Gavin, updating him on their latest crisis. She hit send and offered a silent prayer to the gods of the cellular network as the progress bar slowly ticked across the screen.

"Well?" Adam asked, sliding onto the seat across from her.

She held up a finger. "Hold please."

Only a little bit more to go. *Come on, come on...*

"Yes!" she announced with a fist pump when the text went through with a *whooshing* sound.

Adam's jaw tensed as he swallowed a yawn. "Let's hope the signal stays strong enough to receive any response he sends."

Olivia gulped down her instant coffee and grimaced at the taste. "What's he going to say? Swim there? It's out of our hands."

Adam's eyebrows lifted as he licked yogurt off his spoon. "You seem uncharacteristically chill this morning, considering our current circumstances."

She shrugged, concentrating on her own yogurt so she wouldn't have to watch his tongue sexily caressing his plastic spoon in a way that was probably illegal in the Bible Belt. "It's a new thing I'm trying, in order to keep from going completely insane."

If she let herself think about it, she would seriously lose her shit, and she couldn't afford to do that. Nature had conspired to put them in a temporary time-out, and there wasn't a damned thing either of them could do about it. The only way to bear it was to ignore it.

They ate their yogurt and sipped their coffee while the local news radio station regaled them with tales of flooded roadways and washed-out bridges, and of the next band of storms expected to hit that afternoon.

Since it was their only available caffeine source, they stayed for a second cup of instant coffee before bidding Linda goodbye. She told them to come back at noon, when she'd have some sandwiches for lunch. At her urging, they took a few extra pieces of fruit and fun-size boxes of cereal to snack on later.

Back in Olivia's room, the door closed behind them with an ominous thud.

They were alone again. Just the two of them, in a small motel room with a giant bed and nothing to do.

"I'm going to take a shower," Adam announced, and disappeared into the bathroom with a bundle of clothes from his suitcase.

Thank god. He was changing out of those damned sweatpants. Hopefully that would alleviate some of Olivia's distraction. And it gave her a few minutes alone to breathe without feeling like she was being watched—or having to worry about accidentally being caught watching him.

Only when she heard the shower turn on did it occur to her that Adam was completely naked in the next room. Which of course caused her to imagine the water running in sheets over his smooth, muscled torso and down his legs. His hands lathering up the soap, and rubbing it over his body—

Nope. Stop.

She needed something else to focus on. Something to take her mind off the hot naked man on the other side of the bathroom door.

She got up and dug out her knitting. It wasn't exactly bright in the room, but if she sat on the floor by the window, there was just enough light to knit by. Fortunately, she was far enough along on Penny's shawl that she'd internalized the pattern and could practically do it with her eyes closed.

When Adam came out of the bathroom, all dewy-skinned and damp-haired, wearing jeans but no shirt, Olivia was grateful to have something to look at that wasn't his glistening bare chest.

"Man, it's dark in that bathroom with the door closed. And it gets hot in there fast."

"Uh huh." She breathed in the steamy, shampoo-scented air billowing out of the bathroom and tried not to imagine droplets of condensation collecting on Adam's skin and trickling down the valley between his pecs. Instead, she repeated the shawl's pattern in her head like a mantra: *Knit three, knit two together, yarn over. Knit three, knit two together, yarn over.*

He was walking back and forth across the room, from his suitcase to the bathroom and back again, and he still hadn't put his shirt on. He must be trying to cool off first, but she wished he'd hurry up and do it. She caught a whiff of that spicy, woodsy scent she'd smelled on him before, and glanced up to see him rubbing product into his hair in front of the bathroom mirror.

She lowered her eyes again quickly, but the scent had filled up the small room, and she inhaled slowly through her nose, enjoying the comforting Adam-ness of it.

He came back out of the bathroom and paced to the window, standing beside her as he stared out at the rain. "This weather is bullshit."

"Uh huh," she said again.

His bare foot was next to her knee, his leg so close it was practically touching hers, and the scent of his hair product was making her dizzy. Also, he still hadn't put his shirt on. He had it draped over his shoulder like a dish towel, and it required all her willpower not to gaze up at him wistfully.

"You really lived with storms like this all the time growing up?"

"Not like *this*." Her knuckles were white as she gripped the knitting needles. *Knit three, knit two together, yarn over.* "A storm this bad used to be an every ten to twenty years kind of event. But with climate change they're practically an annual occurrence these days."

She could feel his eyes on her now. He was watching her knit, standing over her all bare-chested and hot in those jeans that hugged his thighs in a way she refused to let herself look at even though his thighs were at eye level and only inches away from her.

Knit three, knit two together, yarn over.

How much longer was he going to stand there watching her?

And was he ever going to put his damn shirt on? Her fingers fumbled the yarn-over, and she nearly dropped a stitch.

Olivia gave up and set her knitting aside. "If you're done in the bathroom, I'm going to shower."

"Yeah, it's all yours." Adam stayed by the window while she dug through her suitcase for clean underwear. "Don't forget to take your phone," he added when she started for the bathroom, clutching her small bundle of intimate apparel to her chest—as if he hadn't already gotten an eyeful of her underwear in the bathroom this morning.

"Thank you." Grabbing her phone out of her purse, she escaped into the bathroom and blew out a relived breath as the door closed between them, plunging her into total darkness.

She used the light on her phone to start up the shower and undress, but turned it off before stepping under the water. Showering in the dark felt weird, but also oddly nice. It was a little like being in one of those sensory deprivation tanks, and it went a long way toward helping her relax.

Until it started to get too hot and stuffy. Adam was right—with the bathroom door closed, the steam combined with the lack of air-conditioning turned the small space into a sauna pretty fast. She decided against washing her hair, which she wouldn't be able to blow dry anyway, and switched the water to cold for a minute to cool off before stepping out of the shower.

It was no fun pulling her clothes on over her damp, sweaty skin, but she didn't have the option of walking around shirtless like Adam, so she sucked it up and got fully dressed. When she pulled open the door, sighing with relief at the influx of cooler air that hit her skin, she found Adam bent over examining her knitting.

He jolted upright, raising his hands like a criminal cornered by the police. "I wasn't touching it, I swear."

"Okay." She carried her dirty clothes over to her suitcase and stuffed them deep inside.

"What are you making?" he asked, edging toward the bed.

"A shawl."

"Is it for your grandmother?"

"No, it's for my best friend for her birthday."

He nodded and sank down on the foot of the bed.

Olivia went back to her knitting, settling down on the floor again with her back against the window. Outside, the rain pattered a steady, lulling rhythm, punctuated by an occasional increase in intensity when a gust of wind blew it against the glass.

Adam pulled out his phone with a sigh, thumbed through it for a minute, then shoved it back in his pocket with another, louder sigh. He got up and wandered over to the minifridge, stooping to examine its contents for a minute before shutting it again. He paced over to his suitcase, stared at it for a second, then paced over to the window to stand next to Olivia again.

"Dude, you're making me nervous. Find something to do."

"I'm bored," he said with a grumbly sigh. "I can't even play games on my phone, because I don't want to run the battery down. Not that I have a cell signal." He glanced at her. "Have you heard anything more from Gavin?"

She set down her knitting and checked her phone. No new emails or texts. "Nope," she said, picking up her knitting again.

It wasn't even ten in the morning. This was going to be one long-ass, unbearable day.

Adam sank down on the bed again. "What the hell did people do before electricity and television and the internet?"

"I think most of them worked themselves half to death just to stay alive."

"Okay, but what about rich white people with servants to do all the work for them? How the hell did they pass the time?"

She thought about all the costume dramas she'd watched. "I believe their lives were so dull they considered a turn about the room entertainment."

His eyebrows lifted in amusement. "So I should go back to pacing, then?"

"Please don't." She tried to recall what else the idle rich in historicals did to fill their time between meals and dressing for meals. "They wrote a lot of letters. There's probably a pen and stationery in the desk if you want to give it a shot."

He made a face. "I'm not doing that."

"Needlecrafts," she said smugly over her knitting.

"Good for you, but I seem to have left my embroidery back in LA."

"Painting, drawing, music, and other artistic endeavors."

"None of which is of any use here in this motel room."

"They read a lot—or read aloud to each other."

"Do you have any books?"

"On my phone."

"Great." He fell backward onto the bed, arms akimbo above his head, and let out another dramatic sigh. "I guess I'll just lie here and contemplate existence, then." Who knew he was such a baby?

"They also played games," she offered.

He swiveled his head toward her hopefully. "Do you have any games?"

"On my phone."

"No deck of cards in your Bag of Holding? I'm disappointed in you, Woerner."

Her stomach did a swoop. It had annoyed her the first time he'd called her by her last name, but she was starting to like it. "Too bad you can't play D&D with just two players."

"You can, actually, but one person has to play the dungeon master and all the other party members and NPCs."

She wrinkled her nose. "Sounds like a lot of effort."

"It'd be pretty impossible without internet access or rule books to refer to."

"Or dice," she added.

He shrugged. "I have a dice app on my phone."

"You really are a nerd," she exclaimed in delight.

"Are you surprised?

"Yes. You're way too hot." The words tumbled out before she could stop them.

He managed to look startled, dismayed and flattered all at once. "I don't know if that's more insulting to me or to nerds."

Olivia concentrated on her knitting, pretending she hadn't just overplayed her hand. "I just called you hot, so it's probably not more insulting to you."

"But it implies you didn't think I was interesting because of the way I look."

"Well that's true." She risked a wry grin and he huffed out a laugh.

His gaze lingered on her, long enough to make her uncomfortable again. "Teach me to knit."

She stared at him in surprise. "You're not serious?"

He came over and sat down next to her on the floor. The spicy-sexy scent of his hair product perfumed the air between them. "Why not?"

She didn't know why not, except it wasn't something she could imagine herself doing.

But she had an extra pair of needles and some worsted waste yarn in the bottom of her knitting bag, so what the hell? At least it would pass the time.

ADAM GROANED in frustration as yet another stitch escaped off his needle. "Why am I so bad at this?"

Olivia reached out and pinched the tiny loop between her thumb and forefinger before it could unravel. "You're doing fine. You should have seen me when I first started."

The thing about teaching Adam to knit that she hadn't previously considered was that it required them to sit very close together. Even worse than that, it required her to touch his hands —a lot. She'd had to show him how to hold the needles, and where to insert the needle into the loop, and how to wrap the yarn around and transfer the stitch from one needle to the other.

Not to mention, there were a lot of dirty-sounding phrases involved in knitting. Every time she had to tell him to "insert the point" or "stick it in there," she felt herself flush. It would be one thing if she was the only one conscious of the double entendre. But every time she said something like that, Adam would give her this *look,* like he was thinking about it too, and then they'd both be thinking about it, and she'd flush even more.

She'd even found herself uttering the phrase "just the tip," which had driven them both into a five-minute fit of hysterical giggles.

"Did you think it would be easy?" she asked as she carefully placed the loop back on his needle.

"Maybe? Easier than this, anyway."

"What exactly about using two sticks to turn a piece of string into clothing sounds easy to you?"

"Well, when you put it like that..."

"Not there," she said when he inserted his needle into the wrong side of the stitch.

He course corrected, the tip of his tongue sticking out as he concentrated on wrapping the yarn around his needle. "I guess I never really thought about it at all, except as something old ladies do."

Olivia rolled her eyes. "And if old ladies can do it, it must be easy?"

"Well...yeah?"

"It's not easy." She nudged his shoulder with hers, only barely resisting the urge to lean against him.

"I'm figuring that out." He sighed and lowered his small knitted rectangle to his lap. "My hands hurt, and it's getting too dark to see."

She turned and looked out the window. Ominous dark clouds were building to the south. The next band of the storm was coming.

"We should go grab some sandwiches from the office," she said, checking her phone and realizing it was past noon. Somehow they'd wasted over two hours knitting.

"Sounds like a plan." Adam stood and offered her a hand off the floor.

She accepted it with only a small hesitation. When his fingers closed around hers, firm and strong, she tried very hard not to feel like Elizabeth Bennett being handed into a coach by Mr. Darcy.

But she did. Oh, she did feel like that. So much so that when he let go of her, she dropped her hand to her side and flexed her fingers just like Matthew Macfadyen in that *Pride and Prejudice* gif she'd reblogged a million times on Tumblr.

Which maybe made her the Darcy in this situation? Because she was the one who'd liked Adam and had her petition rebuffed —even if it had been a request for a professional reference instead of a marriage proposal. And now she was the one who still liked him despite herself, when he didn't like her at all.

Except he liked her a little, didn't he?

He liked being with her better than Gavin. He'd said as much.

He just wasn't attracted to her the way she was attracted to him. But that was okay. That was fine. She only had to keep being normal around him in this absurd situation in this small room they were stuck in together with the giant bed. That was no problem at all.

"Aren't you going to put your shoes on?" Adam asked. "Or do you not want to go for sandwiches after all?"

"No, I do," Olivia said, snapping herself out of her daze. "I definitely want to go."

Chapter Thirteen

The sandwiches were made with Wonder Bread and bright orange squares of American cheese with lots of yellow French's mustard. To go with them there were single-serving bags of chips in a variety of flavors, and packets of Nutter Butters and Chips Ahoy cookies, and a cooler full of lukewarm cans of Coke.

It reminded Olivia of elementary school field trips, eating her sandwich on the bus out of a paper bag on the way back from the San Jacinto Monument or the Museum of Natural Science.

Except instead of a bus she was sitting in the recently renovated lobby of a Quality Inn, listening to a weather radio with a bunch of other stranded travelers. It felt like the setup for a *Twilight Zone* episode where they all realize the world has ended without them and they're the only people left alive—only at the end it turns out it's not the world that's ended, it's just their lives, and they're all trapped in purgatory together.

There was definitely a purgatory-esque theme to this entire trip.

As she ate her ham and cheese sandwich, she watched Adam on the other side of the room. He was standing by the trash can, peeling an orange as he talked to a beautiful, tall brunette. She was dressed in a cute matching workout top and tights like she'd just come from the gym—although there was no gym at the motel—and a full face of makeup. Her hair was pulled back in a ponytail so smooth and bouncy it made Olivia run her fingers through her own disheveled layers that were crying out for the aid of a blow dryer.

For once she hadn't bothered to put on makeup, and now she was regretting it, because Adam was talking to a beautiful woman with perfectly lined lips and he actually seemed to be enjoying himself.

Olivia had never seen him like this. He was lively and engaged, making eye contact and even smiling. But then who wouldn't smile at a woman who looked like that? She had the look of a former beauty queen or cheerleader turned pharmaceutical rep. The kind of woman who probably had an Instagram full of perfectly framed and filtered artistic selfies, and five thousand followers she was hoping to turn into a hundred thousand followers and a spot on a reality TV show.

They made a handsome couple: Adam with his broad shoulders and granite jaw, and Ponytail with her flat stomach and perfect posture. They would have the most amazing, dark-haired, insanely fit babies.

Olivia's eyes fell on Adam's hands, appreciating the confident dexterity of his fingers as he peeled his orange. He freed a segment of fruit and raised it to his lips, meeting Ponytail's eyes and smiling as he popped it into his mouth.

She was gazing back at him with a rapt sort of attention that basically screamed *I want to have sex with you.* Who wouldn't? The guy could make eating an orange unbelievably sexy. Imagine what he could do with those hands and mouth on a woman's body.

Adam said something that made the woman laugh, and she reached out to touch him, her manicured fingers stroking over the length of his forearm.

Olivia's stomach clenched and she turned away, looking out the window where the storm clouds continued to darken. Thunder rumbled a warning in the distance, and she shoved the last bite of sandwich in her mouth, grabbing some extra chips and cookies off the counter before making her way over to Adam.

He turned away from his companion as Olivia approached, and she felt the woman's eyes rake over her the way a rhinoceros beetle sizes up its adversary before a dual. Ponytail didn't know she had nothing to worry about. Olivia was ceding the field.

"I'm going to head back before the rain picks up," she told Adam. "Do you want me to leave you the umbrella?"

"No, I'll come with you," he said before turning back to the woman and bidding her goodbye with a "Nice talking to you" and a "Maybe I'll see you later."

Olivia could guess what that meant. She totally understood if he wanted to spend the night in this other woman's room. What else was there to do in this godforsaken place? What she didn't understand was why he didn't stay and keep talking to his new lady friend.

Adam retrieved their umbrella from the bucket by the door and flicked it open as they stepped outside. He held it over their heads as they hurried down the sidewalk to their room. A gust of wind drove a blast of rain into them, and he reached his free arm around Olivia's shoulders, drawing her closer as he turned his body to shield them both from the sideways rain.

Her hand bumped against his leg, coming dangerously close to his groin, and there was nothing else to do but put her arm around him to keep *that* from happening again. She rested her hand on his lower back, her fingers curling slightly around the thick column of muscle that ran alongside his spine. His T-shirt was so thin she could feel the heat of his skin, and the way his back flexed and shifted with every step.

She stumbled a little, and his hand squeezed her shoulder, steadying her as he pulled her even closer. She was huddled against him now, almost leaning on him, her cheek against his chest as they hurried back to the shelter of their room.

It wasn't until they were safely back inside and he'd let go of her that Olivia realized she'd been holding her breath. That had to be why she felt so dizzy. It was lack of oxygen, and not their clumsy, impromptu cuddle that made it so difficult to catch her breath.

Adam leaned outside to shake some of the water off the umbrella before shutting the door against the driving rain. "We left just in time," he said, propping the dripping umbrella in the corner as a rumble of thunder rattled the window.

"I didn't mean to drag you away from your new acquaintance. Who was she?" Olivia tried not to sound jealous, because she couldn't blame him for wanting to talk to someone who wasn't her after three straight days of forced proximity. They were like two characters handcuffed together in a tropey TV episode.

"I think she said her name was Becca?" Adam replied on his way to the bathroom. "Or maybe Beth. I forget."

"You looked like you were having a good time talking to her."

He shrugged as he reemerged with a hand towel. "She's a sales rep for some kind of health supplement? Sounded like a multi-level marketing scam to me. She was asking me about my fitness regimen, but I think she was just trying to sell me protein shakes."

He finished drying off his arms and offered the towel to Olivia. It smelled faintly of oranges from his hands. In fact, the whole room smelled a little like oranges, which was a distinct improvement over wet umbrella.

She hung the towel up in the bathroom when she was done drying off, and came back out to find Adam staring out the window.

"I guess it's too dark to keep knitting," he said.

"Yeah." It had gotten too dark to do much of anything, even though it was the middle of the day. There was enough light to move around and make out objects in the room, but not enough to read by or see fine detail.

She was tempted to get her phone out, but she needed to conserve the battery. Linda had said the power company had crews out working on the downed lines, but in this weather they wouldn't be able to get much done.

Lightning flashed across the sky outside, and Olivia saw Adam tense at the ensuing crash of thunder.

"Let's play a game," she proposed, both to distract him and herself.

He turned away from the window. "I thought you didn't have any games. Not that we could see them anyway."

"There are games we can play with just ourselves." His eyebrows shot up in amusement, and she gave him an admonishing head shake. "Get your mind out of the dumpster. I was thinking Twenty Questions."

"How about Truth or Dare?" he proposed instead. There was an eagerness in his voice that made Olivia's stomach tingle.

"I don't like dares," she said with equal amounts of trepidation and excitement. "I'm not going to lick deodorant or whatever other stupid, gross thing you come up with." She didn't tell him the real reason was that she didn't trust herself around him. It would be altogether too tempting to dare him to kiss her.

"Fine, then we'll play Truth or Nothing."

"What if one of us asks something the other doesn't want to answer? We won't have any recourse."

He toed off his shoes and sat on the bed, pulling his legs up underneath him. "We each get three passes we can use on questions we don't want to answer."

"And after we've used our three passes? What then?"

"Then you have to answer, no matter what." He patted the mattress beside him. "Come on, what else are we going to do to pass the time? There aren't enough people for 'light as a feather stiff as a board.'"

She laughed to hide her nervousness as she sat on the bed, leaning against the headboard with her legs steepled in front of her. "Are there any ground rules? Any subjects that are off-limits?"

He thought about it. "I don't know. I guess there are certain questions that would be inappropriate to pose to a coworker. We wouldn't want to upset Karen in HR." There was an ironic lilt to his voice, like he meant exactly the opposite. Like he was *dying* to ask inappropriate questions that would make Karen in HR apoplectic.

"I feel like these are extenuating circumstances," Olivia said, unable to help the smile that spread across her face. "We're a little beyond the purview of HR regs at this point, don't you think?"

They were sheltering in place during a natural disaster, sharing a motel room. A few hours ago they'd been spooning in this very same bed they now were sitting on. His erect penis had accidentally touched her leg, for Chrissake. Karen in HR would just have to deal.

"I think you're right." Adam grinned as he leaned back on his elbows. "The HR code of office conduct is pretty much a dot receding in the distance from here."

"Okay." Olivia laced her fingers together and straightened her spine. "In that case, I propose that for the remainder of the power outage, we aren't coworkers anymore. We're just friends hanging out. Agreed?"

"Agreed," Adam said, and a shiver of anticipation ran up her spine.

Let the game commence.

Chapter Fourteen

"Who goes first?" Adam asked.

"I don't know," Olivia replied, struggling to think of a question she wanted to ask him.

"I'll go, then. How old were you when you lost your virginity?" He blurted it out with no hesitation, as if he'd been thinking of it for a while.

"Wow. You really just went for it without any kind of easing-in period, didn't you?"

He shrugged, looking pleased with himself. "You said nothing's off-limits."

"Did I say that exactly?" She didn't recall using those exact words, but she supposed it might have been implied.

"You didn't say anything *was* off-limits. And you're the one who said we're just friends until the power comes back on."

It was true. She had said that. She just hadn't expected him to switch gears so abruptly.

Olivia grabbed her ankles and pulled her legs closer. "And I suppose you know when all your friends lost their virginity, do you?"

"You can't ask me a question until you've answered mine—unless you want to use one of your passes."

If he was starting with first sexual experiences right out of the gate, she could only imagine the questions were going to get even more personal and embarrassing from here, which meant she'd better hold on to her passes for dear life. "I was seventeen," she said. "My turn."

He nodded, displaying no reaction to her confession. "Hit me."

"How old were you when you lost your virginity?" It seemed as good a place to start as any, and turnabout was only fair.

"Twenty-one," he answered, surprising her. "Who was he?"

"What?" She was still digesting the fact that he hadn't had sex until he was in his twenties. A man as hot as this, who could probably have had anyone he wanted, and he'd waited. Why? Was it some chastity pledge, or something else? She wanted to ask, but wasn't sure she was brave enough to do it.

"The person you lost your virginity with," Adam prompted. "Who was he—or she, if it was a she?" His eyebrow quirked inquisitively.

"It was a he." Olivia picked at a loose thread on her pants. This particular chapter of her life made her feel a little ashamed. "His name was Mike."

"I'm gonna need more than that."

"Then you can ask another question on your next turn."

"No, I didn't ask what his name was. You have to tell me who he was to you."

"Fine. He was a senior I dated for a couple months my junior year of high school. We were in theater together, and I did his makeup for *Oklahoma*. He took me to prom, and we had sex in the back seat of his car outside the after-party at his best friend's house. Satisfied?"

She didn't mention that they'd had to split a six-pack of Zima to work up the nerve to do the deed, or that she'd broken up with him a week later, because she'd realized she didn't really like him that much. She'd just been impatient to punch her v-card, and he'd seemed like the most expedient means to an end. She still felt guilty about using him like that.

"Romantic. Sounds like a real Casanova."

She lifted her chin. "Maybe I was the Casanova."

"I can believe it." Something in Adam's expression sucked the air out of her lungs. "Your turn again," he prompted when she didn't speak.

She struggled to think up a question. "Who was *your* first time?" It wasn't very original to copy all his questions, but she wanted to know the full story.

He lay back on the bed and laced his hands behind his head. "Her name was Brie, and we dated for most of our senior year of college." He spoke in a monotone, like he was reeling off facts from a textbook. "Our first time was at her apartment off campus, two months after our first date."

Olivia searched his expression for some hint of emotion, but there wasn't one.

His head swiveled her way. "Most embarrassing moment?"

This one was a no-brainer. "In third grade, Jenny Gleason made me laugh so hard I peed my pants in the lunchroom."

"Poor third-grade Olivia."

"Yeah, it was horrifying. I'm still in therapy over it." She stretched her leg out and nudged him with her big toe. "Why did you wait so long to have sex?"

"Is twenty-one a long time to wait?"

"It is for some people."

He shrugged without quite meeting her eye. "I wanted to wait until I was with someone I cared about. I guess I wanted it to mean something."

Olivia's stomach tightened. She wished she'd waited like he had. Then maybe her memories of her first time would be something she could look back on fondly instead of this unpleasant stew of awkwardness and guilt.

"Why do you wear so much makeup?" Adam asked.

A million different answers danced on the tip of her tongue. It would be easy to say something flip, or offer an easy half-truth. Instead, she told him the real reason: "Because I always feel like people don't notice me otherwise. Like I blend into the furniture or something." She tried to laugh, like it was no big deal rather than something rooted in her deepest insecurities, only it came out sounding hollow.

"I notice you," he said. "Even without makeup. You always stand out to me."

It was possibly one of the most romantic things anyone had ever said to her. Even though he'd said it matter-of-factly, like it was just a mundane piece of information he was sharing. And maybe it was. Maybe he hadn't meant it to be romantic, and Olivia was reading too much into it.

Except his eyes. They were soft and serious, laser-focused on her with an intensity she definitely wasn't imagining. The spark in his eyes burned bright enough to see even in the storm-filtered light, and it sent her stomach spinning into the outer reaches of the galaxy.

He stretched his arm toward her, in what could be considered a completely innocuous way, like he was just trying to get more comfortable—except for the fact that his finger grazed the back of her hand. It was the lightest of barely-there touches, but it seared into her skin, leaving a stripe that felt permanent.

She could barely get out her next question, the one she'd been dying to ask. "What happened to Brie?" She needed to know more about this woman who was his first time. She wanted to know *everything* about her: hair color, shoe size, SAT scores. There were hours worth of questions tumbling around in her head. They could be here all day.

She wanted to be here all day.

The realization was punctuated by a distant rumble of thunder outside. For once Olivia was grateful for the storm and this whole cursed fucking trip. Because she was *enjoying* herself. She hadn't thought about work in hours, and she wasn't in any hurry to get back to the plant. All she wanted was to stay here talking to Adam, just like this.

"She got accepted to a graduate program in Ohio." He was talking to the ceiling again, and he'd retracted his arm. The hand that had touched hers now lay on his chest, right above his heart. "We mutually agreed to end things when she left instead of trying to do long-distance." He paused, and Olivia thought maybe he was going to add something else, but instead he looked at her and said, "Do you have any tattoos?"

"Yes," she said. "Did you love her?"

He rolled onto his side, propping his head up on his hand. "Hang on, I want to know more about this tattoo—or is it multiple tattoos?"

"There's only one, and you can ask when it's your turn again. Answer my question first."

The rain was starting to let up a little—it was no longer falling in sheets, just a simple, steady downpour—and the room wasn't quite as dark as it had been. It made it easier to see Adam's expression.

His eyes gazed straight into hers, and the sadness in their depths nearly took her apart. "Yes, I loved her. It broke my heart when she left. I wanted to follow her, but she didn't want me to."

"Did she tell you that?" It wasn't her turn to ask another question, but she had to know.

"Yes. She said she wasn't that serious about me. She didn't want to be tied down."

A sour feeling churned in Olivia's stomach. "Shit, I'm sorry," she said, both for asking the question and for the fact that it had ever happened to him. It was hard to imagine anyone saying that to him. What was wrong with this woman named after soft cheese that she couldn't appreciate a man like Adam when she had him?

Only the thing was, Olivia knew exactly what was wrong with

her. Because Olivia had been the woman who'd thrown away a perfectly good man before. A couple of times, actually. Just like Adam had been thrown away.

His eyes lowered, his lashes casting deeper shadows on his face. "It was a long time ago. I'm over it now."

He didn't look like he was over it. Olivia could see the pain etched in his face as clear as daylight, and suddenly she didn't want to ask him any more questions about Brie.

All her preconceptions about him had been wrong. She'd always assumed he was as lucky in love as a guy this gorgeous could be. Instead he was a serial monogamist who seemed to love selectively and hard, and who'd had his heart crushed at least twice before.

She wanted to give him a hug. She wanted to give him a lot more than a hug, but her brain intruded to remind her that was going too far. He didn't want her like that.

But a hug she might be able to get away with now that they were friends.

"Now tell me about this tattoo," he said, resting his chin in his hand. "I need to know everything."

She shook her head. "You're gonna laugh."

His eyes crinkled. "I hope so."

"It's on the side of my rib cage." She felt her cheeks color. "It's the White Tree of Gondor."

He didn't laugh, but he did grin. "You're a way bigger nerd than I am."

"Are you actually shocked? After I told you about my cosplay habit? *Lord of the Rings* was my first fandom."

"Cosplay's one thing, but a tattoo's forever. Can I see it?"

"That sounds like a dare."

"It's not. It's just a question. You can answer it however you want."

She bit down on her lip, then reached for the bottom of her T-shirt. He'd just ripped a bandage off his heart for her, so she figured she owed him one.

Slowly, she raised her shirt up to the bottom of her bra, twisting so the tattoo was facing him.

He crawled toward her on the bed for a closer look, peering at it intently. His face was only a few inches from her skin, his breath a warm tickle that sent goose bumps skittering down her arms. He lifted his hand, his fingers hovering in midair like he wanted to touch it, but he didn't.

Something surged beneath the surface of her skin, urging her toward him and craving the touch of his fingers. But she forced herself to hold still, even though it nearly killed her.

He lowered his hand. "It's beautiful."

"Thank you." She hoped it was too dark for him to see her blush as she lowered her shirt.

He flopped down on the bed beside her, cramming his pillow under his head. "Your turn."

"Um..." She didn't have another question ready. Her mind reeled as she curled up on her side, mirroring him. "Do you have any tattoos?" God, she was crap at this, regurgitating all his own questions at him.

"Nope," he answered easily. "My mother would murder me."

Damn. She'd really been hoping there was a tattoo hiding somewhere she hadn't seen. Although, she'd seen a lot of him at this point, so that really only left his ass and his legs.

He chewed on his lip, gazing at her as he considered his next question. "Have you ever sent a nude selfie?"

She only hesitated a second before answering. "Yes." Before he could ask a follow-up she blurted out her next question. "Favorite sexual position?"

His eyes widened slightly before skating away. Ha! She'd embarrassed him.

"You're going to think I'm lame," he said, rolling onto his back.

"Maybe."

"It's missionary."

She snorted. She couldn't help it. It was the most boring, vanilla possible answer.

He gave her a sheepish look without exactly looking at her. "It's because I like the closeness and the eye contact. I told you it was lame."

"That's not lame. It's almost stupidly romantic."

Something like a smile curved his lips, but it was tinged with too much bitterness to qualify as one. "Almost stupidly romantic could be the title of my autobiography."

"Or the title of your sex tape."

It was his turn to snort in surprised amusement. "Tell me about your last boyfriend."

It was an obvious line of inquiry, and she should have been ready for it, but she wasn't. "Pass."

"Fine," he said, and she exhaled in relief. *Bullet dodged.*

Until he asked his next question: "Why don't you want to tell me about your last boyfriend?"

"That's cheating," she protested.

"There's no rule against it. Either answer the question or use another pass."

She chewed on her lip. Technically, she could answer without having to tell him the thing she didn't want to tell him. "I don't want to talk about it because I don't want you to think badly of me."

He rolled onto his side again and propped his head on his hand. "I won't. I swear." He looked so earnest it made her want to confess every bad thing she'd ever done in her life.

Except for this one thing, because she still felt so guilty it made her sick to her stomach. "You don't know that. You don't know what I did."

"Did you cheat?" There was an edge to his voice now.

"I've never cheated on anyone," she told him honestly. That

much, at least, she could claim.

Adam's expression relaxed into a smile. "Did you murder him? Blackmail him? Sell him out to the mob?" He was teasing her now.

"The mob? Who am I? A nineteen fifties movie moll?" She laughed despite herself. "Nothing illegal or violent transpired."

"Then I promise not to think badly of you." He drew an arc through the air that encompassed them both. "This is a safe space. You can tell me anything."

She did feel safe with him. Lying face-to-face on the bed like best friends at a sleepover—or lovers staying up all night baring their souls. Like the two of them were in a cozy little bubble removed from the real world.

"I broke his heart," she said, dragging the admission out of the blackest part of her soul.

Adam's expression didn't change. "How?"

"He asked me to move in with him and I said yes. But then when we started looking at apartments and talking about leases and consolidating our furniture, I chickened out. I realized I couldn't do it—I didn't want to do it. I *wanted* to want it, but I didn't. Not with him."

She'd expected Adam to react with contempt, but instead he looked at her with sympathy.

"You don't owe anyone your love."

She shook her head, remembering how much pain she'd caused. "I strung him along for nine months, letting him think I loved him. He was blindsided when I told him. Seriously, completely gutted." She winced at the memory. "I've never hurt anyone that badly before."

"You didn't love him?"

"I thought I did, but...looking back on it, I think I just wanted to be in love. And I knew he loved me, so it was easy to go along."

"There's nothing wrong with that. You didn't hurt him on purpose."

"But I still hurt him. I'm just as bad as your soft cheese girlfriend."

"Brie." Adam smiled. "Neither of you are bad. You can't choose whether or not you love someone or how much. If you don't feel it, you don't feel it. Pretending's not going to make anyone happy. At least you were honest with him. You did him a favor."

Ryan had definitely not seen it that way. He was still making passive-aggressive comments about her on Instagram. "Is that how you felt when Brie ended things?"

"Not at first. But once the shock wore off, yeah. Can you imagine if I'd picked up my whole life and followed her? If she'd stayed with me out of guilt or obligation? We would have been miserable, and it wouldn't have lasted, and then I'd have been dumped *and* living someplace I didn't want to be."

"I guess."

"The fact that you're carrying all this guilt around over this guy proves what a kind, caring person you are. You should forgive yourself." He reached out, and Olivia held her breath as he tucked a strand of hair behind her ear. "You deserve forgiveness." His fingers brushed her cheek as he withdrew his hand, and her skin tingled as if it had been electrified.

"Do you think people are naturally monogamous?" she asked. "That we're meant to pair off like swans or penguins or whatever?" It was something she'd always wondered. Was her perfect match still out there somewhere waiting for her? Or was she too broken to see a good thing when it was right under her nose?

Adam's brow creased, and she felt an overwhelming urge to smooth it with her fingers. "I don't think people are naturally meant to do anything, and I definitely don't believe in soul mates. Do you?"

"Not if you mean some sort of creepy predestined coupling you have no control over." She'd seen enough soul mate fan fiction to be put off by the whole idea. "But I want to believe it's possible to find someone who fits you perfectly. I think it sounds nice, actually."

His mouth curved in a semi-smile. "So you'd like to find your matching penguin?"

"I'd just like to fall in love." She wasn't sure she'd ever admitted that to anyone before—not even Penny. She'd always tried to pretend she was tougher than that, that she didn't need anyone else to complete her.

"You don't think single people can live a happy, fulfilling life?"

"No, I totally think they can. I just…I'd like to see how the other half lives, I guess."

His face had gone strangely still, and she wondered what he was thinking. Was he remembering happier times when he'd been in love, or was he so scarred and embittered he'd given up on the whole idea? She wanted to ask him, but she was too afraid of poking another sore spot.

"It's your turn to ask a question," she said to break the silence, which had started to feel too weighty. The longer it went on, the more she felt like she was going to explode and do something she might regret.

"Okay." He was quiet for a moment, thinking about it. "Do you still hate me?"

Her insides crumpled themselves into a tiny ball. "I never hated you."

His eyes darkened with disbelief. "You did a little."

"I was pissed at you, but that's not the same as hate."

"Okay, maybe you don't *hate* me, but you don't like me very much."

She swallowed and looked away, so he wouldn't be able to see how very, incredibly wrong he was.

"See," he said in that know-it-all voice of his. "I'm right."

"No." She shook her head. He had no idea, and she desperately wanted to keep it that way. "You're the one who doesn't like *me*, remember?"

"You're never going to let me forget that, are you?" He sounded distressed, and she couldn't make herself look at him, because she couldn't stand to see his face looking the way his voice sounded.

"It's fine."

He touched her wrist. "Don't do that. Don't pretend not to care about something you obviously care about. You *should* hate me. I was an asshole to you."

"I don't hate you." She couldn't. She'd tried to hate him, but it was impossible.

"For the record, I think you're amazing."

Something cracked inside her chest, and she was pretty sure it was her heart. It was like it had been encased in a thin layer of stone, and he'd just reached out and tapped it, shattering the brittle shell into a million tiny fragments. She stared at him, unable to speak or even breathe.

"I was so wrong about you, Olivia. You're clever and decisive and good with people. I think you're going to make an excellent manager, and if you asked me again I'd give you that reference in a heartbeat."

"Oh," she whispered.

"But you don't have to forgive me or lie to spare my feelings."

"I'm not. I do like you." She tried to stop there, but the words spilled out of her anyway. "A little too much."

She thought he'd pull away after that, but he didn't. Instead he said, "Why don't you ever look at me, then?"

"What are you talking about?"

"You look everywhere in the room except at me."

"I don't do that, do I?"

"You're not even looking at me right now."

He was right. She'd gotten into the habit of only looking at him in her peripheral vision, because his face was too lovely to look directly at without being swamped by all sorts of feelings she wasn't supposed to be having.

Like the feelings she was having now that she'd met his gaze directly.

"I like when you look at me," he said without blinking. "I wish you did it more."

She didn't remember deciding to move or making a conscious choice to kiss him, but she was doing it. Her mouth pressed against his, and for one glorious second she felt his lips soften beneath hers, and it was like nothing else existed in the whole world except the two of them in this perfect moment.

Until he jerked away like he'd been shocked, and Olivia knew she'd done a Bad Thing.

She'd read the whole situation wrong. All his soulful stares and nice words hadn't meant he was attracted to her. He was just trying to be her friend—her good buddy, her work pal—and she'd gone and ruined it by putting her stupid mouth on him.

"Shit, I'm sorry," he said, like he was the one who'd just put his mouth on someone who didn't want it. His eyes were big as saucers, as if he'd accidentally googled something really disgusting and now he'd never be able to bleach the search results from his brain.

"No, I'm the one who's sorry." Olivia's stomach churned in horror as she pushed herself off the bed. "God, what the fuck was I thinking?"

"It's okay." He was trying to make her feel better because he was a nice person. But it wasn't going to work. She was never going to get over this.

"Jesus shit fuck Christ, it's not okay." She scrubbed her hands over her face as she paced around the room like a caged cheetah.

"Let me explain—"

"Nope," she said, putting up a hand to stop him. "Please do not try to explain *my* mistake. You don't have to explain anything. I just need—I have to get out of here."

There was nowhere to go but out into the rain.

So that was where she went.

Chapter Fifteen

Olivia heard Adam call out after her as the door slammed shut, but she pretended she hadn't heard and kept going.

The rain drenched her like a bucket of cold water, which was exactly what she needed right now—a shock to the system to wipe away the memory of her epic blunder.

The shoes she'd hastily shoved her feet into kicked up gouts of water as she ran down the walkway toward the far end of the building. There was a picnic table and a sad little play area with a sandbox, a slide, and a set of old swings.

Since digging a hole and burying herself in the fucking ground wasn't a viable option, she went straight for the swings. Maybe she'd be struck by lightning. Except the last thunder she'd heard had been a while ago and far in the distance.

She turned her face up to the sky and closed her eyes, letting the rain run down her cheeks as she clutched the chains of the swing.

What the fuck had she been thinking, trying to kiss him?

He was too handsome. She should have known better than to try something like that with someone like him. Just because he was a little bit nerdy didn't mean a guy who looked like an underwear model was going to be attracted to someone as plain and forgettable as her.

How was she ever going to face him again?

The worst part was how disturbed he'd looked. She'd sexually harassed him. She'd fucking sexually harassed him, by trying to kiss a coworker who didn't want to be kissed.

She was scum. She was that slimy, crusty stuff that clogged up pipes.

God, and they'd actually had a good thing going. They were getting along and enjoying each other's company before she'd fucked everything up.

Or at least it had seemed that way. Maybe he'd just been pretending. Making the most of a bad situation by humoring her and acting like he liked her when really he'd been repulsed all along.

But even as the thought occurred to her, she knew that wasn't right. He wouldn't do something like that. He put too high a premium on honesty, and didn't believe in telling white lies to make other people comfortable.

He wouldn't have told her she was amazing if he didn't mean it on some level.

But obviously he hadn't meant it the way she'd taken it. He'd meant it in more of a *platonic coworkers who are forced to spend time together* kind of way. Or maybe even a *coworkers who have become friends but nothing more than that* kind of way.

But definitely not in a *let's smush our faceholes together* kind of way.

"Olivia!"

Great, he'd followed her.

The sight of Adam walking toward her caused the raw, red burn of rejection to flare up anew. But even though she'd come out here to get away from him, there was still a part of her that was glad to see him. Even though it hurt to look at him and be reminded of her humiliation, she liked him too much to wish him away.

As long as he didn't try to talk to her about what had just happened. She'd rather suck on a battery or gargle jalapeño juice than dissect her mortifying blunder and listen to Adam try to console her for being a bad person.

"Can we talk about what just happened?" he said, coming to a stop a few feet in front of her.

"Let's not," she said, refusing to look at him. Which was pretty easy to do with the rain running into her eyes and making everything look blurry and gray. "It's fine. I just have a new most embarrassing moment, is all."

"Please don't be embarrassed."

Her fists squeezed the swing chains until the metal bit into her skin. "Sure, and while I'm at it I'll just stop having blue eyes too. Because it's that easy."

"It has nothing to do with you."

She barked out a laugh. "Right." So much for his dedication to truthfulness. Now he was feeding her the oldest lie in the book: *it's not you, it's me.* As if.

"I really do like you," he said, but he'd lost all credibility. She didn't have to believe him. "If things were different..." He didn't finish the sentence, which was just as well, because she didn't need to hear him describe the impossible possibilities that might lie ahead if only he liked her the way she liked him.

"You don't have to try to make me feel better," she told him, hoping he'd take it to heart and stop talking. "Really."

But he wasn't going to be dissuaded that easily. He was going to say what he'd come out here to say. "It's not that I don't want to, it's just...I can't get involved with another coworker. I just can't. Not after what happened with Hailey."

She did look up at him then, but she had to wipe the rain out of her eyes before she could focus on him properly. He looked as embarrassed as she felt, which only made her feel worse. His eyes were like two hollow pools as they skittered away from hers.

He claimed the swing beside her and sat down, which was much better, because then neither of them had to look at the other, and there was a nice, defined safety zone between them.

Adam's swing creaked as he straightened his legs out in front of him. "When things blew up between us, it made going to work a nightmare, and I swore I'd never put myself in that position again."

Olivia watched the raindrops bounce off the picnic table in front of them. "I guess I can understand that."

"I'm sorry if I misled you."

"I'm sorry that I wanted to be misled."

"I wanted it too. But I can't. Dating a coworker is too fraught. I won't go there again."

She dared a glance at him and immediately regretted it. He looked like the walking wounded. He was one of those people shuffling around a hospital ward with his IV stand after surgery. Even though the incision had been all stitched up and wasn't bleeding anymore, every step was a painful reminder of the wound that hadn't healed.

"That's okay," she said, trying to make her voice sound light. "It's cool. How about we just forget all this ever happened? Do a reset and roll back the clock like Daylight Savings Time. The last hour is a total wipe."

"Sure," he said. "I can do that."

"Great. It never happened, and we'll never speak of it again."

"Sounds good to me."

The problem was she didn't know how to go on from here. How to get back to where they were before she'd ruined it all. What were they supposed to talk about now? How were they going to spend the rest of the day cooped up together in a tiny motel room? How in the holy cheese-covered fuck were they supposed to sleep in the same bed tonight?

"Do you want to go back inside now?" he asked, giving her a sidelong glance.

"Not really." She pushed off with her feet and let herself swing. The raindrops smacked her in the face as she sliced through the air, and she squeezed her eyes shut.

"Okay. I guess we'll just stay out here in the rain, then." He was pitying her, which was almost as bad as being repulsed by her.

"You don't have to stay," she told him, turning her face up to the sky to let the rain wash her hair back. "I'm fine."

"I'm already wet. I might as well. Besides, I haven't been on a swing since I was a kid."

"Me too. I forgot how much I liked them."

She heard him get up, and opened her eyes as the sound of his feet crunching on the gravel drew nearer. "What are you doing?" she asked in alarm as he positioned himself behind her.

"I'm giving you a push." His hands landed on her lower back before she could prepare herself for it. The contact pressed her wet clothes against her skin, and all the breath rushed out of her lungs as he propelled her forward.

She straightened her legs and leaned back as she flew into the air, her muscle memory instinctively taking over to push her higher. For a moment she hung there at the terminus of the arc, suspended between forward and backward momentum, and felt an exhilarating sort of freedom, like there was nothing tethering her to the earth and all her problems.

When she sailed back toward Adam he pushed her again, harder this time, to send her flying even higher. A laugh bubbled out of her throat as she sliced through the raindrops, and she heard him laugh along with her.

"I really do think you're amazing," he said.

Her stomach clenched, and she jammed her feet into the ground to bring herself to a lurching halt.

She stood unsteadily and rounded on him as she wiped the rain out of her face. "You're not making this any easier by saying things like that. Saying things like that is exactly how I ended up humiliating myself." Her voice was shaking but it couldn't be helped under the circumstances. She was lucky she'd been able to get the words out at all.

He hung his head a little. "I'm sorry."

"We should go inside," she said, and started back to the room.

She made it all the way to the sidewalk before Adam's hand closed around her wrist, bringing her to a sudden halt. She spun and found herself looking up into his eyes, which were so dark and deep she felt like she was drowning in them.

Before her brain had time to register what was happening, he took her face in his hands and kissed her.

Chapter Sixteen

Adam's lips were so warm Olivia could feel them all the way down to her toes. She could feel his kiss everywhere, seeping into her numb limbs and waking them up with tingling pins and needles.

She was kissing Adam. Even better, he was kissing her, and he was doing it like he couldn't stand to do anything else. Hungry and desperate, but still somehow tender and just a little uncertain.

They were kissing in the rain like two people in a goddamn Nicholas Sparks movie, which wasn't something she'd thought happened in real life, yet here they were. He was Channing Tatum and Ryan Gosling rolled into one, and she was Rachel McAdams or that other actress whose name she couldn't remember.

When Adam pulled away, Olivia was so dazed she couldn't move. She couldn't even open her eyes, because she was afraid if she did, it would break the spell and he'd try to take it back. She stood there in stunned silence with her eyes squeezed shut, waiting for him to push her away again as the raindrops slid down her face.

But he didn't.

Instead, he pulled her even closer, and his thumb stroked her cheek as he murmured her name. He was breathing hard, all erratic and shaky like he'd just run a marathon. His forehead touched hers and their noses rubbed. Then his mouth found its way to hers again, and this time she gave herself up completely.

Her hands wrapped around his waist as her lips parted for him. Their tongues slid together in a kiss that was hot and wet and urgent, and he clutched at her with the ferocity of a drowning man who'd found something to grab onto. She didn't know what had happened to change his mind, but kissing him felt too good to worry about that right now.

The pressure of his mouth was bruising as it slanted over hers, and she rose up on her toes, craving even more. Her hands explored the broad plains of his back, her fingernails curling into his wet shirt as she strained against him. He hadn't shaved that morning and his stubble burned as it scraped over her lips, but it only made her kiss him harder.

His teeth caught her lower lip, and it took her moment to realize the moan she was hearing was coming from her. It seemed to excite him, and his hands slid down to her ass, squeezing and caressing as he held her even closer.

And then he was lifting her up, his arms banding around her as he settled her on his hips. She wrapped her legs around him as he carried her back toward their room, not breaking the kiss until they'd made it to the door. He had to set her down then so he could wrestle the key out of his pocket and shove it into the card reader. He pushed the door open, dragging her inside as their mouths crashed together again.

She couldn't believe they were doing this. Her heart was thumping against the walls of her chest, her pulse thrumming with arousal. Their hands were everywhere, like they couldn't get enough of touching each other, but their clothes were sopping wet, sticking to their skin with shiver-inducing clamminess. They were dripping on the floor, leaving a damp puddle on the rug, and

Olivia's drenched hair was plastered to her face, sending rivulets of water into her eyes and down her neck.

Adam broke free long enough to wrestle off his soaked T-shirt and slick his wet hair back out of his eyes. She reached for the broad expanse of beautiful bronze muscles, pressing her palm against his chest. He winced as her cold hand touched him, and covered it with his own.

"You're freezing." His other hand cupped her jaw as his lips grazed hers in a gentle kiss. "We need to dry off."

"We need to get out of these clothes." She was starting to feel claustrophobic, like her wet clothes were shrinking onto her body, and if she didn't get out of them soon she was going to explode out of them like the Hulk.

"Yes," he said. "God, yes."

He took her hand and led her into the bathroom, grabbing a towel off the hook and handing it to her. She dried her face and arms, then wrapped the towel around her wet hair, tying it into a turban before she became distracted by the sight of Adam rubbing another towel over his chest.

He noticed her staring and stopped, a hint of uncertainty flitting across his expression. "What?"

"You're just so gorgeous. Your body is unreal."

She watched a flush creep up his throat to color his face as he glanced away in embarrassment.

"What's wrong? I thought you liked it when I look at you."

"I do." He dropped his towel to the floor and stepped closer, cupping her jaw again as he bent toward her.

She turned her head and his kiss landed on the corner of her mouth. "Why so bashful, then?" It was hard to imagine someone who looked like him being shy about his body. If she looked like a model from a Bowflex commercial, she'd be posting underwear selfies on Instagram every goddamn day.

He kissed her cheek before moving on to her earlobe. "I guess I'm not used to being complimented on my body."

"Come on. I can't be the first woman to notice you've got a slamming bod." She stroked her hands over his upper arms and shoulders.

"I didn't used to look like this." His lips found a sensitive spot beneath her ear, and she shivered as his breath tickled her neck. "It was only after the breakup that I started going to the gym."

"Lucky me." It explained so much about him. How he'd never acted like someone who knew he was hot, and how oblivious he seemed to the interest of the women around him.

He reached up and loosened the towel around her head, letting it tumble to the floor in a spill of damp hair as his mouth closed over hers again. His tongue touched hers, tasting and teasing as his fingers tugged at the bottom of her sodden shirt. "Let's get you out of these clothes."

"Yes, please." She helped him pull her shirt over her head, shivering as the air hit her wet skin.

His big, rough hands roamed over her torso, leaving trails of tingling warmth everywhere they touched her. Then his fingers found the button of her jeans, and he peeled the wet denim off her legs. She stepped out of her pants and kicked them away, feeling like she'd just been freed from a straitjacket. Her hands grasped the waistband of his jeans, and he helped her unbutton them and shove them down.

It was too dark in the bathroom to see well, so they explored each other with their hands. Olivia squeezed Adam's shoulders, wrapped her fingers around his biceps, and slid her palms over his flat stomach. He was built like a brick wall, if a brick wall could be smooth and warm.

It was almost better, finding her way by feel in the dark. It gave her a freedom to touch that she might not have had if she'd been able to see him looking at her.

"Bed?" he suggested.

It was still afternoon. They had hours ahead of them to kill, just the two of them alone in this room. A whole night. The thought of everything they could do to each other sent tremors of excitement shooting down her spine.

"Bed," she agreed heartily. But one step out of the bathroom had her clutching at his arm. "The blinds are open."

It was their only source of light, but it exposed them to the view of anyone who happened to be passing by. And the things she planned to do to him were not fit for public consumption.

"On it." Adam went to the window and drew the blinds, plunging them into near-total darkness.

Olivia fumbled her way to the bed and heard him engage the security latch on the door with a finality that made her blood spark.

"Where are you?" he asked as she slipped between the sheets.

"Over here." She patted the mattress beside her.

"Keep talking to me so I can find you."

"Marco."

There was a scuffing sound followed by a soft thump. "Ow, fuck. Polo."

"Be careful," she warned him. The way the rest of this trip had gone, he'd probably break his leg or give himself a concussion and fall into a coma. She didn't even know where the nearest hospital was from here, or if the ambulance would be able to get to them through the flooding.

"You're supposed to say Marco."

"And you're not supposed to kill yourself in the dark." Her heart was buzzing in her chest, so hard that if there'd been any light, she was certain she'd be able to see it vibrating.

"Polo," he said as a shape loomed over her, a darker blot in the darkness, and she felt his knees depress the mattress on either side of hers. His hands landed next, caging her in, and the weight of his body pressed down on her as his mouth found her neck.

Thunder rumbled outside, or maybe it was inside her head. Maybe it was actually her pulse making that noise in her ears as their bodies slid together in the dark.

He murmured words against her skin, and they were all about her. How amazing she was, how beautiful, and how good she made him feel. She let herself sink into him, carried away by the sound of his voice and the feel of him wrapped all around her.

It wasn't at all how she'd imagined it would be. Not when she'd first noticed him and felt that initial spark of attraction, or even later, after she'd gotten to know him better and understand him. She'd imagined he'd be assertive and straightforward in bed. Maybe even a little rough, but in the best kind of way.

Never in a million years had she expected this tender intensity. He was so gentle, and patient, and sensual. When he touched her she felt it everywhere, shimmering through every pore all over her body, every nerve ending and every cell of brain matter. He turned her inside out, driving her to places she never even knew existed.

It made her wonder what she'd been doing all these years, wasting her time with men who couldn't affect her this way. How had she ever done without this feeling?

And now that she'd experienced it, how would she ever live without it?

Chapter Seventeen

For the second morning in a row, Olivia woke in Adam's arms. Only this time, his hand was cupping her breast instead of her waist.

There was a moment of disorientation, followed by realization. Memories of the night before flooded back, and she felt a moment of uncertainty as she wondered what this would mean for them.

How were they meant to go forward from here? Was last night a one-time thing or something more?

She wanted more, but she had no idea if Adam would. If he didn't, she'd have to find a way to navigate that with dignity. They still had to work together.

Oh god, the job.

Her eyes flew open, and the digital clock on the nightstand flashed at her in the pre-dawn light. The power was back on.

That was when she realized the rain had stopped. That dull roar she could hear wasn't rain, it was traffic on the highway. The roads were open again.

Adam stirred behind her and she froze, waiting to see what he would do. She'd take her cue from him. If he shrank away from her and leapt out of bed, it was probably safe to assume he wasn't interested in a repeat performance.

He didn't shrink away or leap out of bed. Instead, he pulled her even closer, nuzzling kisses into her hair. "Morning," he murmured as his hand roamed over her stomach and down between her thighs.

Her limbs melted into a quivering puddle, and she felt him press against her, hard and eager. She pressed back, wanting it just as much as he did. She could stay here forever in this bed with him, just the two of them in their little bubble, completely separate from the world outside.

But that wasn't practical. The power was back on, and they had a job to do. A job with a deadline of midnight tonight.

"Adam." Her voice came out in a breathy moan, and he increased his attentions, taking it as encouragement.

If only they could spare the time. She'd give almost anything for him not to stop.

Except her job. She couldn't afford to give that up.

"Adam," she tried again. "The power's back on."

"I guess that means I'd better stop." He didn't stop though, and it was making it very difficult for her to remember what their priorities were supposed to be.

"Probably," she managed in a shaky voice, even as she pressed back against him for more.

He withdrew his hand—much to her disappointment—and propped himself up, rolling her onto her back. "Too bad," he said, smiling as he bent to brush a light kiss across her lips.

His hair was ruffled and sticking up, and his lips had a bruised, raw look to them. He looked like someone who'd been ravished. Kissed and fondled and thoroughly fucked for hours. She probably looked the same.

When he kicked off the sheets and climbed out of bed, she couldn't help feeling like she'd lost something. Their happy little bubble had popped, and now they would have to reenter normal time and space. A nagging worry tugged at her that they'd never recapture this moment again. Once the pressures of the real world intruded, they'd lose this fragile thing they'd built.

Adam offered her the first shower, and Olivia took him up on it. When she came out, toweling off her freshly washed hair, he said he'd been down to the office to talk to Linda, who'd told him the roads to the plant were all open again. They were back in business—and another day behind.

"She said she'd have a new room for me tonight," Adam said as he dug his electric razor out of his suitcase.

"Too bad you're not gonna need it," Olivia replied as she ran a comb through her clean, wet hair.

"Yeah, there's a pretty good chance we'll have to work through the night," he agreed as he disappeared into the bathroom.

Which wasn't what Olivia had meant at all, but he was probably right.

They stopped off at the motel lobby to grab coffee and breakfast—which was fresh this morning, thanks to the miracle of restored electricity—and drove straight to the plant.

In the car, Olivia checked her phone and found no less than five panicked emails from Gavin since yesterday afternoon.

"I think Gavin's having an extended panic attack," she told Adam.

"Tell him we're on the job and everything's going to be fine." His knuckles whitened on the steering wheel, making a liar out of him.

"Maybe we should ask for an extension," Olivia suggested. They had two days of testing left to do, and only one day to do it. She couldn't imagine a scenario in which they'd be able to meet their deadline tonight.

Adam shook his head. "I still think we can make it."

"How can you say that?"

"We just have to accelerate the process."

"What does that mean?" she asked. "How do we do that?"

"It means we work smart and prioritize."

"As opposed to every other day when we work dumb and fly by the seat of our pants?"

He threw her a glance. "I mean you might have to skip a few things on your checklist."

She felt her hackles rise. "My checklist isn't just there for fun. Everything on it is important."

"I know you like to have all your i's dotted—"

"It's actually the energy commission that likes that. They're pretty particular about it."

"I just think it's too early to throw in the towel."

"And when might you be willing to throw in the towel?" she wondered. "I'd prefer to warn them sooner rather than later if we're not going to make the deadline."

Painting a rosy picture of a probable imminent disaster went against Olivia's nature. Her preferred strategy was to prepare people for the worst, then hopefully deliver more than they were expecting. Adam's false bravado in the face of likely failure felt like a bad idea.

He glanced at the clock on the dashboard. "How about two o'clock? We work our asses off until then and get as much done as we can, and at two p.m. we reevaluate. If we need the extension, that still gives Gavin plenty of time to smooth the waters with the CIO."

"Fine," she said. "I can live with that." Barely.

She spent the rest of the drive typing out an email to Gavin explaining their game plan and letting him know they'd give him a status update later that afternoon.

They pulled up to the gate just as she hit send.

"Ready for this?" Adam asked after he'd parked the car. She could feel him itching to dive back into work, but she wasn't quite ready to leave their bubble yet.

All morning she'd sensed him pulling away, retreating back into his no-nonsense work persona. He hadn't touched her once since he'd climbed out of her bed. It felt like the Adam from yesterday was disappearing, and she was afraid she'd never get to see him again.

"Is it going to make things weird?" she asked. "What happened last night?"

"It doesn't have to." There was more of his trademark bravado. Maybe he actually believed what he was saying, but it didn't do anything to calm the voices hissing in the back of her head.

She'd felt things yesterday that she'd never felt before. Whatever this was between them, it was visceral and intense, and it scared the shit out of her.

Mostly because she was afraid of losing it.

"Come on," he said, giving her one of his almost-smiles. "We've got work to do."

THEY WORKED their asses off for the next six hours, throwing themselves into testing with grim determination. When two o'clock rolled around, and it was time to make the call on an extension, Olivia was still convinced they needed another day of testing and Adam was convinced they didn't.

They went over the tests they had left, arguing over which could be put off and which couldn't, and how long they'd each take to run. Kurt was off doing one of his regular checks, so they were alone in the office for the first time all day, but there were no fond smiles or affectionate touches as they hashed out their opposing positions.

Adam was right that it would technically be possible to start generating power from the plant at midnight. But Olivia was afraid of staking their careers on the hope that everything was working as opposed to being really certain. The halls of IT history were littered with the bodies of people who thought something would be fine when it wasn't, and the stakes were high because it was power. The regulatory fines for making a mistake were steep. Millions of dollars were on the line, not to mention little things like hospitals and airports and grandmothers who needed their air-conditioning.

"You know they're not going to bid it out to market until Monday," Adam pointed out. "They'll want to do test generation first. And we'd already planned on staying through Sunday in case something barfs. That gives us plenty of time to catch anything we might have missed."

"That's all the more reason not to rush," Olivia insisted. "We're killing ourselves for an arbitrary deadline. Realistically, the board won't care if it's done Friday midnight or Saturday midnight, as long as when they walk in the door Monday morning, it's done."

Adam leaned back in his chair and crossed his arms. "How confident are you that we can go live right now with no failures? Put a number value on it."

She tried to rub some of the tension out of her neck while she thought about it. "Eighty percent? Maybe eighty-five."

"Eighty-five percent is pretty fucking sure." He was starting to sound exasperated. "You know how impressed they'll be if we meet that deadline tonight after all the shit that's gone wrong this week? We'll be superheroes. I thought you wanted to make a name for yourself."

Olivia dug her heels in. "I want another day of testing. I think it's worth asking for the extension."

"You're just resisting because you're allergic to shortcuts. You have to make everything as difficult as possible."

Now she was pissed. "I happen to love shortcuts, when they're actual shortcuts. I'll have you know, I have all the shortcut paths at Ikea memorized. I can move through that store like a goddamn ninja and be in and out in under ten minutes on a holiday weekend. What I don't like is leaving half the work undone and calling it a shortcut, which is what you're proposing. It's sloppy and I won't sign my name to it."

As she glared at him, she remembered his hand sliding through her hair last night, his mouth moving over her body, and his voice, rough with desire, alternately soothing and begging. But today was a brand-new day, and the closeness of yesterday felt like a dream-fogged memory that faded more with every tick of the clock toward their midnight deadline.

Why had she thought anything would be different between them? Just because they'd slept together didn't mean they'd magically start agreeing on everything or even getting along. It was one thing to fall into each other's arms during a moment of boredom in close quarters, but they weren't bored or isolated anymore. They were back in the real world now, and in the real world they were the opposite of compatible.

"Most of these tests are redundant and you know it." His jaw was set and there was a vein standing out in his neck. He looked so frustrated and annoyed, she couldn't bear it—not now that she knew what he looked like when he was telling her he thought she was amazing.

She grabbed the borrowed mug she'd been using and stalked over to the coffee maker. "Redundancies exist for a reason. Every single one of these tests is part of the process because someone missed something one time and they realized they needed to test for it before going into production."

"Fine," Adam said behind her. "We'll play it safe."

She poured a cup of silty black coffee. "Eighty-five percent certain is still a fifteen percent chance of catastrophic fucking failure. The potential benefit isn't worth the risk."

"I said fine."

She turned around. "You did?"

"Call Gavin, if that's what you want. Tell him we need another day."

"Really?"

Adam shrugged. "I'm not stopping you."

"Okay."

He watched dispassionately as she picked her phone up off the desk and called Gavin, who answered on the first ring.

"Olivia? What's the word?"

"We need another twenty-four hours for testing."

The was a beat of silence on Gavin's end. "Is Cortinas there?"

"Yeah, he's standing right here." Adam's eyes hadn't left her the whole time she'd been talking.

"I wanna talk to him," Gavin said. "Hand him the phone."

He could have asked her to put Adam on speaker so the three of them could all talk together, but he hadn't. He wanted to talk to Adam without her being part of the conversation.

Olivia held the phone out. "Gavin wants to talk to you."

Adam took it from her and paced a few steps away, turning his back on her. "Hey, Gavin."

She could hear the faint murmur of Gavin's voice on the other end, but not well enough to make out what he was saying. She could imagine it though. He was second-guessing her. Double-checking to make sure Adam was in agreement with her assessment of the situation.

Which he wasn't.

All Adam had to do to get his way was say the word, and Gavin would do whatever he recommended. Olivia's opinion wouldn't count for anything, just like it hadn't counted for anything in the meeting with the CIO on Monday. Not when rock star Adam Cortinas was there to give them exactly what they wanted. So what if they hadn't finished half the testing? No one wanted to hear things like that. They wanted to hear good news.

Once again, Olivia had been forced into the role of Cassandra with her gloom and doom predictions. Her warnings would go unheeded, and when things blew up in their faces later, you could bet they'd find a way to lay the blame at her feet.

Adam answered Gavin in mumbled monosyllables that didn't

tell her much. "I know," she heard him say, followed by more of Gavin's murmured voice. "Yes... No..." There was a long pause on Adam's end while Gavin spoke again, and then, "No, I don't think that's necessary."

There it was. He was totally throwing her under the bus.

Olivia sank down in front of her laptop.

"I understand completely," Adam said behind her. "Sure... Yep. You got it... Will do. Okay. Bye."

Adam came over and laid her phone down on the desk in front of her. He was standing behind her, so close his stomach brushed against her hair. "We've got another day for testing," he said. "Gavin's smoothing it over with the CIO."

"Wait—really?" She swiveled her chair around and Adam backed out of the path of her knees as they spun toward him.

"Yes." Furrows sprouted across his brow. "What did you think he'd say? No?"

"No, I just..." She stopped, unable to force the rest of the words out, because they suddenly seemed unfair. Worse than that, they were unkind. Adam hadn't thrown her under any buses, and based on the look on his face, he never would have. She probably should have known that.

"You thought I wouldn't back you up." His posture could have been an illustration next to the word *defensive* in the dictionary—arms crossed, spine ramrod straight, glaring down at her. But it was what she saw in his eyes that made her feel sick. He looked hurt.

"Well..." She couldn't lie to him, but she also didn't want to admit that it was true.

She didn't have to. He'd already sussed it out.

She stood up and took a step toward him. Her gut twisted when he edged backward in response. "I'm sorry," she said.

"For what?"

"For not trusting you."

"Why should you?" There was a flatness in his expression that made her feel sick.

She reached for his hand, and to her relief he didn't back away this time. He let her fingers twine around his, but he didn't squeeze back. That was okay. She could do enough squeezing for the both of them.

The door to the control shack flew open and Kurt stomped in, scuffing his muddy boots on the mat in front of the door.

Adam pulled his hand out of hers and went to sit down in front of his laptop.

"Whew, it's mucky out there," Kurt announced. "All this rain's washed away half our gravel. Gonna need to get a crew out here to fill in the low spots."

Olivia sat back down and stared at her laptop screen. She could feel Adam behind her, putting off waves of unhappiness that burned the surface of her skin like a heat lamp.

Kurt went into his office, humming tunelessly to himself, and sat down at the desk facing out at them.

For the rest of the afternoon, Adam barely talked to her unless it was about the work they were doing. When he did, he was matter-of-fact and impersonal, like he was putting distance between them. He was treating her the way he used to when they'd worked together in the office, before they were friends. Before they were something more than friends.

THEY STAYED at the plant testing until eleven that night, when they finally threw in the towel. The test they'd just started would have to run for at least six hours, so there was no point sitting around watching the progress bar inch along.

So far their testing hadn't turned up any major issues. There was still another day's worth to do, but they had a whole other day to do it, and it felt like they'd be able to make the midnight deadline exactly the way Olivia liked—with time to spare.

If only she were half as confident about Adam.

"Is everything okay?" she asked him on the drive back to the motel.

He seemed startled by the sound of her voice, like he'd forgotten she was in the car. Or maybe he'd just forgotten they could talk about something other than telemetry data.

"Yeah." He shifted in his seat and ran a hand through his hair. He'd been doing a lot of that today, and it was beautifully tousled. It made her want to put her fingers in it and sculpt it like Floam. "I'm just tired. It's been a long day." His hand squeezed the steering wheel and the tendons in his wrist flexed.

She longed to uncurl his fingers from the wheel and massage the tension out of them, but even aside from probably causing them to drive off the road, she wasn't convinced he'd welcome her touch. "You'd tell me if something was wrong, wouldn't you? You wouldn't just say you were fine if you weren't?"

He threw a glance at her and his expression softened incrementally. "Yes to the first question and no to the second."

Her brain was clearly failing from her own exhaustion, because it took longer than it should have to parse his response and assign the right answer to the right question. Once she did, she puffed out a breath. "Okay."

He switched hands on the steering wheel and laid his arm across the console, palm up in invitation.

She grabbed onto it greedily, like Violet Beauregarde snatching a piece of Wonka's gum. An electric tingle traveled up her arm from where their palms fit together, and her whole body sighed with relief.

She'd never gotten such a rush from the simple act of holding hands. She could actually feel herself being revived by the connection. Some sort of magical Adam energy was pouring into her body, lighting her up like a neon sign. It was as if his skin was an electronic charging pad that juiced up her battery when it came into contact with hers.

Even as some of her uncertainty eased away, she felt a fresh stab of fear. Never once had she felt anything like this before. Not with anyone.

She'd been craving Adam's touch all day the way a junkie craved her next hit of heroin. His skin was like a drug that brought euphoric highs—or crushing lows when he took it away.

And that terrified her, because he could take it away again.

Their future was far from certain. She had no idea if they were really compatible. They hadn't exactly worked like a seamless team today. And he'd said he never again wanted to get involved with someone at work, yet that was exactly what he'd done. Would he start having regrets when they got back to the office? Was he already having them now?

Even while he was holding her hand, she could tell from the faint frown between his brows that he was thinking. Maybe even about how to let her down easy and untangle himself from this thing that neither of them had expected or even wanted to happen.

And maybe that was for the best.

Chapter Eighteen

When they got back to the motel, Olivia unlocked the door and Adam followed her inside. The room had been cleaned in their absence, the bed made and the wet towels replaced.

Sitting in the middle of the small round table where Olivia set her purse was a room key and a note from Linda:

Room 27 is all yours if you want it.

As Olivia stared down at the note, Adam came over to see what she was looking at. He didn't react as he read it, but the words seemed to hang in the air between them.

If you want it.

That was the question, wasn't it? Did he want to go to his own room? Did she want him to? But even as her mind asked the question, she knew the answer. She wanted Adam to stay.

Maybe they would be better off ending this before it went any further, but she didn't care. She wanted it. Right now, standing here in this room with Adam where they'd been so happy, she wasn't ready to let go of him.

But she needed him to *want* to stay. She wasn't going to beg or pressure him. He had to choose her freely.

He walked into the bathroom, and when he came back out, he was holding his razor and toothbrush. Which pretty clearly answered the question. He'd made his choice, and it wasn't her.

"I'm really beat," he said with this awful, apologetic look on his face. "It's probably best if I sleep in my own room tonight."

"Sure," she said, even though it wasn't what she wanted to say. She wanted to tell him it wasn't best for *her*. That more than anything she wanted him to stay, even if it was only for one more night.

She didn't tell him those things though, because he'd made up his mind already and she didn't want to seem pathetic. If she told him how she felt, he'd only feel sorry for her. Even worse—he might stay one more night as a favor. He might feel like he had to, as some sort of consolation prize. The last thing she wanted from him was a pity fuck.

"We've got another long day ahead of us tomorrow," he added, in case she wasn't convinced. "We'll both be better off with a full night's sleep."

"Yep." She was being so agreeable. No one had ever agreed with anything more, even if it was breaking her heart a little to do it.

She watched as he moved around the room, packing up the rest of his things, and all she could feel was numb. It wasn't the least bit cold in the room, but her feet and her fingers were blocks of ice, sending frozen tendrils to her spine and up into her hypothalamus.

She'd known, on some level, that it would probably come to this. The fantasy had been nice while it lasted, but it wasn't like they could stay here forever in their bubble. She hadn't ever really believed they could go on like this, what with their jobs and reality waiting for them on the other side of the door.

But she'd hoped. She'd let herself hope, and look what that had gotten her.

Adam finished packing and zipped up his suitcase. He was all ready to go, and because she was helpful—so helpful and so agreeable—Olivia went to hold the door open for him.

He rolled his suitcase over and stopped in front of her. She couldn't bring herself to look at him, but he was so big and tall and standing so close, he took up her whole field of vision. So instead she looked down at the floor with a mumbled goodnight.

But he didn't leave. He stayed right where he was.

Then his hand—oh god, his hand was touching her face. He cupped her cheek, and his fingers slid into her hair to tip her face up to his, and he gazed down at her with eyes so black and bottomless they could swallow her whole.

He looked like he wanted to kiss her.

An ember of longing flared to life in her chest. The part of her that still clung to hope couldn't help thinking he'd changed his mind. It sure seemed like he'd changed his mind. He even tilted his head and started to lean in.

But then he just...didn't.

His hand dropped to his side and he took a step back. "I'll see you in the morning." Another step back, and he was on the other side of the threshold now. "Make sure you bolt the door behind me."

All she could do was nod as he rolled his suitcase away.

THE NEXT MORNING came like a boot to the head. Olivia had hardly gotten any sleep—or at least it felt that way. It was one of those nights where you toss and turn and toss and turn, and it feels like you never really fall asleep, but you must, because when your alarm goes off in the morning you're so deeply asleep it hits you like a freight train.

She took too long in the shower, standing under the hot spray waiting fruitlessly to feel human again. So when seven o'clock rolled around—the time she'd agreed to meet Adam for breakfast in the lobby—she still hadn't put on her makeup.

Fuck it, she thought as she hastily twisted her hair into a bun. *I'll wear my real face today.*

Who was going to see her or care? Only Adam, who definitely didn't care, and maybe a couple guys at the plant she'd never see again. She could face the world without makeup for this one day of her life.

Adam was already there when she pushed through the door to the lobby. He turned away from the cereal bar at the sound of the door, and their eyes met across the room.

Jesus shit fuck Christ, those eyes of his.

Did he know what they did to her? How they took her breath away every single time he looked at her?

"I got you a coffee," he said, pointing to a table where two styrofoam cups sat side by side, steaming.

She made a beeline for them, and gulped down half of one, not even caring that it scalded her throat.

Adam watched her, eyebrows lifted in an expression of amusement. "If it'd be easier, we can fix you up with a caffeine IV."

He was weirdly chipper this morning. Apparently not sleeping with her put him in an excellent mood. *Swell.*

"Did you know that bananas are berries but strawberries aren't?" he announced as she examined the fruit bowl at the breakfast bar.

"Are you kidding?" she mumbled, blinking at the banana in her hand. Somehow this information felt like a personal betrayal, as if bananas had been lying to her as part of some vast fruit conspiracy her whole life.

"Blackberries and raspberries—also not berries."

She shoved the banana back in the bowl and went for an apple

Danish instead. "I can't even process that. I'm still too pissed off about bananas being berries."

"You know what else is a berry? Watermelon."

"What the fuck?"

"Also avocados."

"Okay, now I know you're just messing with me." She grabbed a vanilla yogurt—because apparently all berry yogurt was a lie—and took it and her Danish over to the table.

Adam followed her with his two yogurt cups and a tiny box of Frosted Flakes. "Botanically, a berry is defined as a fruit produced from the ovary of a single flower. Which includes grapes, tomatoes, and peppers, but not a lot of the fruits that we commonly consider berries."

Olivia shotgunned the rest of her coffee. "I can't believe you're talking to me about plant ovaries at seven in the morning."

"I thought you'd find it interesting." He looked slightly hurt that she wasn't more impressed by his fun facts about fruit, but she couldn't very well explain that she was in a bad mood because she'd been awake half the night agonizing over the fact that he hadn't wanted to sleep with her.

"I do find it interesting," she told him, trying to sound conciliatory. "I just haven't had enough coffee to have my entire fruit worldview upended."

"Then I'd better get you some more," he said, and took her coffee cup for a refill.

Damn him, why did he have to be so sweet? It was making this even harder on her.

But she'd made it over the hump. She'd faced Adam this morning and come through it with her dignity mostly intact. They could do this. They could interact and work together and be mostly normal.

Only as soon as they were alone in the car together, on the way to the plant, things got awkward again.

"Are you okay?" Adam asked, casting a worried glance her way.

"Yes," she said, turning to look out the window. It wasn't a lie. She was okay. She would be.

"Because it seems like something's wrong," he persisted.

It wasn't a question, so she didn't answer. They were passing a very nice pasture of cows, and she watched them graze on a patch of wildflowers.

"*Is* something wrong?" He really wasn't going to let this go.

"I'd rather not talk about it," she said to the window. There was no point in lying when he could clearly see that something was bothering her. Lying would only make him prod more.

"Okay."

He fell silent, and she breathed out a sigh of relief.

"How about this..." he said after a moment. "How about I tell you what I think is wrong, and you tell me if I'm right or not?"

She could say no. He would probably drop it if she told him she didn't want to play this game right now. But then she'd never hear what he thought was wrong—and she needed to know.

"Fine," she said. Her gaze was still fixed on the window, but without seeing what lay beyond the glass. All of her awareness was concentrated on the inside of the car. On Adam and what he might be about to say.

"I think you were hurt that I went to my own room and didn't spend the night with you last night. I think you think I did that because I didn't *want* to spend the night with you, and I want you to know that's not true at all."

She swiveled her head to look at him, but his focus remained on the road ahead. "Then why?" she asked, feeling that familiar flare of longing again.

"I really was exhausted. I don't know if you noticed, but I didn't get a lot of sleep the night before."

"I noticed," she said, closing her eyes against the memory of his body sliding against hers into the wee hours of the morning.

"Yeah, well I didn't get much sleep the night before that either." He was talking about the first night they'd shared a bed, when the storm had displaced him from his room. His fingers squeezed the steering wheel. "Or the night before that, truthfully." That was after the wrecker had dropped them at that creepy motel.

"Why not?" she asked.

He shrugged. "Too much adrenaline after the flat tire." He hesitated, like he wanted to say something else. And then he said it, and it blew her mind a little: "Or maybe it was because you were so close—right on the other side of that door you'd asked me to leave open—and I was starting to have a lot of feelings that I didn't know what to do with."

"Feelings? About me?"

"Yes. Feelings about you." He glanced over at her, and their eyes caught and held for a second before he looked back at the road. "Anyway, I was pretty much running on empty by the end of the day yesterday, and I knew we still had a lot of work to do today, and I wouldn't be able to focus at all if I didn't get some sleep."

"I want to go back and talk about these feelings you were having about me."

"I like you, Olivia. Haven't you figured that out by now?"

Maybe she had. Maybe she'd known but hadn't let herself believe it.

"I like you," he repeated. "But we work together, and I didn't know what to do. I wasn't sure if you liked me back—"

"I do," she cut in, because she felt like she needed to put that on the record. He'd laid his feelings on the table for her, and she wanted him to know he wasn't the only one out there on the ledge.

He breathed out a long breath, and his shoulders relaxed a little. "I didn't know that, and I didn't want to make you uncomfortable." He paused, and the muscles in his jaw tightened. "And also I really, *really* didn't want to jump into another relationship with someone I work with."

"Right," she said, feeling a knot start to form in her stomach. Of course he didn't. He'd already told her as much.

"If I'm being honest, that's partially why I left last night. I knew if I didn't get out of there, I wouldn't be able to keep my hands off you..."

It sounded like a good thing, but she just knew there was another shoe coming, and it probably wouldn't be as awesome.

"And I wasn't sure any of this was a good idea," he went on. "I thought maybe it would be best not to let it go further." The other shoe dropped with a crashing thud that reverberated through Olivia's chest.

"I see," she said, feeling the numbness creep back into her fingers and toes. "I was thinking the same thing, actually."

He cut a glance at her. "You were?"

"Yeah. Maybe it'd be better if we quit while we're ahead."

His teeth bit into his lower lip and he gave a slow nod. "Well, I don't know what conclusion you came to, but I decided that was bullshit."

She was so startled it took her several seconds to respond. "You did?"

"It was just me being scared of getting hurt again and trying to protect myself. But I'm tired of being scared. You have no idea how lonely I've been."

She had an idea. She'd always assumed he had this whole life outside work and that was why he didn't have any work friends. But now she knew he didn't have *any* friends. And it was all because he'd been hurt, and was so afraid of being hurt again that he'd shut himself away from everyone in his life. Even his family to some extent.

"Fuck being scared," he said. "Let's just try this and see what happens."

It was exactly what she'd wanted to hear.

The words *yes, great, let's do it* hovered on the tip of her tongue, but for some reason she couldn't make herself say them.

Because what if he was wrong? What if they tried and failed, and it ended up causing even more pain and awkwardness that made things hideously uncomfortable at work? He'd already been through that once, and she didn't want to put him through it again. He needed a friendship that wouldn't self-destruct more than he needed a bed buddy.

Olivia was a pragmatist, so she tried to calculate what odds she'd give them. Based on their personalities and past failed relationships, and all their previous interactions, she tried to assign a number value to the chances of them surviving even six months as a couple.

It wasn't a good number. If this were an Oscar pool, she'd put her money on a different nominee.

Adam was still waiting for her to say something. He kept throwing hopeful little glances her way, and she didn't want to disappoint him, but she knew it was better to get it all out in the open now.

"Counterpoint," she said. "Maybe your first instinct was right, and we should put the brakes on things now, before it blows up in our faces."

He nodded slowly. "You're scared too."

"I'm not scared. I'm trying to be logical." She tugged at the cuffs of her shirt, pulling them down over the backs of her hands.

"What's logical about giving up before we've even had a chance to get started?"

"We don't even like each other."

"We both just admitted that we do."

"What if we're wrong?"

"I think I know how I feel."

She shook her head. "You only think you have feelings for me because we've been stuck together like conjoined twins for the past three days. We're both suffering from Stockholm Syndrome." She couldn't stop herself, even though she was arguing against the thing she wanted.

"That's not what Stockholm Syndrome is. If anything, all the stressful situations we've been through this week should make us like each other less, not more. The fact that it brought us closer means something."

"No, it doesn't. It's like one of those wartime romances that burns really hot for a short time and then flames out when life goes back to normal."

"You think this week is what war is like?"

"No, of course not. All I mean is that relationships based on intense experiences never work out."

He glanced at her in disbelief. "Are you quoting *Speed* now?"

"Maybe, but Sandra Bullock was right! Keanu wasn't in the sequel, was he? She was with Jason Patric!"

"Yeah, and *Speed 2* sucked. But I don't see how the casting problems of a failed nineties action franchise have any bearing on what's happened between us."

"All we ever seem to do is argue."

"I love arguing with you."

She loved it too, although it surprised her to realize it. Arguing with Adam wasn't like arguing with other people, because he actually listened to her. Like, super intently. It gave her a rush to have all of his attention focused on her and her ideas. And unlike a lot of people, he didn't play devil's advocate or argue just for the sake of disagreeing. He was willing to have his mind changed, and didn't shy away from admitting when he was wrong.

Arguing with Adam engaged her competitive instincts, but it also got her hot. Even now, arguing about their possible non-future, she could feel the heat pooling in the pit of her stomach. She was staring at his mouth and thinking about how much she wanted to feel his lips on her again.

She made one last attempt to parry. "If we try this and it doesn't work out, it could make work really hard." It had seemed like such a good reason before, but now it felt like a lame excuse.

"Maybe, maybe not." He gave a one-shouldered shrug. "If it

does, I'll get another job. I can work anywhere." He made it sound so easy, like it hadn't ruined his life the last time he'd had to do it.

"I don't want you to have to do that."

"I think you're worth the risk."

A well of emotion burst inside her. How was he just sitting there calmly driving the car and saying such incredible words to her? And why did he have to say them now, when she couldn't climb into his lap and kiss him without killing them both in a fiery vehicular crash?

He dared a glance at her and must have liked what he saw in her expression, because a smile lit up his whole face, so beautiful it made her eyes water.

He laid his arm across the console like he'd done yesterday, with his palm face up and beckoning to her. "Marco."

"Polo," she whispered, and slipped her hand into his.

Chapter Nineteen

Adam was staring at her again. He'd been staring at her for hours, devouring her with his eyes.

Instead of sitting behind her, today when they'd arrived at the control shack he'd chosen a desk farther away, but facing hers. So he could gaze at her with those glorious dark eyes that turned her legs to jelly.

She felt ensnared by every look he cut her way. How was she supposed to survive the whole day with him watching her like a terrier tracking a squirrel? The sensations it inspired in her made it difficult to concentrate. There was some self-consciousness, and some embarrassment, but also something deeper and wilder. Craving. Desire. Excitement.

It was killing her that they couldn't touch. They hadn't even been able to kiss when he'd parked the car, because there were security cameras outside, and they didn't need the weekend shift manager watching them suck face. She was boiling with the need to feel Adam's touch, and from the look in those eyes of his, he felt exactly the same.

It was torture.

But also sort of fun?

Olivia's competitive streak had been activated again. As the hours wore on and the sexual tension crackling across the room between them amped up, she'd turned it into a contest.

They were playing an adult version of the Quiet Game that Olivia's elementary school teachers had inflicted on her and her fellow classmates. In this version of the Quiet Game, they weren't allowed to do anything to arouse the suspicion of the shift manager or his weekend crew. They could share meaningful looks and flirt with their eyes, but only if they could do it without being noticed.

They could even touch, occasionally, but only in the most innocent and unobtrusive ways. The way two coworkers might accidentally touch in the course of conferring over a laptop or sharing a meal from the vending machine. A casual brush of fingers here, a slight press against the thigh there, but nothing an observer would notice as untoward. Which turned out to be far more erotic and intoxicating than she'd imagined it could be.

She'd never fully appreciated the power of a tease before. How the lightest of touches when there was no possibility of follow-through could set her on fire, burning her from the inside out. And how she could do the same thing to someone else.

She propped her elbow on the desk and rested her chin on her palm, gazing across the room at Adam. Until the next batch of tests finished running, there wasn't much for her to do.

Adam pretended not to be aware of her staring, but she knew from the way he reached up to run his fingers through his hair that he was very aware indeed. Christ, she loved his hair. It was unfair that he should have such lustrous, silky waves. She couldn't wait to run her fingers through them tonight.

The weekend shift manager was in his office, eating his lunch. His attention was mostly divided between his club sandwich and his computer screen, but he could look up at any second. He was their ever-present chaperone. The principal standing over the punch bowl, whose presence kept the kids on the dance floor from engaging in too much hanky-panky.

Olivia let out a quiet little sigh of boredom, and Adam's eyes drifted her way. He reclined in his chair and crossed his arms. His biceps bulged, straining at the fabric of his shirt, and she felt a bit of drool collect at the corner of her mouth.

She squirmed in her seat and crossed her legs. It wasn't easy to be seductive in clumpy Doc Martens and a baggy plaid shirt.

There was a pencil cup on the desk in front of her, and she chose a long yellow Ticonderoga, spinning it between her fingers like a student waiting to take the SAT. Adam watched her intently, mesmerized.

She held the pencil up in front of her face and stroked it from eraser to tip.

His eyes flashed in response. Somehow he was grinning without moving his face.

She turned the pencil over and stroked it again, running her fingers slowly down its length and back again. Her heart gave a little leap of triumph when the corner of Adam's mouth twitched.

Invigorated, she gripped the pencil as if she were about to write something, opened her mouth, and touched the tip to her tongue.

It was a powerful high, watching Adam's eyes go black and wide because of something she'd done. She smiled to herself as she reached for a Post-it and wrote out a question.

He was leaning forward, curious to know what she'd written. She held the note up so he could read it.

You OK over there?

His expression was half amused and half something else that made her stomach flutter and her chest feel hot. The two of them were like Jim and Pam on *The Office*, sharing a silent in-joke and communicating across the room with heated glances and smirks.

Olivia tore the Post-it off the pad and wadded it up. Adam's eyes were heavy and watchful as she leaned back in her chair, lifting up her shirt and thrusting her hip forward to tuck the crumpled note into the front pocket of her jeans. His tongue was practically lolling out of his mouth like a salivating Labrador.

That was when she remembered the toy robot she'd gotten in her kids meal at the airport—the one she'd named Tiny Adam. She dug it out of her purse and held it up, smiling. Adam pressed his lips together, barely containing a laugh as she wound the tiny crank with exaggerated movements.

She was enjoying this too much. If she wasn't careful, she'd get carried away.

As she set the toy robot marching across the desk, Olivia glanced at her computer screen and sat bolt upright. "Come here," she said, beckoning to Adam with her index finger.

He lifted his eyebrows in inquiry, trying to decipher if this was part of the game.

"I'm seeing a lot of packet loss coming from the number three turbine."

He pushed himself to his feet, the Quiet Game forgotten as he peered down at her screen. The software was ticking out how many kilowatts were being generated by each turbine, and instead of numbers it was throwing zeros.

"Fuck," he said.

Fuck was right. It could be anything, including a fire, but since none of the plant's alarms were going off, chances are it was a problem with their software and not with the turbine itself.

"Could it be a loose connection?" she asked.

"Maybe." He grabbed his hard hat on his way to talk to the shift manager. "I'll go outside and see what's up."

It took them two hours to identify the problem. It turned out the new network switch Adam had installed was in direct sunlight in the latter half of the day, causing it to overheat. Which of course he couldn't have known when he'd installed it under thick cloud cover on Wednesday.

Once he'd relocated it, they were good to go again. A simple fix for a simple problem, but it could have caused major complications if they'd been interfacing with the market and dropped telemetry like that. One tiny error like that could have cost the company millions of dollars in fines, like a butterfly flapping its wings and causing a hurricane.

A disaster had been narrowly averted, and they both knew it.

Adam had pulled a chair up beside Olivia's desk to watch the sub-second telemetry reporting on her screen. He swiveled to face her, his expression contrite. "You were right about waiting another day." There was an apology in his voice, if not in his actual words. "We would have been in deep shit if I hadn't listened to you."

It was gratifying to hear him commend her for the same caution he'd criticized her for before. But her sense of fair play was too strong to take all the credit for this victory. She wouldn't have been able to pull this off if it hadn't been for him. She wouldn't have even had the courage to try, if not for him pushing her to take a risk and stretch herself.

"Yeah, but you were right that we could do the integration in half as much time as I thought we needed. If it'd been up to me, we would have insisted on a whole extra week, and pissed off the CIO and the board." She spun her chair a little, so her knee bumped against his leg. "So we were both partially right, and both partially wrong."

A smile played across his lips. "The truth was halfway in between. You know what that means?"

"What?"

"We make a good team."

A matched set, her mind whispered.

If only.

It was hard to picture her and Adam ever being as cozy and easy with one another as Penny and Caleb were. But maybe they could make their own kind of cozy.

"We moderate each other's worst instincts and complement each other's strengths." Adam's leg exerted pressure against hers, though from the waist up his posture was all business. They were back to playing the Quiet Game.

The weekend shift manager wandered out of his office with a coffee cup in his hand, and Olivia's gaze shifted to her computer screen. Beneath the desk, she laid her hand on her thigh so her fingers would graze Adam's knee.

Together, they watched the progress bar on their last test tick toward completion, counting down the minutes until they were released from the constraints of professional behavior.

AT NINE O'CLOCK—THREE hours ahead of schedule—the newly acquired Walhalla Power Plant officially went online.

They'd run the last of the connectivity tests, verified the data with ERCOT, and texted the all-clear to the trade floor, giving them the go-ahead to start selling power from the plant.

They stuck around for another hour after that, drinking a round of celebratory beers from the minifridge in the shift manager's office, before heading back to the motel.

Olivia glared up at the security cameras as she and Adam walked across the gravel parking lot. If it weren't for Big Brother spying on them, she'd push him up against the car and kiss him.

A mile down the road, Adam suddenly pulled off onto the shoulder, hit the hazards, and put the car in park.

"What's wrong?" she asked, alarmed.

"Nothing," he said, unclipping his seat belt and turning toward her. "Nothing at all."

When his hand skimmed her cheek after hours of touch deprivation, it set off pyrotechnics on the surface of her skin. She breathed out in relief at the contact she'd been craving all day.

Then his lips touched hers.

Kissing him felt like falling, only it was the kind of free fall she never wanted to come out of. A feeling of completion shuddered through her like an earthquake. She would still be feeling this kiss days from now. She'd be sitting in a plant ops status meeting next week and her lips would still be tingling with the aftershocks of this kiss.

When they finally came up for air, Adam rested his forehead against hers like he'd spent every last bit of energy kissing her. "I've been wanting to do that all day."

"God, me too."

They stayed clenched together for a few dreamy seconds, forehead to forehead, eyes closed, his hand curled around the back of her neck as their breath mingled in shaky puffs.

Then he let go of her and pulled away, as abruptly as he'd kissed her.

"Wait, that's all?" she asked as he refastened his seat belt.

His eyes were dark with barely restrained lust when he looked at her. "I just needed to taste you. The main course can wait until we're not parked by the side of a narrow rural road in the dark."

Olivia grinned, slapping the dashboard with her palm. "Drive like the wind, Bullseye!"

Ten minutes later they were pulling into the parking lot of the motel. Thirty seconds after that they were tumbling into Olivia's room in a tangle of limbs and lips and questing hands.

As they peeled each other's clothes off, desperate for the skin-to-skin contact they'd denied themselves all day, she pushed aside all her worries about the future and gave herself up to the here and now.

THEY HAD to go back to the plant and work for a few hours the next morning. And then they had to drive seventy miles to Austin, turn in their rental car, and catch a flight back to LA.

After that, Olivia didn't know what would happen. Living in the now without worrying about the future was not a natural state of being for her, but it was what she was determined to do. At least for this one day. They could worry about tomorrow when it came.

To be honest, she was too tired to do much else. Adam might have gotten a good night's sleep and recharged the night he'd retreated to his own room, but Olivia had not been so lucky. The stress and emotional ups and downs of the week were catching up with her, and she felt like someone halfway through the transition from human to slow, shambling zombie as she checked the logs for errors.

When they were as sure as they could be that their software was running smoothly, they bid goodbye to the weekend shift manager, climbed back into their trusty Honda Fit, and headed for Austin.

The sky was clear and blue, and as Olivia blinked at the sunlight reflecting off the highway, she felt like Gollum emerging from the lightless depths below the Misty Mountains. Between the weather and the long hours locked up inside the plant, she'd barely seen the sun in days, and the warm rays soaking into her skin felt like a miracle.

A few minutes later, as they were driving through a small town, she saw a sign for a roadside store, and told Adam they needed to make a stop.

"Do you need to pee already?" he asked, sounding more amused than annoyed.

"No, I have to buy something here."

"We don't have a ton of time to waste," he warned, even as he was pulling off the highway and into the crowded parking lot.

"It won't take long," she promised.

He followed her inside Hruska's Store and Bakery, established in 1912, past the registers and aisles full of snack foods and souvenirs and jars of pickles and jams, to the long glass counter at the back.

"Holy shit." Adam's eyes were wide and bright as he stared at the bakery case. "Are those all—"

"Kolaches," Olivia confirmed with a nod. "Even better than the ones at Buc-ee's."

She helped him select a variety of the best flavors—cream cheese and chocolate, apple, peach, and sausage and cheese—and they got back in the car and set out for Austin again. She fed him kolaches as he drove them through the wildflower-covered hills of central Texas, past cattle ranches, pumpjacks, and picturesque small towns. At some point after they'd shared the last kolache, Olivia nodded off to sleep, curled up facing Adam with her hand resting on his thigh.

The next time she opened her eyes, they were turning off for the Austin airport. She sat up and stretched, and Adam reached for her hand and brought it to his lips.

She felt a wistful pang when they turned in their rental car. A lot had happened in that dusty little Honda Fit, and it was harder than expected to say goodbye.

Before she knew it, they were dragging their suitcases through the doors to the airport terminal. The security line was a breeze compared to LAX, and their flight was still scheduled to depart on time.

"I'll watch your bag," Adam said as they approached a restroom, and patiently rolled their suitcases off to the side to wait for her.

Olivia barely recognized herself in the bathroom mirror when she was washing her hands. She'd forgone makeup yet again, and the dark circles under her eyes were verging into black hole territory.

As soon as she stepped out of the restroom, Adam's gaze homed in on her like a heat-seeking missile, and his whole face seemed to light up. He leaned in for a kiss as she reached to take her roller bag from him, like she'd been gone three days instead of three minutes.

They set out for their gate, and detoured again at the sight of a Starbucks. It had been days since she'd had a decent cup of coffee, and Olivia nearly hugged the barista when he handed over her venti mocha latte.

Coffees in hand, they found two seats at their gate, and passed the time identifying celebrity doppelgängers among their fellow travelers.

"Blue shirt over there looks like a young James Earl Jones," Olivia said, nudging Adam's shoulder with her own.

He followed her gaze and nodded with appreciation at her find. "Not bad." His eyes traveled around the terminal. "Middle-aged Miley Cyrus," he pointed out, and she laughed, unable to remember the last time she'd enjoyed herself this much at an airport. It was the two of them against the world, comfortable and carefree and victorious after what felt like an eon of struggle.

Boarding for their flight started five minutes early, and only when they went to line up did she remember that they wouldn't be sitting together. Adam had a seat in first class.

"You can go ahead and get on," she pointed out. "They've already boarded first class."

He shook his head and brushed a kiss across her lips. "I'd rather spend a few more minutes with you."

When it was Olivia's turn to board, Adam followed her onto the plane, but instead of peeling off at the first class cabin, he walked her to her seat and hoisted her bag into the overhead compartment for her.

"Excuse me," he said to the large and very uncomfortable-looking man occupying the aisle seat next to Olivia's middle. "How would you like to sit in first class?"

The man's eyes narrowed with suspicion. "What's the catch?"

"No catch," Adam said, presenting his boarding pass. "I'd just rather sit beside my girlfriend."

Olivia gaped, fish-eyed, as the man in the aisle seat accepted his offer. Not only had Adam just sacrificed the luxury of free alcohol and hot towels in order to ride in coach with her, but there was also the not-so-small matter of him calling her his girlfriend.

Had he actually meant it? Or was it merely for her seatmate's sake? A more expedient explanation than *coworker I've slept with but we haven't really worked anything out yet beyond that?*

She slid into the middle seat as Adam stowed his suitcase, and fastened her seat belt with shaky, fumbling fingers. He sank down beside her and lifted the armrest between them before feeling around for his own seat belt.

"Thank you," she said, choosing to ignore the *girlfriend* of it all. "You didn't have to do that."

His dark eyes flashed as he squeezed her thigh. "Who says I did it for you?"

Twenty minutes later, when the plane began taxiing for takeoff, she felt Adam stiffen beside her. It was subtle, but she could feel the tension radiating through the air between them, like ripples in a pond.

She set her knitting down and reached for his hand.

"Thank you," he said, squeezing her fingers between his.

"Who says I did it for you?" she replied, squeezing back.

As the plane picked up speed, preparing to hurtle itself into the air, Adam closed his eyes and leaned his head back against the seat. Olivia rested her head on his shoulder, and they held on to each other as they left the ground.

She felt a small pang as they left Texas behind. Not because it was home—or used to be—but because it was where she and Adam had found each other.

Even though the trip had in no way been a vacation, she couldn't help worrying that this would turn out to be like one of those vacation romances that fizzled out as soon as they went back to their normal lives.

She was probably just being paranoid and silly, but she wouldn't be her if she wasn't worrying about something.

Chapter Twenty

LAX was perhaps as quiet as Olivia had ever seen it when they stepped off the plane. Sunday nights were apparently not a big travel time.

They rolled their bags through the airport at a leisurely pace, neither of them feeling any particular urgency now that they'd arrived at their destination—miraculously, without a single disaster.

"Did you drive?" Adam asked as a sign for the airport garage loomed ahead of them.

"No, Uber."

"Same."

They struck out for the area designated for rideshare pickups. As they stepped outside, into the blessedly dry and relatively cool air, Olivia breathed a sigh of relief. There might be some things she missed about Texas, but the weather was most definitely not one of them.

"Where do you live?" Adam asked, pulling out his phone. "Do you want to share a car?"

"We can," she said. "Or..." She bit down on her lip, deliberating whether she should even make the suggestion.

He looked up from his phone, eyebrows raised.

"You could come over to my place," she ventured. "Unless you're too tired, that is. It has been a hella long week, and you might just want to get home, which is totally fine too. No pressure or anything."

"I'd love that," he said.

Olivia used her phone to summon a car. The driver of the Camry that picked them up was playing slow, mellow jazz that should have been relaxing, but somehow had the exact opposite effect. On her, anyway.

Adam fell asleep again.

Maybe this was a mistake. She didn't want him feeling like he had to take her up on her offer if all he really wanted to do was sleep. Just because she wanted to hang on to this a little bit longer didn't mean he did.

When they stopped in front of her apartment, she gave him a gentle nudge. "We're here."

He followed her inside and parked his suitcase next to the front door.

"Sorry it's such a mess," she said, looking around at all her clutter and trying to imagine it through his eyes.

"It's great," he replied, wandering over to examine a stack of fabric remainders on her dining table. "It's very you."

"Do you want something to drink?" She went into the kitchen and pulled open the fridge. A week-old Chinese takeout container and a single mushy avocado stared back at her. "I have no food," she said helplessly. She probably should have thought of that before inviting him over.

When she turned away from the fridge, he was standing beside her. "We can order something," he said, and bent his head to hers. "Later," he murmured as their lips met in a kiss that made her stomach do an entire gymnastic floor routine.

"Much later," she agreed, and led him to her bedroom.

OLIVIA WOKE in the morning alone in her bed. It took her sleepy brain a while to remember that wasn't how she'd fallen asleep last night.

She opened her eyes and saw Adam across the room buttoning up his shirt. From the faint gray light coming in through the slats in her blinds, it couldn't be much past six a.m. She sat up and rubbed her eyes. "You're leaving?"

He nodded as he finished the last button on his shirt. "I'm all out of clean clothes. I'm going back to my place to shower before work." He bent to brush a kiss across her lips. "I'll see you at the office in a couple hours, okay?"

This was it, their bubble was officially broken. No more hiding from the real world or putting off the inevitable. Reentry was upon them.

"What's wrong?" he asked, sitting on the edge of the bed. "You have your worried face." He reached up to stroke her cheek, and her stomach dropped through the floor to the apartment below. "Don't look like that," he said with a deepening frown. "You're freaking me out."

"Sorry." She tried to will the worry lines off her face. "I'm just nervous about today, I guess."

"Why?"

"I'm afraid it will be weird."

"What will?"

"Us. At work. What if we revert back to our old selves as soon as we set foot in the building?"

"My geographical location has no bearing on how I feel about you." There was a hint of reproof in his eyes, as if she'd disappointed him by having doubts.

She reached for his hand and interlaced her fingers with his. "A lot's happened in a really short span of time. We haven't even had time to process it."

"What's to process?"

"How we feel about each other when we're not stranded in the middle of nowhere. What's to say we won't step back into our regular lives today and realize we don't like each other that much after all?"

"Nothing at all," he said mildly, which wasn't the reassurance she'd been hoping for. "You want some kind of guarantee or contingency plan." He knew her so well.

"Yes, exactly. That's what I want."

He smiled and turned her hand over in his. "There isn't one. Not for this." His thumb stroked over her palm like a fortune teller. "You have to take a leap of faith."

"You don't believe in faith."

His eyes met hers. "Maybe I do now. Maybe you've rubbed off on me."

"Do you really have faith in this?" she asked, pressing her hand against his, palm to palm. "Tell the truth."

"I always tell the truth," he said. "And yes."

THE FIRST THING Olivia did when she arrived at work two hours later was remove Tiny Adam the toy robot from her purse and give him a place of honor among the other assorted toys at her desk. Now, whenever she looked down at him, sitting there between Baby Groot and the TARDIS, she'd be reminded of Adam.

Her Adam.

The word sent a thrill racing through her. Her eyes drifted across the open workspace to Adam's cubicle. He'd gotten in before her, but his back was to both her and the elevators, so he probably didn't know she was here yet. All she could see was the top of his head, but even that was enough to set off a swirl of butterflies in her stomach.

Yeah, this wasn't going to make it hard to focus on work at all.

And she'd thought her crush on him had been distracting before. That was nothing compared to this overpowering urge to go over there and talk to him, which was made worse by the fact that she knew he'd welcome her company.

Well, she was just going to have to cope. It was going to be like this every day—except when he was out of the office traveling for work.

She downed the last of the coffee she'd brought for the commute this morning and started up her computer. Only then did she notice the piece of paper someone had left on her desk.

It was a recommendation letter from Adam.

Olivia's eyes pricked with tears as she read it. It wasn't just complimentary, it was *glowing*. He described her with phrases like "determined problem-solver" and "brilliant mind." He said she had the best people skills of anyone he knew at the company, was deserving of more responsibility, and would shine in a management role. He recommended her wholeheartedly for the Future Leader Development Course.

But even as her heart soared to read his words, she felt a stab of doubt.

He'd only written her a recommendation after they'd slept together. She didn't doubt he meant every word—he wasn't the sort of person to lie for the sake of flattery or personal connections. But was it ethical to use his help for her professional advancement now that they were in a relationship?

They hadn't talked about when or if they'd let people at work know about them—although she realized now they probably should have. She assumed they'd opt for discretion, at least for a while. The optics of coming back from a business trip and suddenly being a couple were not great.

But presumably people would find out eventually. They'd probably need to disclose to HR at some point. Gavin would find out, and the CIO. And if anyone happened to remember she'd used a recommendation from Adam to bolster her application to the leadership program, they might think things about her.

She might think things about her. She wanted to be able to look back and know she'd earned this on her own merits. She'd rather not have it at all than get it with an asterisk beside her name.

She stood up, reference letter in hand, intending to go talk to Adam about it. To thank him for writing such an incredible recommendation, and explain why she wouldn't feel right about using it anymore.

As soon as she stood up, however, Gavin caught her eye and beckoned her over. She weaved through the cube maze, still carrying Adam's letter, and stopped in the open doorway of Gavin's glass-walled office. Even the managers important enough to have offices with walls and doors weren't allowed any real privacy.

"Hey, welcome back!" He leaned back in his chair and saluted her with his coffee mug. "The victorious hero returns!"

"Ha ha," she said, putting on her amiable work smile. "Yeah."

"You guys had quite a week. But you pulled it off! Tell you the truth, I wasn't entirely sure it was possible. And then after all the stuff that happened, I thought we were sunk for sure. But you and Cortinas worked a miracle and pulled off a win for us. You obviously make a good team."

"Yeah, I guess we do," she said, smiling for real.

"And to think, he didn't even want you on the trip."

Her smile froze in place. "What?"

"Yeah, he came to me after the meeting with the CIO and asked if I could send someone else from the commercial systems team instead."

"He did?" Her limbs felt numb.

"Mmm." Gavin nodded as he sipped his coffee. "But I told him you were the only one I trusted to do the job in my place. And since I couldn't go, he was stuck with you."

Stuck with me.

"Anyway, you proved him wrong, hey? And it sounds like you two got along fine. Talk about a trial by fire."

Gavin went on talking, but Olivia barely heard a word he said after that. All she could think about was Adam, going to her boss behind her back and asking that she be taken off a project.

She'd known, obviously, that Adam hadn't been her biggest fan before. He'd made that pretty clear. But she hadn't known his dislike of her had run so deep, that he'd had so little faith in her abilities he'd actually tried an end run to avoid taking her with him to Texas.

"Hey, you okay?" Gavin must have realized she wasn't paying attention because he was frowning at her.

"Sorry." She shook her head, tuning back in to the present. "Just tired."

"Yeah, I'll bet." He gave her a sympathetic look. "Listen, the CIO's out today, so the postmortem on Walhalla's gotta wait until tomorrow. If you want, you can work from home for the rest of the day."

"Okay." She rubbed Adam's reference letter between her fingers. The corner she was holding was becoming felted from the friction. "Thanks."

Gavin waved his hand in friendly dismissal. "Go on. Get out of here."

As Olivia walked away from Gavin's office, her eyes went automatically to Adam. He was hunched over his computer with his back to her still. She stopped, unsure where to go or what to do next.

Adam's head swiveled around, as if he'd sensed her watching him. When his gaze found her, he did that thing where he smiled with only his eyes.

Olivia turned away and headed for her desk. She retrieved her purse and shoved the reference letter inside, not caring if it got crumpled. While she was packing up her computer, Adam came over.

"Hey." He stood just outside her cubicle, resting his forearms on top of the partition. "You leaving?"

She didn't look at him as she shoved her laptop into her bag. "Gavin told me I could work from home today."

"Nice. Did you get the reference letter I left on your desk?"

"I did. Thank you." She grabbed her travel mug and started for the elevators.

"I'll walk you out." Adam trailed along behind her, his long legs easily keeping pace.

When the elevator came, he got on with her. She jabbed the button for the lobby and stared straight ahead, facing the doors.

"What's wrong?" he asked as soon as they were alone. "Did Gavin say something to piss you off?"

"In a manner of speaking."

"Olivia." Adam's fingers brushed her arm. "Talk to me."

She turned to face him. "Did you go to Gavin after the meeting with the CIO last Monday and ask him to send someone else on the trip instead of me?"

He looked confused. "Yes."

"You told him you didn't want to work with me."

"I asked him if there was someone else he could send instead of you."

"Why? Why would you do that?"

"I thought traveling together would be awkward after I'd declined to give you a reference."

"You thought it would be awkward," she repeated in disbelief. "So you decided to torpedo my credibility with my boss to save yourself the inconvenience of a little social discomfort?"

"I told him it didn't have anything to do with your job performance. That it was an interpersonal conflict that would make things tense between us."

"Oh, well, that's fine, then. I'm sure it won't affect my professional reputation at all that you couldn't stand to work with me because of an interpersonal conflict. Jesus, Adam!" She dug into her purse for the recommendation letter. "You can take this back. I don't want it." She shoved it at him, but he refused to take it.

"Don't say that. Come on—"

She ripped the paper in half. "I'd rather get a reference from someone who actually believes in me."

His whole face seemed to sag as he stared at the shredded letter in her hands. "I apologize. In hindsight, it was a shitty thing to do."

"You think?"

"I realize now that you're treated with a double-standard that means a comment like that can have repercussions beyond what I intended."

"Well, as long as you realize that *now*."

He scowled at her sarcasm. "I regret it, Olivia, just like I regret not giving you that reference when you first asked. But I don't understand why you're so mad about this now. You knew how I felt before." He sounded frustrated, like he expected her to just get over this. Like it hadn't felt like a knife in her heart to find out he'd done that to her.

"You told me that you didn't have any confidence in my management potential, but you didn't mention that you disliked me so much you went behind my back to try and get me taken off this assignment. Christ, what do you think the CIO would have thought if Gavin had actually gone along with it and replaced me? He would have thought it was because I couldn't hack it."

The elevator doors slid open and she rocketed into the lobby. Adam followed silently as she tramped across the wide expanse of polished tile and through the door to the parking garage.

As soon as they were alone in the echoey garage, he surged ahead of her, bringing her to a stop. "I fucked up, okay? I was wrong in every possible way. But I've made a complete one-eighty in my thinking. From now on I'm Team Olivia."

"Great."

"You're still mad." He actually looked surprised.

"Of course I'm still mad! I don't get over being mad the second you apologize. Apologies aren't coins you feed into a vending machine in exchange for instant forgiveness."

"What more do you want me to do?"

"I don't know. Nothing."

He reached for her hand. "Olivia—"

She pulled her hand out of his grasp. "Don't. I need to go. I don't want to talk about this here anymore."

"But we can talk about it later?"

"Fine." She stalked off toward the garage elevators. Thankfully, Adam didn't follow this time.

"I'll call you later!" he called out.

She kept walking.

Chapter Twenty-One

Olivia couldn't remember the last time she'd cried over a man. Maybe when Cody Briggs had called her a booger-eater on the playground, come to think of it.

But she was crying when she got home, and what was that even about? Crying over a guy she barely even knew a week ago. She shouldn't care enough to cry over him yet.

But here she was, nevertheless, blubbering into a pillow that still smelled like him.

She should have done a better job of protecting her heart. She should have fortified the walls she'd built around it, instead of letting Adam dismantle them stone by stone. Now her heart hurt like it had been torn in half, and it was all his fault for making her care about him.

The really annoying thing was that he was right. She'd known he'd disliked her before, so what was the big deal? Why did it hurt so much to be confronted with the evidence of his past antipathy?

She shouldn't care. But she did. So much it scared her.

Because the thing was, she wasn't simply attracted to Adam. It wasn't just his body she craved, or his touch. She wanted to *know* him. Even more shocking—she wanted him to know her.

That had never happened to her before. Even with Ryan, when she'd convinced herself she'd been in love, she'd still been reluctant to open up. It had been a persistent point of contention between them. He was always accusing her of being too closed off and uncommunicative.

But with Adam, she felt the strangest urge to confess all her hopes and fears and sins—all the secret insecurities she usually worked so hard to cover up.

It was crazy. The exact opposite of sensible. It went against all her instincts for self-preservation.

She'd thrown caution to the wind and let him make a space for himself in her heart, when he was probably the last person on earth she should lower her drawbridge for.

That was why it hurt so much to find out he'd gone to Gavin behind her back. To be reminded of how strong his dislike of her had been, and how little he'd cared for her feelings.

Adam had changed his mind about her so fast—in just a couple of days. It was *too* fast. If he could do a complete one-eighty that easily, what was stopping him from doing it again?

Would he realize in another week he didn't like her so much after all?

Olivia sat up and leaned across the bed for a tissue. After she'd finished blowing her nose, she reached for her phone, intending to call Penny. But it was the middle of the day, and even though she teleworked, Penny still had to actually do work when she was supposed to be working. Plus, Olivia hadn't talked to Penny all week, so she'd have to start from the very beginning of the story. She'd have to explain how she and Adam had gotten together before she could explain why she was upset now.

The thought of it exhausted her. She wasn't up to that much talking right now. She wasn't up to anything.

Instead of calling her best friend, she switched her phone to Do Not Disturb and climbed under the covers to take a nap.

WHEN OLIVIA WOKE a few hours later, it felt like her eyelids had been welded shut. She'd fallen asleep with her makeup on—after crying half of it down her face—which she never, ever did.

She pushed herself upright and groaned when she saw she'd gotten smears of black eyeliner and dark red lipstick all over her pillowcase. A halo of yellow-orange light glowed around the blinds in her bedroom. It was nearly evening; she'd slept away the whole day.

Feeling like she'd been hit by a truck, she went into the bathroom and scrubbed her face clean. Her skin looked raw and ruddy in the bathroom mirror. The skin under her eyes was so translucent they looked hollow and sunken, like a skeleton.

She hadn't just fallen asleep in her makeup, she'd fallen asleep in her work clothes. Her bra was like a band of nails around her rib cage and her shirt had turned into sandpaper. She clawed at the offending garments, stripping them off like they were trying to kill her.

Her suitcase lurked in a corner of her bedroom, still waiting to be unpacked, so she dug through her dresser until she found an old T-shirt and a pair of plaid boxer shorts she'd had since college.

In the kitchen, she was confronted by the remnants of the takeout she and Adam had ordered last night, and it felt like a punch to the chest. Ignoring the mess and the pain in her heart, she poured herself a glass of water and guzzled the whole thing down.

She'd just started cleaning up the takeout containers when there was a knock on the door. That was when she remembered her phone was still on Do Not Disturb—and discovered all the text messages from Adam she'd missed.

I'm sorry.

Are you okay?

Are you there?

Are you ignoring me?

Olivia, please.

I'm coming over, okay?

I hope it's okay because I'm on my way to your place right now.

She wasn't sure what to expect as she went to answer the door. Would he be angry? Worried? Relieved? Happy to see her?

The one thing she hadn't envisioned was what she got: total blankness.

His face betrayed no detectable emotion. He stood on her doorstep wearing an expressionless mask, the one he used at work and around people he didn't want to engage with.

It hurt. She felt it like a needle sliding between her ribs—and not a tiny little flu shot needle you could barely feel, but a big-ass scary needle, like the one they used on Uma Thurman in *Pulp Fiction*.

But even while it was hurting her, she felt a little twinge of familiarity. This was the Adam she remembered, the one she'd known for the two years before last week. *Oh, hello,* she thought. *There you are. You're still in there after all.*

He was still capable of being that Adam with her, rather than *her* Adam.

But then he spoke, and his voice was so quiet and unsteady she knew it was all an act. He was hiding behind his mask, pretending not to feel anything, but the emotions were leaking out through his voice.

"I've been trying to call you," he said, betraying himself. In those six little words she could hear reproach and relief, trepidation and a hint of resentment, and over all of it a layer of exasperation.

"I had my phone off. I was sleeping."

"Can I come in?"

She nodded and stepped back. As he moved past her into the apartment, she caught a whiff of the blissful Adam scent of his skin, and it made her want to throw her arms around him.

But she didn't.

He stood in the middle of her living room, hands shoved awkwardly into the pockets of his work slacks, still wearing his leather messenger bag across his chest.

"Look, Olivia—" he started, but she held up her hand to stop him. There was something she needed to say to him first.

"You were right."

"I was?" He seemed wary, like he was waiting for the other shoe to drop. Which was smart, because she was juggling a whole closet of shoes, and she was trying her best to keep them in the air, but any second now they were going to start crashing to the floor around her.

"I overreacted earlier. You're right that what you said to Gavin before shouldn't change anything between us now."

"Okay." He nodded, slightly mollified. "Thank you."

"Maybe what's wrong now has always been wrong."

His face didn't move. Not even a twitch. "Is that what you think?"

"I think it's a sign."

"A sign," he repeated. The fact that he just sighed wearily instead of insisting there was no such thing as signs was probably another sign. A bad one. He couldn't even be bothered to argue anymore.

"I'm just not sure intense mutual dislike is a great foundation to build a relationship on," she ventured.

"I don't care how you felt about me before." He'd removed his hands from his pockets and was squeezing the strap of his messenger bag.

"But I do," she said. "*I* care. And I don't know how to stop caring about it. I want to, but I don't know how. Maybe it's my Rejection Sensitive Dysphoria, or just a lifetime of insecurity, but I don't know how to get past it, and I'm afraid it's going to keep cropping up, and every time it's going to feel like this, until eventually we both get sick of trying."

He looked down at the floor, and she wished she had a mirror she could lay at his feet so she could see his expression. Whatever emotion he was experiencing so strongly he needed to hide his face from her while he steeled himself, she wanted desperately to see.

But then he looked up, and he hadn't steeled himself at all. The emotion was still on his face plain as day. It was anguish. He looked utterly anguished, and it was because of her.

"Don't you get it?" he said, his voice coming out rough and cracking a little. "I didn't like *anyone*. I didn't feel any differently about you than I felt about everyone else in that office. I never let myself think about you or know you because I didn't want to know anyone."

She could almost believe it. As much as the voices in her brain were trying to tell her it was all about her, that he must have harbored a special dislike for her because she was obviously The Worst and always would be, she could remember well enough how distant he'd been with everyone. How he'd never joined in on group lunches or after-work drinks, never chatted in the break room or showed up to the holiday party. How she'd never once seen him acting chummy with anyone or talking about anything but work.

"But...why?"

"Because I hated myself and I hated everyone around me. I had completely closed myself off from everything and everyone. After Hailey, I was so miserable, all I could do was go through the motions every day. I put all of my energy into doing my work and going to the gym, even though I hated it, and I acted like kind of an asshole, because it kept people from trying to be my friend. I was miserable for so long, I forgot how to be anything else." He shifted his messenger bag, hugging it against his stomach. "So it didn't have anything to do with you. It wasn't you that I disliked—it was myself."

"But you asked Gavin to send someone else in my place." Why

would he have done that if he'd despised everyone just as much? That had to have been about her specifically.

"Because I felt guilty for refusing to give you a recommendation. I wouldn't have liked whoever else he sent any better, but at least they wouldn't have been looking at me all week like I'd taken a dump on their birthday cake."

"I didn't look at you like that."

"No, you looked at me like you wanted to kick me in the nads."

"That's because I did."

"I know." The corner of his mouth twitched. "It was hot."

"Seriously?"

He shrugged. "Everyone at this job is always trying to kiss my ass. No one ever calls me on my bullshit, because I'm the CIO's golden boy. All I ever hear is how great I am."

She couldn't help how salty she sounded. "Must be terrible for you. What a hardship."

"See? I love that you call me on my bullshit."

She shook her head. "You hate my sarcasm."

"No, I fucking love it. When I showed up at the airport, I was expecting you to be all meek and crestfallen and spend the whole week shooting silent recriminations at me like a kicked dog. I didn't expect you to stand up to me like you did. I'd never seen that side of you before. The more you challenged me, the more it made me want to poke back, to bring out more of that fire inside you."

She didn't know what to say. None of this sounded like any better starting place for a relationship. She'd thought she was the broken one of the two of them, but it turned out they both were. How were they supposed to navigate all this baggage?

Adam looked down at his messenger bag, which he was clutching like a life preserver. "But I understand if you can't forgive me for who I was. For how I treated you and everyone else. You didn't deserve it." His fingers worried at the buckle on his bag. "Maybe you're right. Maybe it's better to quit while we're ahead—while we can still part friends."

She'd thought it was what she wanted to hear. It was exactly what she'd been saying and thinking. But it hurt more than she expected to hear him actually agree with her. "I mean...with our jobs, I just...I don't know."

He looked up, and when his eyes met hers they were defiant. "I don't give a shit about my job. I'd rather have you than this job."

It was like he'd dropped a stun grenade into the middle of the room. All Olivia could do was blink at him, dazed, as her ears filled with a ringing sound.

Adam dug around in his messenger bag and pulled out a yellow notepad, which he thrust into her hands. "This is what I did at work today instead of my job."

"What is it?" she asked, too disoriented to focus on the handwritten black scrawl on the top page.

"It's a list of everything I like about you."

"But..." She thumbed through the pages of the notepad. "Every page of this is full." Page after page, every single line was covered in his cramped, messy handwriting.

She heard the apartment door close and looked up. He'd left. Just handed her this ridiculous, wonderful, unbelievable thing and then walked out without a word.

She stood rooted in place as she flipped through the notepad, reading the exhaustive list of things he liked about her, which ranged from the silly to the unbearably sentimental.

Your sense of humor

Your cute butt

The way you swear

Your brain

How much you care about your job

How much you care about so many things

That you play D&D

Your eyelashes

The sound of you typing
When you steal my food
The smell of your hair
The freckle by your left eyebrow
The way your eyelids flutter when I touch you
Your big heart
That you're smarter than anyone else I know
That you're smarter than me

There were tears in her eyes. It just went on and on. Hundreds of lines. Hundreds of little things he'd noticed about her. Hundreds of arguments to prove how much he cared.

Hundreds of reasons not to give up on each other.

And he was gone.

He'd told her he wanted her more than his job, handed her the evidence to back it up, and then disappeared on her.

What the *fuck*?

She had to stop him before he got too far. She ran across the apartment and grabbed her phone off the kitchen counter.

"Hi," he said when he answered the phone, like he hadn't just walked out on a conversation seconds ago.

"Come back." Her voice sounded like it was coming from the bottom of the ocean. "Please come back."

"Open the door," he told her, and when she did he was standing on the other side like he'd never left at all. "Marco."

"What? How?" All of this was too much. She was experiencing so many emotions at once, she didn't know what to feel first, and it was impairing her ability to process information at her usual speed. All she knew for sure was that she needed him not to leave again.

"You're supposed to say Polo." He gave a sheepish shrug. "I couldn't make myself walk away. So I just waited, in case you changed your mind."

"Asshole." She grabbed his arm and dragged him inside. "Don't leave like that again." This time she locked the door, in case he tried to make another escape.

"Okay." A ghost of a smile drifted across his lips. A shimmer of escaping hope. "Does this mean you've changed your mind?"

Instead of answering, she hurled herself into his arms.

Nothing else mattered except how fiercely he held on to her, and the way his chest hitched as she pressed her face into it. His scent enveloped her, that sweet, fresh Adam smell, and it was like coming back home after being away on a trip.

She still clutched the notepad in her hand. It was making it hard to touch him the way she wanted to, but she couldn't let go of it—not yet—so she held on to it and she held on to him, like they were the two most important things in the world.

"I can't believe you wrote all that stuff," she said. "It must have taken you hours."

"It was the easiest thing I've ever done."

"Shut up."

"I was so awful to you before, I just needed you to know how I feel about you now."

"I do."

He cradled her face in his big, warm hands. "I see you," he said, and the way his dark, piercing eyes were looking down at her, she felt the truth of his words like never before—right down to the very bottom of her soul. "Sometimes it feels like I can't see anything but you. I know you feel like people don't see you, Olivia, but I see you. With my whole heart."

"Goddammit," she said, blinking furiously. "Stop making me cry."

He touched a finger to the underside of her chin, tilting her face up. His eyes raked over her like they were drinking her in. She strained toward him, and their lips met in a kiss that turned her inside out, leaving her shaky and defenseless.

But it was okay. She didn't need her defenses around him

anymore. She could lower the drawbridge and let her walls crumble a little. The man at the gate was a friendly.

When they parted, Adam was breathing almost as hard as she was, and he clutched at her like she was the only thing holding him up.

"I see you too," she said, and felt a tremor run through his body. "I see the real you. The one you try to keep hidden from everyone." She curled a hand around his neck and tried to bring him back for another kiss, but he evaded her lips.

"I feel like I've been in a coma for the last two years. And then you walked in and woke me up." He leaned away from her so he could untangle himself from his messenger bag.

She tugged him back toward her as soon as he'd lowered his bag to the floor. "By yelling at you?"

He smiled in response, and she laughed. "It felt more like a kick in the head." He extricated the notepad from her fingers and dropped it on top of his bag.

"Some Prince Charming I am."

His arms wound around her again. "It was exactly what I needed. *You* were exactly what I needed."

Their mouths came together like two magnets attracting. A force of nature. Their opposite poles perfectly aligned, creating a magnetic field that forced the world to change around them.

He was there with her. He wanted to be there, and that meant something.

It meant everything.

Epilogue

SIX MONTHS LATER

LAX at Christmastime made Dante's vision of hell look like a trip to Disneyland.

Apparently everyone in the greater Los Angeles area was traveling out of town today, lugging packs of whiny, overstimulated children and shopping bags full of presents home for the holidays. Olivia had already seen two near-fights break out—one at curbside check-in and another over the last empty table at the airport McDonald's. *Merry fucking Christmas.*

She was glad she'd gotten there early. Even with the extra-long security lines, she'd made it to the gate with enough time to stock up on snacks and bottles of water in one of the airport shops.

Still no sign of Adam anywhere, but that wasn't a surprise. She'd known what she was in for when they'd agreed to meet at the airport. They were both coming straight from the office, but Olivia worked in an office in El Segundo these days.

A few months after finishing the Future Leader Development Course, she'd taken a job with another company: leading a team building wind farm optimization software for Sauer Hewson's wind energy division. It was challenging, and scary, and hard, but she loved it.

As the minutes ticked toward their scheduled boarding time, Olivia swallowed down a bubble of nerves. She couldn't do this without Adam. The only reason she'd even agreed to go home for Christmas this year was so he could meet her family. For some reason it had been important to him, and she hadn't had the heart to say no.

He'd introduced her to his family months ago, and they'd welcomed her with open arms and plates of homemade Mexican food and endless intrusive questions. It had been intimidating and overwhelming, but also pretty wonderful. She'd never felt anything like that before—like being smothered with attention.

If it had been up to Olivia, they'd have spent Christmas with Adam's parents and sisters and nieces and nephews and cousins in Riverside. Or used his frequent flyer miles to book a mini vacay on some tropical beach somewhere, just the two of them.

If Adam missed this flight and made her face her family alone, she swore to Christ—

"Hey, Woerner," he said, elbowing his way through the crowd toward her.

At the sight of him, Olivia's heart swelled like a balloon attached to a helium tank. Sometimes she still couldn't believe he was hers.

Adam propped his bag next to hers and wrapped his arms around her, dropping a light kiss on her mouth. "I made it."

She tugged at the hem of his henley, and her knuckles grazed his stomach. Where there had once been a six-pack, he'd developed a soft little pooch. He still went to the gym, but only three days a week instead of seven. He had better things to do now, like spend time with his girlfriend.

Olivia loved his little pooch, because it was physical evidence of how much happier and more relaxed he was. His body was softening along with his personality. He wasn't half as brusque as he used to be, and he smiled all the time, even at people who weren't her. He'd even been making more of an effort to make friends. He showed up for after-work drinks with her new coworkers most weeks when he wasn't traveling, and had even made a few appearances at her knitting group's weekly meetups. His knitting skills hadn't progressed much, but he'd scored massive points with her friends for being the first boyfriend in the group to even make the attempt.

"I was only a little worried," Olivia admitted.

"I wasn't going to miss the plane," Adam said, gently admonishing. "I wouldn't do that to you."

"I know, but you know I can't help worrying."

"I do know, and I love you for it." He rubbed his nose against hers. "How long have you been here?"

"Only about ten minutes."

"That's not bad. Did you get snacks? I assume you got snacks."

"I did." She wriggled out of his embrace and opened her purse to show off her haul from the airport newsstand.

He shook his head as he peered at the selection of candy bars and chips. "You know we're not going to need any of that, right?"

He'd used his miles to upgrade both of them to first class. Soon they'd be reclining in luxury, sipping free alcoholic beverages and enjoying hot towels and warm nuts on the flight to Houston. It would probably be the highlight of the entire trip.

"This is for stress eating at my parents' house," she said, repositioning her bag on her shoulder. "I'm going to start drinking my weight in champagne just as soon as they let us on the airplane."

The crowd around them was getting pushy, and Adam draped an arm around her shoulders, pulling her into the shelter of his body. "It's going to be fine."

She pressed her hand against his cheek, imagining the two of them kissing in the surf or soaking up the sun on one of those big deck chairs made for two, and let out a wistful sigh for what could have been. "You're so sweet and naive, and you're going to eat those words, buddy."

"Come on." He laid his hand over hers and nuzzled a kiss into her palm. "They're not monsters. How bad can it be?"

She snorted. "Well, my dad probably won't talk at all unless it's about the glory days of my brother's football career, my mother will talk incessantly about my perfect sister's perfect husband and perfect career, my brother will do everything in his power to push my buttons, and I'll revert to the emotional maturity of a sulky teenager. If you still love me after this trip, it will be a miracle."

"I'll always love you," Adam said, brushing a kiss against her temple. "And it won't be that bad this time because you won't be alone. You'll have someone on your side. Team Olivia all the way."

She rose up on her toes and kissed him long and hard on the mouth, ignoring the disapproving looks it earned from their fellow passengers. Adam's lips parted for her as he tugged her against his body. Just before things veered into socially inexcusable, Olivia broke off the kiss.

"Goddamn, do I love you," she said between breaths. Every time they kissed it set her heart racing in her chest. Apparently she was never going to get over that electric thrill. She'd be eighty and still gasping at every kiss like it was their first.

"Not as much as I love you," he said, beaming down at her with adoring eyes. He really meant it, of that she was one hundred percent certain. Whatever small indignities her family inflicted on her were meaningless compared to that.

The gate agent announced that pre-boarding for their flight would begin in a moment, and Adam laid a hand in the small of Olivia's back to guide her through the swelling crowd.

"You ready?" he asked as the gate agent scanned their boarding passes.

"Ready as I'll ever be."

Adam reached for her hand as they stepped onto the jetway, and a sudden surge of happiness drowned out the last of her apprehensions.

Whatever happened, she knew it would be fine, because they were together. The unknown didn't scare her nearly as much anymore. She knew she could survive anything, because the person she loved most in the world had her back.

Everything else would work itself out, one way or another.

Acknowledgments

Readers familiar with Texas geography may notice I've taken some liberties for the sake of plot. In spirit, however, I hope I've been true to my beloved home state.

As always, thanks are owed to my wonderful husband, Dave, for being my biggest cheerleader and number one fan. Also to my beta readers Mer and Jo, for encouraging me and saving me from myself. And to my excellent editor Julia, for being so amazing at what she does.

A special shoutout goes to Siobhán Nevin in my Facebook reader group for giving me Adam's name.

This book wouldn't exist if not for the support and encouragement of a wonderful community of indie authors who've been with me on every step of this incredible journey. In particular, I need to thank the following:

Melanie Greene, for taking me to an RWA meeting three years ago.

K.L. Montgomery and everyone at IAS, for creating a welcoming community where we can all learn from each other.

Annika Martin and Penny Reid, for holding out their hands to lift me up.

Skye Warren, for sharing her wisdom and helping me make sense of this business we're in.

And finally, to everyone who picked up my first book and took a chance on an unknown author. If it weren't for the confidence you gave me, I'm not sure I would have made it to book six.

About the Author

SUSANNAH NIX lives in Texas with her husband, two ornery cats, and a flatulent pit bull. When she's not writing, she enjoys reading, cooking, knitting, watching stupid amounts of television, and getting distracted by Tumblr. She is also a powerlifter who can deadlift as much as Captain America weighs.

www.susannahnix.com

CPSIA information can be obtained
at www.ICGtesting.com
Printed in the USA
LVHW042314151019
634269LV00011B/883/P

9 781950 087020